Praise f
KASIE W

"Hits all the right notes."
—*Kirkus Reviews* on *Sunkissed*

"Light, frothy, swoony!"
—*SLJ* on *Sunkissed*

"This is a perfect romance for reading on a road trip or at the beach."
—*The Bulletin* on *Places We've Never Been*

"Sweet teen romance."
—*SLJ* on *Places We've Never Been*

"*Borrow My Heart* is a sweet treat you won't want to put down."
—*Cultures* on *Borrow My Heart*

"Fun and lighthearted."
—*Booklist* on *Listen to Your Heart*

"Kasie West books are our kind of comfort food— romantic, light and cute!"
—*Justine Magazine* on *Lucky in Love*

"The perfect romantic comedy."
—*VOYA* on *P.S. I Like You*

ALSO BY KASIE WEST

Better Than Revenge

THAN

Revenge

KASIE WEST

**Delacorte
Romance**

Text copyright © 2024 by Kasie West
Cover art copyright © 2024 by Jess Miller

Delacorte Romance and the colophon are trademarks of Penguin Random House LLC.

GetUnderlined.com

Educators and librarians, for a variety of teaching tools, visit us at RHTeachersLibrarians.com

Library of Congress Cataloging-in-Publication Data is available upon request.
ISBN 978-0-593-64329-7 (tr. pbk.) — ISBN 978-0-593-64330-3 (ebook)

The text of this book is set in 11-point Adobe Garamond Pro.
Interior design by Megan Shortt

Printed in the United States of America
10 9 8 7 6 5 4 3 2
First Edition

To Taylor Swift, whose music and lyrics
have kept my imagination whirling and my
heart soaring for many years.
You are truly an inspiration.

Chapter
one

THE CENTRAL CALIFORNIA COAST FOG CLUNG TO THE hills that March morning, which was why I had pulled on a flannel and beanie before leaving the house. I should've taken the fog as a bad omen, but I was oblivious, aside from the nervous energy coursing through me. I stood in a line, two people in front of me, seven behind, outside our high school's recording studio—a small building near the front office—waiting for my audition.

I pulled off my hat and shoved it in my pocket. Ava, two steps ahead of me, was practicing, mouthing words to herself. My script was on my phone, and I reviewed it silently.

A set of arms snaked around my waist, surprising me. I let out a squeal and tilted my head up to see Jensen's smiling face.

"Hi, boyfriend," I said, leaning back against him. "Come to wish me luck and help me relax?"

He was wearing his football jersey. Even though football season was long over, there was going to be a rally today where the football players did some sort of relay.

"Hey, babe." He took in the line and the closed door of the studio. "This is it, huh? The moment of truth."

"This is it." I drew a deep breath. It was finally time. Only seniors hosted the school's podcast, and they were in charge of auditions. I'd been waiting since freshman year for this. Two and a half years of broadcasting classes where I learned about soundboards and soundproofing and advertising and creative segues. About hot-button topics and interviewing. All to prepare me for this moment.

"Did you finish writing your pitch thingy?"

I held up my phone, where my notes app was open. "I decided on the student highlight feature." This audition wasn't just to see how well we could speak on microphone under pressure, but also to see what creative ideas and topics we might bring to the team. One of my ideas was to interview a different student each week to learn more about the people we went to school with.

"Really?" he asked.

"You didn't like that one?" I'd practiced in front of him the night before on my at-home setup. He'd nodded and laughed and clapped for me, like the perfect boyfriend he was.

"No, it's good. I liked the weekly puzzle idea too." That idea had been to give a short but difficult brain teaser or puzzle at the beginning of each week, and the first student to solve it and turn in the correct answer won a prize or extra credit or something. I liked that idea too but didn't feel like it would better our school the way learning the stories of those around us would, and that was important to me.

"Yeah, those were the two I was deciding between. You think the other one would be better?" I asked, trying not to get in my head now, in the eleventh hour.

"No, the interview idea is great." His eyes traveled to the top of my head, and he reached out and ran his hands down my long light brown hair. It had a slight wave to it, so it was always frizzy when there was extra moisture in the air.

"I was wearing a hat earlier," I said, helping him in the smoothing process. "And it's not fair that you can see the top of my head better than most." I was pretty tall, but Jensen was taller.

He smiled and kissed my forehead. "You look cute."

"Thanks." I shook out my hands as the line moved forward.

Lincoln came out of the building, his face a little pale.

"How was it?" I asked. I knew everyone here. We'd gone through the last couple years together. Sure, we were now competition, but we'd always known that would be the case. Only two people would be picked to be the voice of the podcast, and I was dying to be one of them. Not only was it good experience, it led directly to an internship at the community college as well.

"Brutal," Lincoln said. "I stammered through several words."

That was my main worry. That I'd trip up on words. Use too many fillers. I didn't have the ability to edit my performance after the fact like I would in a normal podcast. "I'm sure you did better than your brain is telling you," I said to him now, and maybe a little to myself.

He held up crossed fingers, then kept walking. "Good luck, Finley!" he called over his shoulder.

"Thanks!" I returned.

Ava, now the last person between me and the door, turned around and gave me a nervous face. I reached out and squeezed her hand. "You got this."

She looked up at Jensen, then at his football jersey. "You're the kicker, right?"

"Yes. I'll be the starting kicker next year." He was proud of that, and his face beamed when he said the words. He'd been the backup kicker for three seasons, only got to play the final game of last season because Theo, the starter, had been injured. And now, Theo would finally graduate in June. I was happy about that. Theo was arrogant and unhelpful and constantly criticized Jensen's ability in front of the whole team. He was a bully and a jerk, and next year would be so much better without him getting in Jensen's head. They were supposed to be on the same team; I didn't know why he tried so hard to bring Jensen down.

"And how do you feel about your future starting spot?" I said, holding up a fake microphone.

He rolled his eyes and pushed my hand down. He didn't like it when I played reporter. Especially in front of other people.

"Didn't you used to play soccer?" Ava asked, looking at me. "You both like to kick things."

"Balls. We both like to kick balls," I joked back.

"Finley," Jensen said in a low, reprimanding voice.

"Sorry," I said, even though I thought it was funny.

I used to be a defender on the girls' soccer team. But it took a lot of time away from what I really loved—podcasts. That's what I wanted to do with my life, so I had quit soccer after sophomore season to focus on that. Plus, my parents needed me at home more. "I probably couldn't kick a soccer ball twenty feet if my life depended on it these days."

Jensen let out a sharp laugh. "Anyone can kick a soccer ball twenty feet, babe. That's not very far. Plus, a soccer ball basically rolls all by itself." He winked at me.

"Oh, right, I forgot, a football is *so* much harder to kick," I said, heavy with sarcasm.

"It is," he returned. "The shape alone—"

I held up my hands, stopping him midsentence. "I get it—you're a stud."

He squeezed me into a hug. "I try."

The door opened, and Lisa came out.

"Here I go," Ava said.

That left me staring at the door.

"How are you feeling?" Jensen asked.

"My stomach hurts." I hugged his waist, resting my cheek on his chest. Even though the last few years of my life had been preparing me for this moment, something in the back of my mind told me that I still wasn't good enough.

Jensen held me for several long minutes as I stared at the door, which was red with rust streaks near the hinges.

"Did you know Marcos could juggle?" I said, trying to focus.

"How do *you* know that?" he asked.

"When I was preparing for this pitch over the last several months, I asked a few people in my classes to tell me their hidden talents." That was why I loved this idea so much. It allowed me to learn about people.

"That's cool," he said.

"Maybe you could be one of my student interviews. Like a real interview," I said, waving my pretend microphone in the air. "Not one of my fake ones. I can ask you about your rise to starting kicker and how it felt to wait in the wings for years." Assuming I was chosen. We'd find out today at lunch.

"Nobody wants to hear me complain," he said.

"Everybody likes a good underdog story, Jensen," I said.

"I guess."

The door whined as it opened, and I let out a surprised yelp.

"So jumpy," Jensen said.

"Kiss for luck?"

He pulled me against him and gave me a passionate kiss in front of that whole line of students, leaving me a little lightheaded. Cheeks flushed, I stumbled into the studio.

MY PITCH WENT WELL. REALLY WELL. I WAS WARM AND my voice was smooth and I even got in a witty aside on the spot. My transitions were on point, and as I stood and smiled at the senior interviewers and our broadcasting teacher, Mr. Whitley, I felt pretty confident.

I stepped outside, where Jensen still stood near the front of the line. I was surprised to see him. First period had started ten minutes ago.

"You didn't have to wait for me," I said, but it was sweet that he had.

He studied my face. "How did it go?"

"Great."

His brows shot down, and I got the weirdest feeling he was disappointed by that answer. I reached out my hand, ready to lead him away to where I could tell him all about the audition and then try to make it until lunch without losing my mind.

"Actually"—he pointed at the door, not taking my offered hand—"I think I'm going to try out."

"What?" I said, my heart jolting in my chest. It seemed to understand his meaning more than my brain did. I was so confused.

He didn't clarify; he just disappeared through the door with one small smile over his shoulder.

Mason, who was next in line, pointed at the closed door. "He totally cut the line."

Chapter
two

"YOU LOOK LIKE YOU'RE GOING TO PUKE," MY BEST friend, Deja, said when I found her in her first-period class. I waved to Mrs. Burns and pointed to Deja, asking without words if I could take her. Mrs. Burns nodded, probably thinking I was here on some official school business. I was not. This was absolutely personal.

I pulled her out of her seat and toward the door.

"What's happening?" she whispered as we went.

I didn't speak until we were all the way out of the room, down the hall, and outside under the nearest tree—a tall eucalyptus, its bark peeling off in strips.

"Is your grandma okay?"

I nodded and wanted to use that question to snap my focus back into perspective, but I was on the verge of tears. "Do you know where Jensen is right now? Well, he's probably done. It took me a while to get to this side of campus from the studio."

I swung my backpack to my front and dug my phone out. I wanted to see a message, any message, from him explaining what just happened.

"You're not making any sense," Deja said.

There was no message. "Sorry." I pointed in the general direction of the front office. "He tried out."

"Still not following."

"For the podcast. Jensen tried out for the school's podcast."

"Does *try out* mean something different than I think it means in the podcast world?"

"No."

"Tell me you're lying!" Of course Deja would be as shocked and confused about this as I was. As my best friend, she knew how long I'd been preparing for today. My preparation predated Jensen. It almost predated Deja. I'd met her in sixth grade when we both joined soccer. Unlike me, she was really good at it and had not quit last year. And although she wasn't happy with my decision and constantly tried to convince me to rejoin the team, we were still as close as ever.

"I'm not lying."

"Are you sure? Maybe it wasn't him. Maybe someone heard wrong . . . saw wrong."

"Me. I was the eyeballs on the scene. He literally walked in after me and said, *I'm going to try out.*" I said that last bit in a deep, stupid voice.

"A joke?" she said, still trying to make it make sense. "He's pranking you."

Was he? My sinking gut rose with that thought. "Maybe . . ." He wasn't a big prankster, but occasionally we played jokes on each other. "Do you think he's pranking me? Our one-year anniversary is this week. Maybe it's some anniversary joke?" I pushed my knuckle under my nose to relieve my burning eyes.

"It would be a good one."

"You're right." I sniffled, kicking at a strip of tree bark on the ground. "It would be. That has to be it. There is no other logical explanation."

"I mean, the only other logical explanation is that he's a terrible boyfriend, and person, but he's not. He's been decent."

"A ringing endorsement," I said.

"Well, anyone who hogs half my best friend's time isn't my *favorite* person."

He was one of *my* favorite people, though, and I needed what she was saying now to be true. He wouldn't do this to me.

My phone, which I was loosely holding in my hand, buzzed with a text from Jensen.

Where did you go?

"What is he saying?" Deja asked.

I turned my phone toward her.

"Hmm. That doesn't read like *Just kidding. Gotcha. You should've seen your face.*"

"If this is a joke, he'd play the long game. It's a joke."

To class, I typed back. *Why?*

Deja laughed. "You're going to pretend his joke is no big deal. I like it."

"He deserves it," I huffed. "I don't find this very funny at all."

"It's a little bit funny." She squeezed my arm. "Tell me how it plays out. I need to go back to the class you just pulled me from."

"Right . . . class. See you later when we can both laugh about this."

IT WAS LATER. I WASN'T LAUGHING. AT ALL.

It was lunch hour, and we, the group of juniors who had tried out that morning, sat outside the studio under some big shade trees. The studio was too small for us all to squeeze inside. Probably another reason the senior team was pretty small—two behind the mics, two on the soundboard, two researchers. Six people. I quickly counted the people sitting around me. There were twenty-five of us. I had about a one in four chance of making it on the team and a one in twelve chance of making it into my dream spot as one of the hosts.

Jensen, who was apparently going to play out this joke to the bitter end, was sitting next to me. He took my hand in his. When I saw him on the break between second and third period, he spent the whole ten minutes complaining about how his English teacher made them write poetry today and not a single word about his audition or why he decided to try out. Since I was not going to give his joke the satisfaction of a huge reaction, I didn't say a word either.

The six outgoing seniors stood in front of us. Nolen, the leader of the group, held a paper in his hand. He was well loved by the entire school, one of the voices we heard every morning and afternoon over the announcements and twice a week on the podcast, which was broadcast after school hours and I'd listened to religiously for the last five years.

"This year was very competitive. I know you've all been thinking about this moment for years, and it's not a decision we've taken lightly. We've analyzed and rearranged and debated. But we've finally come to a *nearly* unanimous decision."

Susie, the cohost, added, "We *almost* had two girls hosting the podcast next year. It was this close." She held up her pointer finger and thumb millimeters apart. "But we decided to go another way. We decided to think outside the box, perhaps bring a new audience to our show."

New audience? As in, they hoped some of the students who didn't listen to the show now would start listening because there was new blood involved? My stomach felt like it was collapsing in on itself.

A smile broke out on Nolen's face. "Jensen Ballard, dude, you made it as one of our hosts."

Jensen dropped my hand to pump his fist in the air and let out a loud whoop. The rest of the group clapped. One of the senior soundboard techs, standing on the far right, kept her hands firmly in her pockets. She looked angry. Guess I knew who kept the vote from being unanimous.

And I guess I knew this most definitely wasn't some elaborate prank Jensen had thought up. My stomach was sinking again. The only thing that could salvage this now was if I made it too. Jensen and I hosting the podcast our senior year together *could* be epic. Maybe Jensen had pitched some sort of love hotline where we could dole out relationship advice. Our sister school had done that

12

a couple years ago on their podcast. We'd be pretty good candidates for something like that. We had been rocking our relationship . . . until today . . . maybe.

I felt eyes on me, as if my friends thought one less hosting spot was my fault. I wanted to assure them that I was just as shocked as they were. That the big guy sitting next to me with the wide smile on his face had not run this by me first.

"Ava Lester," Susie said. "You made the other hosting spot. Congrats!"

Even though my stomach was now rock hard, I smiled over at Ava through the pain. Would it have been me and her if not for Jensen?

He mumbled something from beside me, but I couldn't hear him because blood seemed to be pumping a direct route through my ears. My eyes were stinging again. I was not going to cry over this. At least not in front of everyone.

Nolen said my name, maybe announcing another spot filled, but I didn't hear any recognizable words beyond that. There was more clapping as someone behind me gave an excited shout. My head throbbed to the beat of my pumping blood. Jensen grabbed my hand and squeezed. I pulled it free.

He gave me a confused look. Was he really confused?

Oh no. I was going to cry. I couldn't be here anymore. I stood. Nolen had obviously been in the middle of a sentence because he stopped.

"Finley?" he asked, waiting.

"Nothing, sorry, I have an appointment."

"Okay, thanks for your time."

I gave a short wave and left the group. I half walked, half stumbled my way over a grassy hill that led to the main corridor. Near the closest building, a group of students sat around eating lunch. The girls were showing each other videos on their phones, and some guys in their football jerseys were throwing empty chip bags and watching seagulls chase after them. Theo, the starting kicker, and Jensen's mortal enemy, leaned against the building, one earbud in, as if he was only barely interested in being with his friends. As if he was too good for everyone.

His eyes danced around me but never landed. I was invisible to him. Not that I cared.

I clenched my teeth, the football jersey he wore making my stomach even tighter. I pulled out my phone. *It wasn't a prank*, I typed into a text message to Deja as I walked past the squawking seagulls.

He's dead to me, she responded back fast. Then just as quickly added, *Wait, does this mean he actually made it?*

Yes.

My phone buzzed with another text. This one from Jensen. *Congrats on the research spot.*

I had made the team. I was one of the two researchers. This meant they liked my idea, just not the way I presented it? I wasn't good enough. This meant my senior year would be spent researching and developing potential podcast ideas for someone else. Would I feel just as upset if that someone else wasn't Jensen? The first tear escaped my eye and trickled down my cheek.

Another Jensen text buzzed through. *I know this was all unexpected, for me too, but I hope you can be happy for me.*

I stared at those words he had typed into his phone while sitting under that tree, surrounded by *my* friends. Was I being selfish? Jealous? Definitely that last one.

Is this something you even want? Like really want? I finally typed back.

Yes.

I released a sigh. Maybe I could eventually be happy for him. Just not today. Today I was sad for me.

NOPE. I COULDN'T BE HAPPY FOR HIM. EVER. THREE things happened that afternoon that made it impossible.

Deja and I had seventh period together, and next to me, she was bouncing between scoffing and quietly cursing. We were listening to the afternoon announcements, where the current podcast seniors were introducing next year's podcast team. Apparently, I was supposed to be there in the booth, but had fled the scene earlier so didn't get those details. And Jensen hadn't thought to tell me. Why would he? Secrets were his new thing, apparently.

That was the first thing that made happiness for his newfound success an impossibility.

The second thing was happening now while they interviewed him, the whole school, including Deja and me, forced to listen during the last fifteen minutes of our last class.

Susie had just asked him, "Tell the school, Jensen, the interesting idea you tried out with."

"Well, Susie," he said, "we thought it would be fun for the school to be given a weekly puzzle or challenge. It won't be some easy brain teaser. It will be something you really have to think about. The first person to solve it will have a chance to win prizes like maybe signed football gear or extra credit points for classes. If you have cool teachers, that is." He said this last bit with a charming laugh.

My fingers were curled around the edge of my desk, my knuckles white with the pressure.

"Am I just angry, or was that your idea?" Deja whisper-yelled next to me.

"Not the football gear stuff," I mumbled. But the rest, yes. That jerk tried out with my idea. My sadness from before was slowly bubbling up into anger, making my eyeballs hot and my chest burn.

Over the speakers, Susie laughed, then directed a question to Ava. Our class was losing interest, and low-speaking voices filled the room. Mr. Vasquez, sitting at his desk up front, looking at his phone, didn't seem to care.

"I hate him so much," Deja said.

My first instinct was to defend my boyfriend, but my clenched teeth made that impossible.

Nolen's voice rang out over the speaker, "Thanks for listening, everyone. I believe we have a killer team for next year."

"But you're stuck with us," Susie said. "For the rest of this year. Tune in today after school for our regular podcast hour!"

"Have a great weekend," Nolen said, and the others in the studio chimed in with goodbyes as well.

Deja turned her entire body toward me. "That was torture. I don't believe we'll have to hear his stupid voice every day next year."

"Yeah," I said, and was about to say more when the words "You all did great" came in Susie's voice from the speaker in the corner of the classroom.

"Turn off the mics," I said, as if Nolen or Susie would be able to hear me.

"Was it everything you always dreamed of?" Nolen asked.

"Yes," Ava said with an excited squeal.

"Never thought about it until now," Jensen said. "So not really."

Mr. Vasquez was staring at the speaker too, probably wondering if there was a way he could disable it from our end. There wasn't. It was controlled by the main panel in the studio.

"Did you and Finley break up or something?" Susie asked.

My heart jumped as I heard my name and registered the question. The rest of the class had quieted as well, suddenly interested in this unscripted conversation.

"No. Why?" he asked.

"Why?" Deja snorted from next to me. "Idiot."

"She's wanted this since freshman year," Susie said.

Seventh grade, I corrected her in my head. *I've wanted this since seventh grade.*

"I figured since you . . ." She trailed off, and now all eyes in the room were on me. I could feel them drilling into me from all sides.

Jensen laughed a little. "It's not my fault she doesn't have the voice, charm, or quick-thinking skills to host a podcast."

And there was the third thing. The nail in the coffin where our relationship would now lay to rest.

I wasn't sure how Susie reacted to Jensen's declaration, because everyone in the classroom, as though at once, let out a collection of noises: grunts, gasps, sighs, laughs.

17

"Settle down," Mr. Vasquez said while giving me an assessing look. I wondered what he thought I was going to do. Cry? Scream? My face felt hot, so I knew that at the very least I was bright red.

"Yep," I said aloud to lighten the mood and play this off like I wasn't crushed. "I'm known for my troll voice."

The class laughed, and I forced a smile.

"Hot mic," the deep voice of Mr. Whitley rang out over the speaker. Finally.

Jensen cussed right into that hot mic; then there was a pop, followed by several seconds of complete silence. Everyone in the class burst out laughing again. Except me and Deja, of course.

"Emergency meeting after school where we plot our revenge?" I said.

"That or murder," Deja said.

"Let's start with revenge."

Chapter three

REVENGE: THE MOST EFFECTIVE WAY TO GET OVER SOMEONE.

I had written those words at the top of a page in my notebook and held it up. We were sitting in a diner in Old Town called the Purple Starfish. It did not sell fish, and nothing was purple, not the walls or the booths or the tiles, not even any of the food. But Deja's parents owned the place, so she was the only one allowed to make fun of the name and she did, often.

The ocean, out the windows to my right, was rough today, the choppy water churning in the bay. I appreciated its support.

"I don't think that's how the saying goes," Lee said. His boyfriend, Maxwell, sat next to him, leaning forward, elbows on the table. The four of us had become friends freshman year when we were grouped together for a project in biology. The project consisted of explaining a science concept in a creative way. Most of the class did picture essays or science experiments. Maxwell had suggested we write a song explaining evolution to the tune of "Look What You Made Me Do" by Taylor Swift. I swear, Lee fell in love with him in that moment. We all did, really.

"Direct your negativity at ideas for payback," I said now, cradling my notebook. "Not at my very correct page header."

"What did Jensen say?" Deja asked, mopping a fry through a pile of ketchup from the basket of fries she'd collected from the kitchen herself. She was supposed to be working, but it was slow today. "Did he try to talk to you? Call you? Text you? I want to know how he attempted to defend himself."

I swallowed. I didn't want to share what he said; it's why I hadn't up until this point. I was embarrassed.

"Whatever he said," Deja added, seeming to sense why I wasn't sharing. "It's BS. It's his way to make *himself* feel better."

She was right. I pulled out my phone and cleared my throat, trying to muster up even more anger to outweigh the hurt. "He said, and I quote: *It was both of our ideas. Remember? We brainstormed. And I told the seniors that, by the way. It was the only reason you got picked for research and not left out completely. Because they thought you came up with two pretty solid ideas.*"

"No, he didn't," Maxwell said. "That's messed up."

"It's not true," Deja said, putting her hand on my forearm. "You know that, right? That was *your* idea. You told me about it weeks before you brainstormed with Jensen. And today you told me they almost picked two girls for the hosting spot. The other girl was you, Finley. He shouldn't have tried out, period, let alone stolen your idea to do it."

"Maybe the other girl wasn't going to be me," I said, my eyes on the window again. Pelicans were diving just off the boardwalk, taking advantage of the fish a group of sea lions must've corralled.

"It was," Lee said, pulling my attention back inside.

I wasn't so sure. Regardless, the thought fueled my anger.

"Did you talk to Nolen or Susie?" Deja asked. "Tell them he stole your idea?"

"And come off like the sore loser who wasn't chosen?" I asked. "You really think they'd believe me?" The idea of getting rejected again made me want to bury my head in the sand.

"Yeah, probably not," Deja said.

"What I can't believe is that he's trying to take credit for your research spot while at the same time stealing your dream spot," Max said.

I couldn't believe any of this. That my boyfriend, of all people, had done this to me. "My boyfriend," I said out loud. "He's still my boyfriend."

"You don't think he knows it's over?" Lee asked. "I mean, I would."

"You should definitely make it official," Maxwell said. "But no in-person meeting for him. He didn't follow any sort of social protocol in what he did. You shouldn't either. First on the revenge agenda, break up with him over text."

"I have the best friends," Deja said.

"To friends who love pettiness," I said, holding up my Coke, trying to bring some levity to this situation because otherwise I was going to burn from the inside out.

21

Lee and Maxwell bumped my cup with theirs, and Deja bumped with a fry.

The front door of the diner opened, and a group of four guys walked in. The seagull-teasing football players from school earlier. They had changed out of their jerseys. I was glad to see Jensen wasn't with them. Not that he would be, because his nemesis, Theo Torres, headed the group. He had the slightest limp, reminding me of his injury from four months ago. Something to do with his knee, if I remembered right. Whatever it was, it had allowed Jensen to score a much-needed field goal in the last game of the season. That clutch play, along with the fact that Theo was graduating, pretty much secured Jensen's place as the starting kicker next year.

Jensen really was going to have a perfect senior year. His dream, my dream, he got it all.

"Theo is so hot," Maxwell mumbled.

"Hello, I'm sitting right here," Lee said.

"You know he is," Max said.

Lee nodded. "Everyone knows he is."

Deja gave Theo an assessing look. "Yes, I think everyone does . . . including him."

I'd met him once before at a party I went to with Jensen, but we talked for less than ten minutes. I was sure Theo, Mr. Popular, didn't remember. I gave him a quick glance. "*I* don't think he's hot. And you're right—he's super cocky." That was one of the many complaints from Jensen over the last year. He was cocky and spoiled and selfish with his time and not as good as he thought he was and on and on.

"Exactly," she said.

Theo and his friends walked up to the counter, where Deja's mom took their order. He wasn't super tall, like Jensen, but he was strong. He had dark hair that he kept long all over. His skin was a golden brown, and he had thick lashes that curled up, making his eyes look like they were always smiling, mocking. His teeth were a bright white. And he didn't dress like he was about to work out at any moment like so many of the football players, including Jensen, did with their athletic shorts and sloppy tees or muscle shirts. He wore jeans and a purple tee with Vans.

"I would be cocky too if I looked like that," Maxwell muttered. Max was cute, but in a boyish way. He had a round face and a round body. A mop of red hair and freckles. Lee was handsome too: an Asian guy with spiky hair, kind eyes, and full lips. And Deja was gorgeous. She was Indian, with straight black hair and striking eyes.

"He thinks he's the king of his friend group, the king of school," I said.

"Isn't he?" Lee asked. "I don't really know Theo."

"He doesn't want to be known. He keeps his group small and acts like everyone else is beneath him. I don't even know if he likes his own friends," I added, picturing him with his earbuds in earlier . . . well, one earbud, but still. "And he could've been a mentor to Jensen, but instead he kept him down." I took a sip from my Coke.

"Retroactively, I've decided Jensen deserved it," Deja said.

I nodded slowly. "Yeah, maybe." I didn't know why it was hard for me to think of Jensen's past self as the same person who just screwed me over, but I needed to start. "Be right back. I need to pee."

In the bathroom, I shut and locked myself into a stall and took a deep breath. I hated thinking about Jensen and the fact that I could be so wrong about someone I'd been making out with for the last year. About someone I had genuinely cared about. What did that say about *me*?

As I was laying the seat protector on the toilet, I took in the graffiti lining the door and walls of the stall, written in colorful markers or ballpoint pens. *Yoga is life. The cow's name was Fred. I sell curses.* I gave a breathy laugh as I used the toilet, then flushed. After washing my hands, I joined the others at the table.

"How do your parents feel about all the bathroom graffiti?" I asked Deja.

She shrugged. "It's a never-ending battle, so they've stopped trying to clean it up. They only make me scrub the super-vulgar ones now."

"Then come be my lookout," I said. I had a couple markers still in my purse from the posters we'd made for the last football game of the season, which was over four months ago now. I really needed to clean out my purse more often.

"Your lookout for what?"

"I need to write a message in the boys' bathroom about Jensen."

Maxwell laughed. "Yes! With his phone number, right?"

"For sure," I said.

"What are you going to write?" she asked.

"Don't worry, you won't be on scrubbing duty."

Deja slid out of the booth and followed me to the bathroom.

I glanced around. "Don't let anyone in," I said, and kicked open the door with my foot. "Hello?"

I was met with silence, so I stepped in, letting the door swing shut behind me. I beelined it past the urinals and straight for a stall. I found an open space on the back of the door and wrote: *Looking for a good time or the love of your life? I could be either. I make dreams come true (mostly my own). Text me.* I added his number to the end and was starting on a little heart when the door creaked open.

"Don't rush me," I loud-whispered to Deja. "I'm writing a masterpiece."

When she didn't respond, I peered around the corner and locked eyes with Theo, whose brows rose in surprise. I would kill Deja later.

"Did I make a wrong turn?" he asked, but he didn't back out to look at the sign. He just stared at me, knowing full well that I was the one in the wrong place, not him.

I capped the Sharpie in my hand and channeled my embarrassment into snarkiness. "No, just posting some ads for the general public."

He strode to where I stood, and his gaze went to the door.

Okay, fine, if I disregarded Jensen's stories and the things I had witnessed, I could see that Theo was hot. Even more so up close. The ends of his hair brushed along his sharp jaw, and his shoulders seemed even wider this close. And he smelled good too, like soap and vanilla.

"Wouldn't joining an online dating site be easier?" he asked.

I forced my gaze back up to his eyes. "It might. But this is a gift for my ex, Jensen. This is his number." Technically not my ex but on his way to being my ex for sure.

25

"Jensen Ballard?"

"I only want the highest-quality people contacting him."

"Patrons of the Purple Starfish . . . bathroom?"

"Exactly." I cleared my throat and shut the bathroom stall. "He's told me a lot about you, by the way. Good to meet you."

Theo let out a scoffing laugh and looked around like this was the oddest place to meet someone. It probably was. "Did you say your *ex*?" he asked.

"Yeah, after what happened today . . ." I trailed off.

"What happened today?"

"You didn't hear?" Had he not been there for the end-of-school announcements? Even if he hadn't, the whole school was talking about it. The comments I'd gotten on the way to my car earlier threatened to redden my cheeks now.

"No. What?" he asked. I couldn't tell if he was serious in his ignorance. His expression was completely neutral.

"Nothing. We just broke up."

"And I should've heard about this?" he asked in a condescending way.

I sighed. "Can I help you?"

He let out a single laugh. "You're the one in the guys' bathroom writing sex ads for your ex-boyfriend."

I gasped. "It's not a . . . It's just an *I want him to get spammed* ad."

"Nice." He was judging me. He thought I was a bitter ex. And I was, but for perfectly reasonable reasons!

I held out the Sharpie. "Want to add anything?"

He smirked. "You seem to have it covered." With that he headed

26

to a urinal. "Are you going to stay for the show or . . . ?" He reached for the button on his pants.

"I'm leaving." I walked to the door.

"Oh, and by the way," he said as I gripped the handle, "we've met before, but Miss Soccer Star probably doesn't remember."

My mouth fell open as I rushed out the door. First, I wasn't a soccer star. Obviously, having quit. And even when I had been on the team, I was just average. Deja was the star. So he was probably mocking me with that title. Second, I had no idea he knew any facts about me at all, let alone that I had been on the soccer team. Third, this interaction didn't really change my opinion about him or his personality.

Deja was back at the table. I gave her a *why did you abandon me?* face as I approached.

"Sorry," she said. "I had to help my mom with drinks for a second. Nobody was coming."

"Theo came in," I said.

She laughed so hard she snorted.

"It's fate, karma," Max said.

I slid into the booth, gripping the notebook I had left on the table. "What does it have to do with fate *or* karma?"

"Fate is telling you that you should try to date him," Maxwell said. Then he waved a finger at my notebook. "He's your ex's nemesis. That should be top on your list of revenge ideas. Jensen would be crushed if you dated Theo."

"No," Deja said. "You don't need any more jerks in your life."

"Seriously," Lee said.

Max shrugged. "I'm just saying. . . ."

I thought about it for a second. He was right—Jensen would be crushed. But even if Theo *wanted* to date me, which was a very low possibility at this point, I decided that using someone to hurt someone else wasn't going to make the list. "No, this list will only include ways to stick it to Jensen. No collateral damage." Not that I thought I could damage Theo, probably the exact opposite, but still.

"I have a revenge idea," Lee said. "How about you only suggest terrible ideas for the podcast. Since you're the research specialist now and since he has no original ideas."

"Yes, absolutely." I wrote that down.

Theo and his friends across the diner laughed about something. When I looked over, our eyes met. I raised my eyebrows in a challenge, and he smirked back. Great, he was probably sharing the bathroom story. As if I needed another reason for the whole school to be talking about me. I turned my attention back to my friends. "First things first. I have a text to compose."

My phone was on the table, and I picked it up. It felt weird to break up with Jensen over text. But why shouldn't I? He'd told the whole school I wouldn't make a good podcast host. I had spent hundreds of dollars on equipment and many years trying to be just that.

"Compose it out loud," Lee said as he watched me staring at my phone.

"*Dear Jensen,*" I said.

"No *dear,*" Deja interrupted.

"*Jensen,*" I said, deleting the *dear.*

28

"Jerk face?" Maxwell suggested.

"Selfish pig?" Lee offered.

I smiled. "I think I'll stick with *Jensen*—that way he doesn't know what's coming right away."

"Good call," Lee said.

I turned my attention back to my phone. *"Jensen, after today, I don't think—"*

"Too nice," Deja said.

I grunted. *"Jensen, you know what you did."*

"And you know what I have to do," Max said in a deep voice.

Deja laughed.

"You know what you did," I repeated. *"Don't pretend I should've seen this coming. Don't pretend that me feeling blindsided makes me a bad, unsupportive girlfriend. You are the one who destroyed anything we could've had. . . ."* I trailed off, not sure if this was what I wanted to say at all. It was too little and maybe too much. He didn't deserve to know I felt destroyed. What I really wanted to write was something sarcastic like *Jensen, it's been real but apparently not real enough because who knew you were such a jerk.*

"It's good," Deja encouraged, getting me out of my head.

"Can you add *buttface* to the end there?" Maxwell said.

Lee reached out and patted my arm. "How about you just add *it's over.*"

I nodded, typed those two words to the end of my text and pushed send.

It was over.

My eyes pricked, and I clenched my teeth to keep the tears

at bay. I looked at my notebook full of half-baked, not-nearly-big-enough ideas for revenge. "He stole my dream," I said out loud. "I need to figure out how to *obliterate* his."

"Football?" Max whispered reverently.

I nodded. "Somehow, we have to take football away from him."

Chapter four

I FIGURED.

"I figured." I read it out loud this time to see if it sounded different when spoken than it did in my head. It didn't. That was Jensen's response to my breakup text. Not him defending himself, not him trying to explain why he did what he did or that he was sorry or that he would quit the podcast because he loved me so much. That he was destroyed because he'd destroyed us.

I figured.

"Ugh!" I should've sent the jerk text I'd composed in my head. I hit the steering wheel with both hands.

I was in my car, parked on the street in front of my house after coming home from the diner. I had just pulled up and turned off the ignition when I got the text. I screenshotted the response and sent it to the group chat Maxwell had started titled *Petty Queens*.

He did not! Max responded first.

Deja was next: *There are no words to describe how much I hate him right now!*

Sorry, babe. That was Lee.

Lee was picking up on my hurt side more than the others, and even though that was so him of him, I didn't want to be hurt. I wanted to be angry. I *was* angry.

Don't you dare respond to him, Deja added.

Wasn't planning on it. If I could delete him from my brain, I would. I settled for blocking him on my phone. After that I gave a satisfied nod and climbed out of my car.

I grabbed my backpack off the passenger seat and walked through the front door to find my mom scooping something up off the floor and dropping it onto a plate.

"Hi," I said, closing the door behind me. "Grandma?"

She blew at a strand of hair that had fallen across her eyes. "Yes."

My grandma was one of my favorite people in the whole world. She was also becoming less and less like my grandma. She was in the beginning stages of Alzheimer's, and some days were harder than others. My mom took care of her, along with a nurse who came in the mornings while my mom went to work.

She took care of me the first twenty years of my life, I'm going to take care of her the last twenty years of hers, my mom often said. I hoped Grandma had twenty years left. I thought that was optimistic, but hope never hurt anyone, including me.

"What can I do?" I picked up a carrot that had somehow ended up by the front door. I tried my best to help Mom when I could because my dad worked a lot and my older brother had moved out several years ago to go to college, but I knew Mom handled the majority of the work.

Mom pointed at the plate she held. "Will you go make sure Grandma is in her bedroom? That's where she went after spilling this."

"Okay." I set the carrot onto the plate as I walked by.

Mom called after me, "Did you go somewhere after school?"

"Yeah, sorry, I should've texted. I went to the diner with Deja and the guys."

"It's fine," Mom said. "Glad you had fun."

I hadn't said anything about fun. But I also hadn't said anything about revenge, and I would keep it that way too. Mom was all about forgiveness and moving forward with dignity. And sure, that was all good in theory, but in reality, sometimes people deserved a little karma. And sometimes, karma needed a little help.

I threw my backpack into my room, the first door on the right, as I walked to my grandma's room, last door on the left, across the hall from my parents.

"Hey, Grams," I said, letting myself into her room.

She was pacing back and forth mumbling something about how Mom should've known she hated carrots. How she'd always hated carrots.

"Hey, Grandma," I tried again.

She stopped pacing and looked at me for a beat too long. I braced myself. She had yet to forget who I was, but one day she would and I couldn't handle that day being today. Today was already terrible enough.

"Oh, Finley," she said, and I let out a relieved breath. "Hello, my lovely girl. How was school?"

"Just okay today."

"Where is Jensen?" Grandma loved Jensen. He always told her how beautiful she was and would often sneak her little chocolate treats because my mom limited her sugar intake. She would recount old movies to him, and he would tell her about the comic books he'd read as a child. I did not want to tell Grandma her boyfriend broke up with us. Well, I broke up with him, but he pretty much made the decision the second he walked into that studio to steal my dream.

But I needed to just get it over with. "We broke up, Grandma."

"What? Why?"

"It's a long story. I guess I didn't know him very well."

She clucked her tongue in disappointment but aside from that was calmer than I expected her to be. "That's too bad. I wanted to show him my nails." She held up her hand. "Betsy did them." Betsy was her nurse.

"You can show *me* your nails."

"I *am* showing you."

I laughed. "You are. They're pretty."

"I know," she said.

"Are you up for an interview?" I had started a podcast about six months ago called *It's About Us* where I interviewed my grandma about her life. Next to nobody listened to it, but it was good to get her stories down while she remembered them. And it was good practice for me. It's what ultimately gave me the idea for my audition. An idea that had obviously done nothing for me.

"Not today, honey. Is that okay?" She lowered herself into a chair by the window.

"Of course." I wasn't exactly up for the reminder of my failure either. "Can I get you anything?"

"My book." She pointed to her nightstand, where books were stacked.

Her room was relatively clean, but there were also things from when she lived in her own house scattered throughout: an old clock that chimed every hour; Styrofoam faceless heads holding her wigs, which she rarely wore anymore; stacks of old magazines that she refused to throw away and would often flip through; a basket full of oils and balms that she rubbed on her knuckles every night to help with her aching joints. It wasn't a lot, though.

About five years ago, Grandma started a fire in her house after forgetting about a pan of hot oil she'd left on the stove. She ended up losing almost everything in that fire, including her ability to live by herself.

I plucked the top book off the stack and handed it to her. "What's it about?" I asked.

"Love," she said wistfully. "Like the best ones always are."

My grandpa had died over ten years ago. Most of the time she remembered that. Sometimes she didn't. On both sides of the memory fence, my grandma was still a hopeless romantic. Another reason I wasn't going to tell her about the jilted tale of revenge I was now embarking on.

I left Grandma reading in her chair and made my way to the kitchen, where my mom was loading the dishwasher.

"She is in her room safe and reading," I said.

"Good. Thank you." She added a plate to the bottom rack of the dishwasher. "How did your audition go?"

"I made it onto the team as one of the research specialists." I tried to say it with as much excitement in my voice as I could, but it was a poor showing.

She turned off the faucet and faced me. Her hands were dripping water down to her elbows, then onto the floor. "Honey, I'm so sorry."

I shrugged, a lump suddenly in my throat. "What can I say? They only want me for my brains, I guess."

"Good thing you have your own podcast," she said.

I let out a fake laugh. "My podcast that has two consistent listeners? One of them being *you*. No way I'm going to get that internship now."

"Not with that attitude," she teased.

What other attitude was there? I'd worked toward this for years, and now I was facing reality. I didn't get what I wanted. The host spot directly led to the internship at the community college. It was just a fact. It had for as long as both programs had been in existence. And that internship spot often led to the UC hosting spot. Jensen had more than derailed my senior year today. He'd derailed my future. "It's been a day, Mom. Can I just whine about it for a little bit before you expect me to save the world?"

She shook her head, a guilty look coming onto her face. "I'm sorry. Of course. Whine away." She winked. "Then save the world."

"Maybe an opportunity will come up next year where I can fill in or something. I'm on the team." Maybe Jensen would get sick . . . or move. A girl could dream.

36

She stood there, elbows dripping, studying my face. Probably looking for a crack, wondering if I was going to break. I wasn't. And if I kept telling myself that, it would be true.

She finally grabbed a dish towel from the counter and wiped her hands and arms. "You eating dinner with us, or did you eat with your friends?"

I let out a breath, glad she was moving on. "I only had fries."

"Will Jensen be joining us for dinner as well?"

I couldn't hold back the long sigh that escaped my body. We were going to get all the hard topics out at once. "We broke up," I said.

Mom, who had turned back to the counter, adding some utensils to the dishwasher, whirled around. "What?" She was holding a fork in the air, and her eyes were wide. "Why?"

"I don't feel like talking about it right now." Or ever, really.

How could I explain to my mom that not only did I fail at making it into the position I'd been working so hard for, but that it was stolen from me by my boyfriend who had zero experience and, before today, zero desire? What did that say about my ability? What did that say about my *relationship*?

"Are you okay?" she asked.

"I will be."

"Grandma is going to be so sad."

I laughed. "She seemed fine, but she probably did like him more than I did." My eyes found a Zelda mug on the counter. My Christmas gift to my older brother, Corey, who had come home for the holidays. Corey must've forgotten it. A flood of hurt washed over me about how easy I was to dismiss, how underwhelming I felt in all aspects of my life.

It's just a mug, Finley.

"You had a really tough day," Mom said.

I cleared my throat so I could speak normally. "I did."

"And yet you seem . . ." She studied my face.

I smiled to sell it.

". . . okay about all this?"

That's because I was going to be. I had a goal, a good one. It had taken over every other emotion and thought in my body. Revenge. And I needed to make sure I wasn't underwhelming at it.

Chapter
five

NOW THAT I'D MADE THE PODCAST TEAM, INSTEAD OF the normal broadcasting class I'd been taking the first part of the school year, I got to switch over to the mentorship program with the podcast seniors for the rest of the year. I walked the hall now, heading toward the library conference room where that program would be held. Had things happened differently, I would've been practically skipping down the corridor in happy anticipation, but as it was, I was trying my best to keep my head down.

It wasn't working. People were calling out things like *Let's hear that terrible voice* or *Charm is overrated* or *Think fast.* All in reference to the things Jensen had announced to the entire school about my subpar abilities. I was not looking forward to seeing Jensen for the first time since Friday.

Jensen. What class was he going to have to drop to slide into this hour? He hadn't taken a single broadcasting class in his life.

"Now I understand the bathroom ad," Theo said, falling into step beside me.

"What?" I had been so in my head that I hadn't seen him approach. *Had* he approached? Or had we just both been walking in the same direction?

He tucked his earbud into his pocket. "Next time I visit that particular bathroom, I'll add a line or two."

"What?" Was that the only word I knew how to say now? My brain wasn't quite understanding what he was implying with this conversation. Was he just making fun of me about the bathroom graffiti again?

"Theo!" someone called from across the way. "The rally Friday was epic."

He raised his hand like he was a celebrity who couldn't be bothered to respond with words.

"So epic," I said sarcastically. "You stood off to the side and watched your teammates table surf."

"You know exactly where I was standing?" he asked, that mocking glint in his eyes.

I was mad at myself that, yes, I had noted where he was standing. "You too good to participate in school-sponsored activities to unite the student body?"

"We all are, Finley."

"Most of us aren't asked to," I said. Only the elite.

"The bathroom ad," he said, bringing us back to his initial topic, apparently the only reason he was talking to me, and the one thing I didn't want to discuss. "I heard the story of why you broke up. Brutal."

Of course he had. This was even more embarrassing than being caught in the bathroom with a Sharpie. "Yeah, it's no big deal."

"No big deal?" Theo asked, confused or appalled, I couldn't decide. "The guy publicly skewered you to the whole school. Spelled out all your weaknesses. That's no big deal?"

I stopped and whirled on him. Somebody walking behind me nearly ran me over but avoided me just in time, adding a "Good thing I'm a quick thinker, Finley" to his sidestep.

My face burned red, but I tried to ignore it. Theo had stopped as well and stood there with an innocent expression.

"Those aren't my weaknesses. I would've killed it as the podcast host. He has zero experience," I tried to say with confidence, but I sounded like I felt, defeated.

"He hasn't even started, and he already has the whole school talking about the podcast. Maybe experience doesn't matter."

"Obviously," I said, and continued walking, so over this conversation with a person who I thought would've been on my side about this. Maybe Theo didn't hate Jensen as much as Jensen had claimed. Or maybe Theo was just trying to irritate me. It was working.

The late bell rang overhead, and I glanced around to see the once-busy halls were now empty. I would have to walk into my first day of mentorship late. Great first impression.

"Good luck!" he yelled.

I flipped him off even though it really wasn't Theo I was mad at. I was frustrated at the entire situation Jensen had created for me. Theo, I could ignore.

He just laughed as he walked away.

"Nice of you to join us, Finley," Nolen said when I slipped into the conference room in the library. Headphones and microphones not plugged into anything sat on the table in front of him like we were going to do a mock podcast today.

There was an open chair by Ava on the end of the long table closest to me, so I took it. "Sorry. Got held up."

"We missed you at the end-of-day announcement Friday too," Susie said.

"Yeah, I didn't know we were supposed to be there. Sorry." My eyes drifted to Jensen with a cold stare.

Surprisingly he was staring straight back and his eyes seemed soft, apologetic even. That confused me more than if I'd been met with an equally cold stare. His actions to this point hadn't indicated any form of remorse. Maybe he'd analyzed things. I quickly averted my gaze and pulled out a notebook. I turned back the front cover, only to see my revenge list. I shut it and looked around to see if anyone noticed. Everyone was focused up front.

Nolen smiled. "Since we have some new people in the group, for the next week we're going to cover some basics of podcasting, to help get everyone up to speed."

"Basics?" I asked, unable to keep my irritation inside. For the *one* new person in the room?

Nolen stopped and looked at me. "Everyone benefits from a review session."

This time I did keep my words in my mouth.

"We'll make it fun," Susie said. "Please partner up, and we'll hand out a review sheet."

No joke, Jensen met my eyes again. That was not happening.

I turned to Ava. "You want to partner?"

"Absolutely," she said.

"Actually," Nolen said to Ava, "I want you and Jensen partnering for most projects. You need a jump start on some chemistry with each other and more practice interacting since Jensen hasn't been part of our group for the last several years. I promise you'll thank me when it helps you interact more naturally on air."

"Sorry," Ava whispered to me.

"It's fine." It wasn't her fault Jensen was a ruiner of all things.

"We'll walk around and give you tips and tricks for some of the concepts on the sheet."

Susie passed out the review, and Ava stood and tentatively made her way over to Jensen at the other end of the long table.

I hadn't noticed before, with the seniors filling in seats, but there was an odd number of juniors today, which left me partnerless.

I leaned back in my chair and opened my notebook again. I was still working through exactly how I was going to accomplish the goal of taking football from Jensen. But in the meantime, I'd been adding smaller ideas for revenge to the list as they came to me or when Deja, Maxwell, or Lee suggested something good in our Petty Queens group chat. Even though the list was decent, I'd yet to actually do anything on it aside from the bathroom thing, which had been more of a whim. It was time to change that.

"OUR REVENGE CHOICES TODAY, FRIENDS," I SAID. "ARE the following . . ." Deja, Maxwell, Lee, and I were sitting in my car in the parking lot after school. "We can sell all his things that he's left at my house for a couple dollars online and then send him the receipt of what we sold."

"That was my idea," Deja said proudly. "I still like it a lot."

"Could I get arrested for that?" I asked, curious.

"I don't think so," Maxwell said. "He left them at your house. Assumed property?"

I wasn't sure if that was true at all, but I continued to read, *"Make an online post about his wrongdoing and hope it goes viral."*

"We'd kind of just have to pray to the social media gods for that one," Lee said.

"Yeah," I agreed. "Plus, the whole story makes me feel stupid. I really don't need everyone knowing. It's bad enough the entire school does. Theo even heard the story today and approached me about it."

"Speaking of gods, what did he have to say?" Maxwell asked.

Lee smacked his arm, and Max laughed.

"He just wanted to point out that since the whole school was talking about it, Nolen and Susie made the right choice putting Jensen as the host."

"Ew," Deja said, her dark eyes flashing irritation. "Stay away from him."

"What about Jensen?" Lee asked. "You never said how the first time seeing him again went."

"He gave me puppy-dog eyes like he was actually sorry."

"He *should* actually be sorry," Lee said.

"But if he was actually sorry," Deja pointed out, "he would've quit the podcast once he realized what he'd done. He's not actually sorry. He wants his cake, and he doesn't want you to be mad at him for eating it too."

"That made zero sense," Lee said.

"I understood," Maxwell said.

"What else is on the list?" Lee asked.

I scanned the page and settled on *"Call his work and pretend he gave me bad service?"* He worked at a tire repair place in town.

"You can't call," Deja said. "They'll recognize your voice."

"I'll call," Maxwell said. "I am happy to assist in his downfall." He pulled out his phone and dialed.

Chapter
SIX

"NO, GRANDMA, JENSEN WON'T BE COMING OVER TODAY. Remember, we broke up?"

"You broke up?" Her eyes went glassy. "Why?"

We sat in my room at my desk. I hooked up the headphones and microphones and powered them on, making sure everything was properly plugged into the soundboard.

"Long story, Grandma." And regardless of the things I was doing to get back at him, like the call Max had placed after school on Monday, leaving a bad review at his work, making him pay was still the first thing I thought about when I woke up. It didn't help that the gossip and comments hadn't settled at school even though it had been almost a week.

She flipped the headphones over but didn't put them on. "I like long stories."

It hadn't occurred to me at first, but I now realized that at this stage in my grandma's illness this would be a story I was going to have to tell over and over again. So far, I had told her every day since Friday. It was now Wednesday. And yet my stomach still clenched as I said it. "He didn't care about me. That's the bottom line."

"Of course he did, honey. He told me he did all the time."

"But at the end of the day, when he had to show it, he proved that words are just words. Actions are more important."

"Actions are very important," she said.

"Let's talk about you now," I said, ready to change the subject. Maybe this would help me forget about my problems for at least a little while. I put my headphones on, and she followed suit.

My interviews with my grandma were a history of her life. We'd talked about her parents and their love story and what she remembered about them; then we'd moved on to her and her childhood. Her early school years. We'd left off with her moving with her family to California from the Midwest when she turned fourteen and how out of place she'd felt.

"How long did it take you to make friends once you were here, Grandma?"

"We moved into this little yellow house by the beach. You've seen it." Grandma always played with the cord of the headphones when she talked. Sometimes it made a scratchy sound on the recording that I had to minimize in edits.

"I have. It was so cute."

"I miss that house."

"Did you love it right from the start?"

"I didn't love anything about this place from the start. I missed my friends and my grandparents. I missed the trees and how it would get so cold in the winter that I could feel it in my bones. I didn't feel that here. Every day I would go out to the beach and wish I was back at my old house in my old life."

"The Pacific Ocean is very offended by that," I said with a smile.

"The ocean got over it years ago," she joked back.

"What happened to change your feelings about this place?"

"Time, I guess. And exploring. I'd spend hours in the rocks and tidepools. Sometimes the sand on the hill was smooth like glass and I'd slide down it on my bare feet, leaving trails behind me. During off season, I'd sit on the deck of one of the locked lifeguard towers and watch the surfers. It was there I met a surfer named Andrew for the first time. He walked over, his board tucked under his arm, and asked if I was ready to save him should the need arise."

"And what did you say?"

"I said, *I'm not equipped to save anyone. We'd both end up drowning.* Then he said, *So you'd just watch me go down.* I responded with *I'd scream, at the very least.*"

I laughed. "A very morbid first conversation, Grandma."

"He liked to joke around, I learned. It was part of his personality. Everyone seemed to know and like him. He'd secure us free baked goods from the shopkeepers and free boat rides."

"You went on boat rides with strangers?"

"Yes, especially during whale-watching season. The wind was cold and would whip through my hair as I stood searching the water for them. We once went on a fishing boat too and helped pull up traps. It was a different time."

"Not that different. Never go on boat rides with strangers, listeners."

"Who is listening?" Grandma asked. "Anyone we know?"

"Basically Mom," I said. "Maybe Corey if he's not too busy for us."

"Hi, Corey," Grandma said. "Come visit me."

"He was just here," I said.

Grandma was thoughtful for a moment. I'd edit out her silence later. It was interesting to me how she could remember her childhood in detail but last week was hard for her. The doctor said that was typical of her illness.

"Tell me more about this surfer," I prompted. "It sounds like you became friends."

"Yes, we did. He was a firecracker."

"Like you?" I asked.

She patted my hand. "Like you, baby girl. Keep your explosive spirit. It will help you make your dreams come true."

I swallowed, a lump rising up my throat. Maybe I wasn't like my grandma thought because all my dreams seemed to be slipping through my fingers. Maybe I'd never had a tight hold on them to begin with. "I'm trying, Grandma."

"I know you are."

I shifted the subject back to her. "So, uh, Andrew?"

"That first meeting was an entire year after we moved here. I was fifteen. I would walk the beach as the sun rose, and he was out there nearly every morning. I'd end up at that lifeguard tower, watching. He was like a skater on ice, graceful and athletic."

"Sounds like he was a pro or something."

"He was very good. I didn't think he noticed me. But then he came out of the water, asking me if I'd save him. Months later, he approached me again with his board and said, *Do you want to take it for a spin?* I said, *I don't know how to surf.* He said, *You learn things by trying them, not by watching them.*"

I took her hand in mine because she was twisting the cord again and I didn't want the feedback. "What did you say?"

"I said, *I learn things faster with a teacher.*"

"Grandma, you were a flirt," I said with a laugh.

"He was very handsome and I hadn't experienced much rejection yet, so I was bold."

"Is that what makes us less bold? Rejection?"

She met my eyes, and it was like her soul could see into mine. "It certainly has the ability to make us second-guess ourselves, doubt our abilities. Don't you think?"

I nodded, which was such a rookie podcast move. Listeners couldn't hear a nod. "Yes, I agree," I said, finding my voice.

"But I was fifteen and I thought I could conquer the world," she said.

"What did he say when you implied he should teach you?"

"He said, *I'm an excellent teacher.* And he was." She pointed to some pictures I had up on my wall of me and Deja and Lee and Maxwell. "Can you get my pictures, hon? I have some from that summer."

I cringed. I hated reminding her of this fact, but she forgot often. "Um, you had a house fire and lost your pictures." She seemed to be having a good memory day today, so I thought she could handle that news.

"Oh . . . right. My surfboard? That wasn't in the fire. I can show you that."

"Uh . . . I don't think you had a surfboard," I said. I didn't even know my grandma had ever surfed. This was the first I was hearing about it. "Did you actually learn how to surf that summer?"

"I did have one," she said. "Andrew gave it to me. He'd painted on it. It was beautiful. I had it."

Sometimes she went from zero to agitated really fast, and I sensed that was going to happen now. "You did," I said, trying to appease her. "I don't know where it is."

She settled a bit. "I better go ask Debra if she's seen it." Debra was my mom. Grandma took off her headphones and left me sitting there at the desk.

"That's it for today," I said. Her exit might've been abrupt for me, but I needed to make it a little less so for my audience. "Thanks for listening. If you have any questions you'd like to ask my grandma, feel free to DM me on my linked socials." I almost felt stupid saying that. My family could text me if they wanted Grandma to answer specific questions. They'd yet to do that.

I stopped the recording, then went back and listened to it from the beginning to make edits. The episode was about ten minutes. Keep them short to match people's attention spans was my thinking. But that strategy obviously hadn't helped. No new listeners were adding my podcast to their queues. Nobody was stumbling upon it. Not that I thought my grandma's story was a gripping tale, but I did think, even by accident, that it might get a few more listens.

My stats hadn't budged, though. Two whole listeners had heard the last episode.

I sighed as my recorded voice said another *uh*. I needed to curb my use of filler words. And when had I started laughing like that?

There was a knock at my door followed by my mom stepping into my room. "What's so funny in here?" she asked, obviously having heard my attempts to rerecord the perfect laugh.

"How come nobody told me I laugh like a hyena?"

"What?"

I pointed to my recording equipment.

"I love your laugh. It's cute." She kissed the top of my head.

"Real-life cute, not on-air cute."

"Not sure what that means," she said. "But Dad made dinner. It's ready."

"Okay, I'll be right there."

She walked back to the door. "Don't fake your laugh," she said, and then was gone.

I listened one more time to the replacement laughs I had recorded. I decided on one, then meticulously blended it into the existing dialogue. "Yes, better," I said when I listened this time.

I stared at the publish button, ready to release the episode into the world, but I paused. What was the point? I could just email it to my mom and brother. They were the only ones who cared.

I closed my computer without pushing publish.

Chapter
seven

"A PARTY," I SAID THE NEXT DAY AS I INTERCEPTED DEJA getting out of her white Honda in the school parking lot.

"What?" she asked. "It's too early to read your mind."

Lee and Maxwell had parked close as well, and Maxwell called out while heading our way, "You better not be discussing plans without us!"

"We need to find or throw or be at a party where all the football players are," I said when they reached us.

"Why?" Lee asked.

"Oh!" Maxwell said. "So you can look hot and Jensen can see you and you can make out with another guy?"

"No." I sighed, adjusting my backpack on my shoulder. "I told you I'm not going to use someone else to punish Jensen."

"Just be up front with said other person. Say, *Can I make out with you because of what Jensen did to me?* I guarantee anyone would say yes."

"You *cannot* make that guarantee."

"Then why the party?" Lee asked, bringing us back to the point.

"I need to infiltrate the team, somehow turn them against Jensen."

"Can the team vote him out?" Lee asked.

"I wish," I said. "No, the coach makes those decisions." Even though I didn't know much about the inner workings of football, I knew this was true from soccer. "But if the whole team is against him, maybe he'll quit or at the very least be completely miserable. And that will make me happy right here." I pointed to my heart.

"He'll be so embarrassed when the whole team hates him," Max said with a giddy look of anticipation.

The first bell rang.

"Yes, I agree with your party idea," Deja said. "Make that happen." The guys nodded as well, and since our classes were in different directions, like every morning, we went our separate ways.

As I walked across the parking lot, I must have been in my head, not paying attention, because a car squealed to a stop inches from my leg. I met Jensen's eyes through the windshield. One hand had flown up out of instinct and was now resting on the hood of his car. My other hand was on my chest in surprise.

He threw his car into park, right there in the middle of the lane, and jumped out. "Are you okay? Did I hit you?"

I took several deep breaths and straightened up, assessing. Had he? My heart was racing, but my body felt intact. Untouched. "No, you didn't. I'm fine."

Relief poured down his face. "Sorry, babe. I mean Finley. I didn't see you."

"You *do* know how to say that word," I said. My backpack felt tight on my shoulders, and I wondered if I was sucking in too much air. Again, I tried to slow my breathing.

"What?" he asked. Someone laid on their horn behind him. He looked back, and his face went dark. I wasn't sure why. To me, he said, "*Sorry?* Is that what you're saying? That I should apologize for the podcast thing?"

"For saying I was terrible to the whole school? For stealing my idea? Yes!"

"I don't think that's what you're really mad about. You're really mad about me earning your spot. The other stuff doesn't matter to you."

Anger coursed through my veins. How dare he tell me what I was *really* angry about. And how dare he be so wrong. The car behind him, a black BMW with tinted windows, backed up and parked.

"All of it matters, Jensen," I said.

"Well, I'm sorry," he said in a quiet voice.

If I thought those words would help at all, I was mistaken, they didn't.

Theo exited from the BMW and on his walk past us said, "Move your scrap metal, Second String—it's in everyone's way."

Jensen shot him a look but didn't reply. A week ago, Theo's dig at Jensen's place on the football team would've made me mad. Today, not so much.

Jensen's eyes were back on me and he said, "I should . . ."

"Go," I said. "I don't want to talk to you."

His shoulders rose, then fell. "Once you're done being angry, can we just—" He took a step forward, attempting to brush my arm.

I stepped back before his hand connected. "Never. I will never be done."

He sighed, climbed into his car, and, since I was now out of the way, continued down the lane. I whirled around. Ahead, I saw Theo. I increased my speed, not to catch up with him, but because I was going to be late. We stepped onto the curb from the parking lot at the same time. His soapy vanilla scent invaded my space.

He gave me a sideways glance. "You get back together with your boyfriend?"

I gasped. "After what he did? Never."

"Didn't you say what he did was no big deal?"

"I lied because you were annoying me."

He let out a surprised laugh.

I pushed ahead but then hesitated, slowing until he was by my side again. "You're not throwing a party this weekend, are you?"

"This weekend? As in tomorrow?"

"Or the day after."

"You looking to party?"

I was so not *looking to party*. "Something like that."

He was thoughtful for a moment before he said, "Yes, there will be a party at my place this weekend."

"Can I come?" We walked toward the science building. I wasn't sure what he had first period, but that's what I had.

"Didn't you flip me off the other day?" he asked.

"Yes, I did."

He smiled. "And now you want to come to one of my parties?"

And now I needed to be in a place where a large number of football players would be gathering. "Yes."

He tilted his head toward me, giving me the once-over, as if deciding if I was worthy enough to attend. "Just don't announce it on the podcast. I'm not inviting the world."

Of course he wasn't. "One, I don't announce anything on the podcast. I don't speak. Two, that's not the kind of thing we would put on the podcast."

"What would you put on the podcast?" he asked as we rounded the first building and entered the covered corridor.

"You've never listened to it?"

"Is it good? Should I?"

"I don't know your taste. Some years are better than others. I like it."

"You've been listening to it for *years*?"

"No comment." I didn't want to discuss just how deep Jensen's betrayal went with Theo, of all people.

He didn't seem to need me to elaborate. "That's some serious dedication for someone to come along and steal it out from under you."

"Are you the king of unhelpful statements?"

"Just keeping it real."

"Well, don't," I said. "My life is already real enough right now." Who knew that one decision a year ago, the decision to date Jensen, would change so much of my future. In the alternate universe of my life where I didn't date him, would he have still tried out for the podcast without my idea, without seeing me practice? "Today would've been our one year," I realized out loud.

"Really?" he said. "Do you want me to say happy anniversary or . . . what's the protocol on this?"

"Definitely no."

"At least you dodged a bullet, right?"

"Did I, though?" It felt like I'd been hit right in the heart. My future self bleeding everywhere.

He reached out, without thinking, it seemed, and squeezed my arm, as though validating my pain. Then, just as fast, his hand was back at his side. So fast, I thought maybe I imagined it.

"What was your idea for the podcast?"

"What?" I asked, still confused over the unexpected contact.

"You said Jensen tried out with one of your ideas. What was the one *you* tried out with?"

Had I said that? I didn't think I had told him that Jensen tried out with my idea. Whoever ended up telling him the story of what happened must've known. "I wanted to interview a new student every week. Get to know our classmates better." I shrugged, feeling a little embarrassed by the idea now. It obviously wasn't as good as I thought.

"They thought that was too boring?" he asked, as if those were *his* thoughts on why I didn't make it.

I held back a sigh. "Guess so." I stopped outside the science building wondering if he was going to follow me in, but right when I grabbed the handle, he turned the other way. "So the party?" I called after him.

"Tomorrow at seven, Soccer Star!"

"A SEGWAY?" JENSEN ASKED. "ISN'T THAT ONE OF THOSE two-wheeled electric scooter things? Finley and I rented one of those over the summer. Right, Finley?"

The heads around the table swung in my direction.

When I didn't answer, Susie said, "No, Jensen, a *segue*. A smooth transition from one subject to the next. You should have some in your arsenal for when you need to change topics quickly so it won't be so jarring for the listeners. Eventually they'll come to you more naturally, but for now, memorize a few."

"Oh, right. Okay." He was wearing the headphones that weren't plugged into anything. "Which ones do you suggest?" He smiled at Ava, and I swear I watched her swoon. She'd been slowly softening to Jensen since she'd been assigned his partner on day one.

They'd been practicing for the last thirty minutes. Going over the basics, like we'd been doing all week. The rest of the class was filling out forms with terminology related to their specialties. It was hard to concentrate, though. Jensen's voice was so loud that I kept getting distracted.

"He doesn't know what a segue is?" Rachel, the girl sitting next to me, asked under her breath.

"Sure he does. It's an electric scooter," I responded sarcastically.

"You have the patience of a saint, Finley," she said. "Not sure I could've stayed on the team if I were you."

Little did she know that my rage ran deep. "I couldn't let him take it all from me." But really, he already had.

My attention was drawn back across the table, where Ava was looking at Jensen's phone now. "You've been getting these weird messages all week?" she asked.

"Yes, I must've gotten added to some spam list."

My entire body went still. He was getting messages from my bathroom ad. He was going to be embarrassed in front of the whole class. I'd get to see some karma play out right before my eyes.

Ava read a message out loud: *"Sitting in the not-so-purple bathroom thinking of you."*

"I liked that one," he said.

"Why would they say what color the bathroom *wasn't*?" she asked.

"I have no idea," he said.

Ava barked out a laugh as she read another. *"I'm glad I ate dairy today so I could find you.* These are funny. We could totally use these as a short feature on the podcast. We could call it *Messages from the Spam Folder.* Or something like that."

"Who Likes Spam," Jensen suggested. *"On the Menu for Today: Spam."*

"That's not half bad," Ava said.

Karma, I wanted to scream, *you're supposed to be on my side!*

Chapter eight

"AND THEN HE SAID, *ON THE MENU FOR TODAY: SPAM*," I said the next day as we pulled onto Theo's street. Deja was driving, and she glided to a stop two doors down from his house and shifted her car into park.

"Ugh," Lee groaned.

"And people liked that? They were eating up his Spam puns?" Max asked.

"I see what you did there," I said.

"I couldn't help myself."

After realizing the bathroom ad hadn't brought him even the tiniest amount of payback, I had spent the past twenty-four hours at half-hearted and mostly failed attempts at revenge. Like stealing Jensen's mints from his locker, which I still had the combination for (he didn't notice), contacting his ex via DM and asking for any dirt (she had none—"He was very nice to me," she'd said), and asking Deja's parents if they'd put up *Jensen can't eat here* on their marquee (they wouldn't, even after Deja said, "But, Mom, he is the worst and completely humiliated Finley, please!"). They didn't budge.

"Maybe I really should make out with a random stranger tonight if it means Jensen will actually feel some kind of sting," I said. I wasn't going to, but I was beginning to think more and more that he wasn't going to feel anything no matter what I did. That he didn't care enough about me to have anything I did make any kind of difference to him.

"Yes!" Max said from the seat behind me. "I support this."

"No," Deja said. "I do not. I thought tonight was the night you were going to infiltrate the football team and see if you can turn them against him."

"It is," I agreed. I needed to focus on that. It was the only thing that might work. "Oh!" I lifted the Target bag I'd brought full of the things Jensen had left at my house over the last year. "I brought a bunch of his stuff to burn in the bonfire. Do you think Theo will have a bonfire?"

Deja shrugged. "I've never been privileged enough to come to one of his parties. Did he have one last time?"

"Yes, he did," I said. "But I've only been to the one."

"Were we even invited to *this* one?" Lee asked.

"Wait," Deja said, eyes wide. "Were we *not*?"

"He had to expect I'd bring my friends, right? I wasn't going to come alone."

"That would've been madness," Maxwell teased.

"What are we waiting for?" Lee asked as we all sat in the car, no one making the initial move to exit the vehicle.

"People," I said.

"What?" he asked.

"There are hardly any cars." I pointed at the street. "We must've come too early."

"I thought we were late—fashionably late," Deja said, checking the time on her phone.

The neighbor's house that we had parked directly in front of was dark, the shades drawn, the porch light off. But I could still tell it was a fancy house. This whole neighborhood was nice oceanfront properties. Theo was obviously loaded.

"We should've brought something besides this bag of burnables. An appetizer? Chips?" I hadn't thought much of it before because I'd assumed a lot of people would be here. Parties like that didn't require contributions. Ten-car parties? That was a different story. "Let's go get something . . . or, you know, go somewhere else entirely. I heard the drive-in is playing *The Purge.* That sounds very cathartic right now."

"No, it's fine," Lee said. "It will be fine. We're not leaving."

"Jensen isn't here," I said, noting the cars on the street. He often ended up at parties where the rest of the team was, regardless of who was throwing it.

"That's a good thing, right?" Lee said. "You don't want him here if you're trying to get in good with the rest of the guys."

"She looks hot," Maxwell said. "*I* wanted him here."

"You *do* look hot," Deja said with a nod. "Like a rave goddess."

"I don't know what that means."

"It means you look like you're ready for a dance party, all wild wavy hair, smoky eyes, and flared jeans. I love it." Max opened his car door, making the final decision for all of us. "We can't let that go to waste."

Lee gripped both my shoulders from behind. "You got this."

I took a deep breath. I had this. Make friends with the football players. Turn them against Jensen. Make football the least fun part of his life. Mission accomplished.

"I bet more people will come later," Maxwell said. "That's how these parties work. They last all night."

He was probably right. We weren't exactly the party type. I'd been to a total of two parties my entire high school career so far, both while dating Jensen. Our *fashionably late* was most likely everyone else's *way too early*.

I pushed my door open and stepped onto the sidewalk.

"The bag," Maxwell said, pointing to the floor of the passenger seat, where I had left it.

"Shouldn't I leave it here until later?"

"If you leave it here, you'll never do it!" Deja called, already several steps ahead.

"Fine." I scooped up the plastic Target bag by the handles and shut the door.

"Did Jensen have any backlash from that message Maxwell left at his work?" Lee asked.

Theo's house was lit up from the path carved through the lush grass to the wide porch adorned with rails and colorful potted plants.

"I've heard nothing," I said. "Knowing my luck, he probably got a promotion from it."

"How?" Lee asked.

"Who knows. He seems to have a wish granter waiting in the wings of his life."

"I want one of those," Maxwell said.

"We all do," I said.

"I feel like we should knock," Deja whispered once we made it to the porch.

"As opposed to?" I asked.

"As opposed to walking in without knocking," she said. "Like I would've done if double the cars were out front."

"It's definitely a knocking situation," Lee agreed.

The door was very tall, made of some dark wood with iron accents. Maxwell pounded on the door with the side of his fist. A couple minutes later, the door swung open and a well-dressed woman stood in front of us. She had smooth dark hair and red lipstick.

"Hello," she said. "Can I help you?"

"We're here for . . . um . . . the party?" I said it like a question. "Theo invited us."

Her eyebrows popped up into an expression I'd seen on Theo's face before. At first, she had looked at us with mild interest, but after my statement, she studied each of us, from the top of our heads down to our shoes. Now was not the time to look like a rave goddess or to be gripping a Target bag, like I'd just come from shopping. The expression on her face told me she agreed with my internal thoughts. She stepped back from the door anyway, opening it wider. "Come in. I'm Theo's mother."

She was definitely not a *call me by my first name* type of mom.

She was an *I will run for president one day and you will not be surprised* type of mom.

"I'm Finley." I stepped inside first. My friends followed, introducing themselves as well.

"Should we take off our shoes?" Lee asked.

Mrs. Torres was wearing shoes, but I completely understood why he asked. It felt like we needed to take off our shoes.

"No, please," she said, looking at our feet. I sensed we'd just been insulted, and I wasn't sure why.

She closed the door softly and led the way through a tiled entry, which housed a table topped with a large flower arrangement and a huge piece of contemporary art on the wall. We walked down a short hall and into a massive great room. On one end was the biggest kitchen I had ever seen in my life. On the other end was a heavily-furnished-and-yet-still-had-plenty-of-space living room. In between those two spaces was a long table. And at that table was what must've been Theo's entire family and extended family. That was what it seemed. There was nobody our age. Just many adults, probably aunts and uncles, even a grandparent or two, and a few kids.

On the island was a large cake with the words *Happy 75th Birthday, Abuela* on top. Definitely not the kind of party we were expecting.

"Theodore," Mrs. Torres said as we all came to a stop. "Your guests are here."

Theo glanced up from his plate of food, then did a double take, his eyes traveling over my outfit and back to my overly made-up face. He said something in Spanish I didn't understand and the whole table laughed. A smirk played on his lips. That little punk.

He had done this on purpose. Was he bored? Had he done this to entertain himself? A surge of rage pulsed through me. Like I needed more humiliation in my life right now.

"Sorry we're late," I said to the oldest-looking woman at the table. Because even though Jensen had claimed over the hot mic to the entire school that I didn't have good enough quick-thinking skills to host a podcast, I thought I did. "Happy birthday." I dug into the bag of Jensen's stuff I held and pulled out a Harry Styles vinyl. "A gift." I set it on the table in front of her.

The woman gave me a wide smile. "Thank you so much."

Theo stood now. "Abuela, this is Finley and her, uh . . . friends." He obviously didn't know their names. Why would he have bothered to learn those?

"Nice to meet you," she said.

There were no more chairs at the table, but Theo pointed to a breakfast nook tucked at the back of the kitchen and raised his eyebrows at his mom. She gave a small nod.

"This way," he said to us.

"Do we get the kids' table?" Maxwell said under his breath as we made our way through the kitchen to the second table. It was surrounded on one side by bay windows. I could make out the ocean in the distance, the moonlight glowing on the surface of the water, but that was about it.

For a second, I thought Theo was going to drop us off at the table and rejoin his family, but he sat down. We did too. The noise at the other table, which had gone completely silent when we were announced, picked up again, a low vibration of voices.

"Theodore, huh?"

"Yes." Theo laughed a little. "You actually came."

"I thought it was a real party," I said with narrowed eyes.

"You asked if I was having a party," he said. "You didn't ask what kind."

"The word *party* implies what kind," I said.

Max popped his eyebrows. "If you were looking for an excuse to get *us* here, you just had to say so." When saying the word *us,* he put his hand on my arm.

I batted it away.

"I'm Max, by the way," he said. Deja and Lee introduced themselves as well. Deja had a look on her face that said she wasn't happy. That this just confirmed he was a jerk and I needed to stay away from him. I agreed.

"Nice to meet you," Theo responded. "Do you want to eat? There's food on the island. You can help yourself. The plates are on the end."

Lee and Maxwell exchanged a look, then rose simultaneously and headed for the food.

"They're dating, right?" Theo asked.

"Do you have a problem with that?" I asked.

"No, I don't. It was just a question."

I took a deep breath. I was not going to let him get to me. Or at least not make it so obvious that he was.

"I'm getting food too." Deja stood. She tried to pull on my arm, take me with her, probably not wanting to leave me alone with Theo. But she didn't need to worry—there was no danger in leaving me with him, my irritation toward him was only growing. I gave her a slight nod, and she let go.

Then it was just me and Theo. He leaned against the back of his chair and nodded toward the Target bag I still clutched. "My grandma looked like a Harry Styles fan to you?"

"Believe me, it was the most appropriate gift in here."

A lazy smile came onto his face. "Should I be worried about what else is in there?"

"It's some stuff Jensen left at my house. I was going to burn it in the bonfire I assumed you'd be having."

He chuckled. "Nice." He sounded like he meant it. Like he was happy I was burning Jensen's things.

"Why do you hate him?" I asked.

He narrowed his eyes at me like my question was some sort of test. Instead of answering, he asked, "Why does *he* hate *me*?"

"You hogged his spot for three years. Didn't even have a single sick day . . . until that last game. Are you the healthiest high school student on earth?"

Theo's eyes flitted to the table behind me full of his relatives, then back to me. He held his arms out to the sides. "I mean, look at me."

"I don't think viruses care how hot you are."

He let out a single laugh. "I was referring to my peak physical condition, but thank you."

"*That's* what Jensen said . . . about you."

"He appreciated my peak physical condition?"

I shook my head. "No. He said you were full of yourself."

"Who else am I going to be full of?"

"Said you thought you were better than you are."

"I was definitely better than him."

"And now? Are you better?" I asked. "From your injury?" My eyes drifted down to his knee, covered by his jeans.

His eyes went hard. "What do you know about my injury?"

"Just that it knocked you out of the last game of the season." I had seen him on crutches a few times at school directly following that game, and he still limped a little . . . although I hadn't noticed a limp since that time in the diner, so maybe he didn't. "And that Jensen got to play in a game for the first time."

"Yeah . . . ," he said, looking at me like he wanted to say more, but before he did, Maxwell and Lee returned with plates of delicious-looking enchiladas, rice, chips, and guacamole.

"This is the kind of party *I* like," Maxwell said as he sat. "Just saying."

"Excuse me for a moment," Theo said, all formal, seeming to forget we were his peers and not the people across the room. When he left and reclaimed his chair at the big table, I was sure we'd lost him for good. He started what looked like a heated conversation with his mom. Probably telling her that he hadn't meant for me to come and that he was sorry I had ruined their night with my presence.

"So for real," Deja said, "do you think he did this just to embarrass you? Are you a jerk magnet? Should we leave?"

"I don't know," I said as an answer to all her questions.

"We're not leaving before I finish my food," Maxwell said.

Lee narrowed his eyes in Theo's direction, his fork full of enchilada, cheese stretching from the plate to the tines. "I say we stay. I sense he might surprise us."

Chapter
nine

ABOUT FORTY-FIVE MINUTES LATER, THEO'S FRIENDS started arriving in clusters. Two or three or four at a time. At least twenty people from school and the football team were here.

"He lied to us," I said, standing on the patio of the now-lit-up backyard. It was an amazing yard. I'd seen it before—this was where the last party of his I attended had taken place. A large pool was steps from the patio, surrounded by resort-quality patio furniture. Beyond that was an expanse of grass where some guys had started a pickup football game. Past the grass was a rock garden, swirly patterns twisting along the ground made with different colors of rocks and interspersed with succulents and potted plants. Vines, dripping with flowers, climbed up an arbor that arched over a section of the stone path. There were side fences separating them from the neighbors, but the back of the yard transitioned straight to the sandy beach, making it look like the ocean itself belonged to them as well.

"He told us the wrong time," I said. "This was the party he knew I wanted to go to. He *wanted* to make me uncomfortable."

"He's an evil genius," Lee said.

"Or just plain evil," Deja amended.

"He's something," Maxwell agreed, wiggling his eyebrows as he watched him catch a football.

My mind drifted back to the last time I'd been here. We'd come in through the side gate. Jensen had immediately left me to go throw the football with some friends. I'd sat on one of the lounge chairs by the pool and watched the lights under the water change colors.

"There's no hidden pattern," Theo had said from where I hadn't noticed him sitting alone ten feet away. "It goes red, blue, green, purple, red, blue, green, purple." If he knew the order so well, I'd wondered what life events he'd contemplated while staring at those lights.

"Are you sure it's not blue, green, purple, red, blue, green, purple, red?" I'd said.

He'd chuckled. "I guess it depends on when you started paying attention."

"At just the right time," I had said with a smirk in his direction.

"More like a little too late," Theo had said.

"Because your opinion is the most true?" I asked, narrowing my eyes.

"Mostly because this is my pool."

Our conversation had been cut short by a football landing in the pool and splashing water all over the two of us.

"My bad!" Jensen had called.

Theo had gotten up and brushed off his jeans. His eyes lit up

72

as he looked at me. "Is it just with me, or does he always feel threatened?" With those words, he'd walked away.

"Earth to Finley," Max said, shaking my arm and pulling me out of the memory I'd nearly forgotten. "When does Operation Infiltrate the Football Team begin?"

I looked at the guys in their pickup game, suddenly not sure what exactly I was going to do or say to them but knowing I needed to do something. "Soon."

"What's up with the funky soccer net?" Deja asked.

On the far right of the yard was one of those freestanding nets kickers used to practice. I'd never seen one in a backyard, just in the stadium at school. Jensen definitely didn't have one. Maybe that's why he stayed the backup kicker all those years. "It's for kicking a football," I said.

"Let's go check it out," Maxwell said.

Next to the net was a large storage cabinet, its doors open. Inside were all sorts of football gear: pads and orange cones and more footballs, even one of those rolling sticks that distributed chalk powder into straight lines.

"Theo's kind of obsessed," Deja said, running her hand along a shelf.

Maxwell retrieved a ball and ran twenty feet away from us. "Ready?" he called.

"For what?" Lee asked.

"I'm going to throw it to you." It was less of a throw and more an underhand lob that landed at my feet.

I picked up the ball and twisted it in my grip. Maxwell jogged back to us. I held a fake microphone to my mouth. "Maxwell, how does it feel to have thrown an unreceived pass that lost the game?"

He ignored my microphone like he usually did and twirled around with his arms outstretched. "It feels amazing."

"I think it's called an uncompleted pass," Lee said.

"That doesn't sound right either," Deja said. Then she pointed. "Try kicking the ball into that net."

I made a show of putting my fake microphone on the ground. "Like Jensen told me numerous times, kicking a football and kicking a soccer ball are two totally different things," I said, eyeing the net. "Soccer balls basically kick themselves."

"I'm sorry, what?" Deja said. "I'm beginning to think he wasn't hiding his jerk at all. You just didn't recognize it."

"No," I said defensively. "He meant that a soccer ball is round and it's easy to put in motion."

Deja scoffed. "So easy. I basically tell it where to go and it does my bidding."

"I guess he *was* making it seem like it took no talent to play soccer."

"Not cool," Lee said.

Had he done that with other things? Nice-guyed his insults? Tried to one-up me in everything? Felt threatened when he wasn't the best? How had I not seen it before? Was that why he tried out for the podcast too? To prove he was better than me?

"Am I blind?" In my indignation I held the football out in front of me and drop-kicked it, like I used to do with the soccer ball.

I could tell right when the ball hit my foot that it wasn't going to go where I'd intended it to go—in the net. My foot struck the ball at an odd angle. It veered to the left, flying through the air, much farther than I realized it would go. It hit some guy all the way across the yard, who was standing next to Theo, on top of the head.

The guy looked around confused. So did Theo. He picked up the ball, then glanced up at the sky like God himself wanted to join their game.

The guy with the ball they'd been using held his up as if to show he hadn't done it.

I rolled my eyes and decided to solve the mystery for them. "Sorry!" I screamed, cupping my hands around my mouth. "Can we have it back?"

At the sound of my voice, Theo searched the yard directly surrounding them until he finally discovered us beyond where he'd been looking.

I held up my hands when he saw me like I was really going to catch the ball if he threw it from there. Could he throw it this far? Obviously not, because he said something to the other players and headed our way. The rest of the group resumed their game.

"You throw that, Soccer Star?" he asked, but he was really looking at Maxwell and Lee as he approached, like they were the only ones he believed could've accomplished the feat.

"She kicked it," Deja said, collecting the ball from him. "What do you think about that, Mr. Starting Kicker?"

"You kicked it?" That seemed to be even more unbelievable to Theo. "From here?"

I pointed at the net, ready to admit it wasn't as amazing as he seemed to think it was. "I was aiming for that."

His eyes drifted to the net, then back to me. "Yeah, accuracy takes some work. But your power"—he raised his eyebrows—"that was impressive." He gave me a nod of respect.

Maxwell raised his hand. "What's it called when you throw a ball to someone and it hits the ground?"

He furrowed his brow. "An incomplete pass?"

"Oh!" we all said at the same time.

He chuckled, then turned to rejoin his friends.

"You think I could be better than him!" The words came pouring out as if some subconscious part of my brain thought them up, because the fully functional part of my brain was shocked by them. This was the first time I'd kicked any sort of ball in nine months. Who did I think I was? "If I practiced."

Theo stopped, turned slowly, then gave me a once-over almost as intimidating as his mom's.

Deja made a weird noise I couldn't interpret. Did she think it was a terrible idea?

Max gave a surprised "Huh."

And I just stood there as Theo assessed me from head to toe, seriously considering my question. He closed the distance between us and asked in a serious voice, "You want to be the kicker for the school football team?"

"What? No. I don't know if I could get *that* good. I just want to show him up. March onto the field one practice, kick a field goal in front of the whole team, and then shrug Elle Woods style and say, *What, like it's hard?*" Maybe it would humiliate him so much that he would quit football.

"Epic," Maxwell said.

"Why *not* try out to be the kicker for the team?" Lee said. "It would accomplish your goal of taking it from him. And his suffering would last all year, just like what he did to you."

Could I?

Theo stood there silently, as if waiting for me to make the decision. But I wasn't sure if it was so he could laugh in my face or tell me how to make it happen.

"When are tryouts for next year's team?" I asked.

"Second Saturday in April," Theo said.

That was only a month away. Not nearly enough time.

That's when I saw Jensen, over Theo's shoulder, join the football players on the grass. He gave fist bumps and said something with a laugh like he was perfectly fine. Like his whole life hadn't been yanked out from under him last week. Instead, he was acting like he was about to claim his crown as king of the school and wear it our entire senior year. In his hand was my Target bag and he was digging out his stuff like it was Christmas morning. *How did he get that?*

"Yes," I said. "I want to try out to be kicker for the football team. But I will only try out if all of you objectively tell me after I practice for the next four weeks that you think I can make it. I am not going to set myself up to be embarrassed again."

Maxwell raised his hand to the square. "I swear on my life I will tell you if you suck."

The others nodded. "*And* this plan . . . this goal . . . this whatever"—I looked at each of them—"it doesn't leave this circle. If I'm going to fail, this time, I'd like it to be in private. Or at least as private as a failure kept between five people can be." My eyes stopped on Theo. He was the wild card. I trusted everyone here except him. He could march over to the group, that now included

Jensen, this second and share the news like it was the joke that he probably thought it was.

"Are you kidding?" Theo said. "I'm not going to tell anyone. But promise me I can be there when you earn the spot from him."

I nodded slowly, remembering what my grandma had asked that surfer boy all those years ago. There was one more necessity to this plan if it was going to work. Jensen used to tell me Theo was selfish with his time. Never wanted to help him when he'd ask for pointers. But it was the only way. I couldn't see myself getting good enough fast enough without him. "Will you teach me?"

Theo didn't hesitate at all when he said, "Absolutely."

Chapter
ten

"WE COULD'VE HELPED YOU," DEJA SAID AS WE ALL drove home together from the family dinner party turned real party turned secret-keeping party.

I left minus Jensen's stuff, not because I'd burned it in the non-existent bonfire but because he'd marched in and took it without asking like he seemed to be doing with everything in my life. Did he just go around looking in bags, or did someone tell him? The only person who knew outside our group was Theo.

"You didn't have to ask the devil himself," she said.

"I could *not* have helped," Max said. "I know nothing about kicking anything, really, but especially a football. The devil will be a better teacher, what with all his devil powers."

"*Jensen* is the devil," I said. "I needed to recruit a helper to take him down even if that helper is—"

"A devil as well?" Deja said.

"In your world there are multiple devils?" Maxwell asked.

"I'm hoping he's a lesser devil," I said. "A demon maybe?"

Deja laughed. "As long as you know who you made a deal with."

"Believe me, I know," I said, pulling a wipe out of my purse and scrubbing off the remains of my lip stain.

"I think you made a deal with someone who wants to see Jensen suffer as much as you do," Lee said.

"Does he, though?" I asked. "And why? Because he was a little annoying on the football field? It doesn't make sense." Deja was right—could I really trust someone I hadn't trusted for so long?

"Whatever the reason, five . . . ," he said, pointing at all of us and then back toward the house to indicate Theo, "like-minded people can accomplish a lot."

"Did Jensen try to talk to you tonight?" Deja asked, looking over her shoulder and switching lanes.

"Didn't even look at me." I dropped the pink-smudged wipe back into my purse.

"That you know of," Maxwell said.

"It's going to feel so awesome to march in there and take his football position." I tried to say those words with confidence, but I was feeling far from confident.

"I guess that's the one silver lining in this deal," Deja said. "When did Theo say he could help you?"

"Tomorrow. He said we are starting tomorrow." I tugged on the top of my seat belt, lengthening it, then letting it slide into place.

"Motivated," Max said. "I like it."

"We don't have a lot of time." I was sure that was the only reason he suggested tomorrow. He knew that four weeks was pushing it as I much as I did.

"Apparently I'm still going to have to share you with a boy for a while," Deja said.

"Yeah, but I think you support it more now than you ever did before."

She let out a long laugh. "If Jensen suffers as a result, I do."

"YOU'RE UP EARLY," GRANDMA SAID THE NEXT MORN-ing. "Isn't it Saturday? Time to sleep in and procrastinate homework or surf."

"I don't surf, Grandma. Apparently, that's you." I sat at the kitchen table eating oatmeal coated in brown sugar and sliced bananas. I had a feeling Theo was going to kick my butt today, and I wanted to make sure I ate enough to support a butt kicking.

"You should. It's fun." Grandma sat next to me eating her own bowl of oatmeal. Hers had bananas but only a small sprinkle of brown sugar.

"Tell me more about your surfing. How long did it take to learn?"

"Andrew Lancaster taught me nearly every day for an entire summer."

"Every day? Did you get really good at it?"

"Not particularly, but I had fun."

That wasn't the pep talk I needed this morning. "I'm going to pretend you became a competition-ready surfer."

"Why would you pretend that?"

"Because I have big plans, Grams, and I need some inspiration."

"You're good at everything you do," she said.

Good was the right word. I was pretty much *good* at things I tried. But good didn't make me a star soccer player. Good didn't make me the host of the school's podcast. And good would definitely not turn me into the starting kicker. I needed to be beyond good. I needed to be exceptional.

"Wait. Andrew Lancaster?" I asked. "Isn't that the famous painter?" The Andrew Lancaster I'd heard of was a pop painting icon. Especially famous around here because he grew up on the Central Coast. He'd died about five years ago, but his art lived on. An art installment of his works traveled the country. He painted on surfboards and tires and old road signs and records and anything he could get his hands on, it seemed.

"Yes, he painted. I told you that. He painted my surfboard. Mine was the first one."

"Really?" Could that be true? My grandma had owned the first piece of art painted by Andrew Lancaster? "What happened to that surfboard again?"

"I don't know."

"Is it part of his art installment?"

"No, my friend borrowed it, and I never got it back. She lost it, I think," she said, like I hadn't just asked her what happened to it and she hadn't just told me she didn't know.

"Huh. Maybe we can find it somehow."

"Maybe," she said.

"I have to go." I kissed her cheek, rinsed my bowl out in the sink, and loaded it into the dishwasher.

"Bye, honey."

82

"Mom! Dad! I'll be back later."

Mom poked her head out of her bedroom on my way to the front door and gave my outfit—running shorts and a tee—a once-over. "Where are you going?" she asked.

"To work out with a new friend. And then maybe grab lunch." I only said that last part because I had a feeling this would take a while. I wanted a cushion of time to work in. I didn't want to tell my mom what I was really doing until I knew it was even the slightest possibility.

"Okay," Mom said. "Also, I'd like to meet this new friend soon."

"Sure." Not happening. I wasn't even sure if Theo thought of me as his friend. I certainly didn't think of him as mine.

My phone buzzed with a text to our group chat as I left the house. *Kill it today,* was the message from Deja. She must've had to work if she was up this early.

Lunch tomorrow? I typed back.

I'm in and I'm sure the guys will be too when they wake up.

Sleeping, Maxwell responded. *Your buzzing woke me up.*

Put your phone on do not disturb, goof, I quickly texted back, then climbed in my car.

My drive over to Theo's house was uneventful. Yes, we were doing this at his house. Yes, I felt like I was imposing. But he'd been the one to suggest his place and it made the most sense because he had the net and the gear and it wasn't as public as the school where anybody could wander in and see what we were doing.

His house seemed even bigger during the day. We'd exchanged numbers before I left his party the night before, and I shot him a text as I walked the path to his front door.

Here.

Above the text was the one he'd sent last night: *Okay, see you at eight-thirty.*

The clock on my phone said eight-twenty-eight.

I scrolled up to read the whole exchange that had landed me on his porch.

He was the first to initiate contact at 10:43 p.m., right as I'd gotten home: *Were you serious about stealing the kicking spot?*

I had texted back: *So serious.*

Ready to start training then?

So ready.

My house tomorrow still work?

So there.

Am I going to regret this?

Probably.

Okay, see you at eight-thirty.

I knocked on his door, hoping he'd beat his mom to answer it since I'd warned him with a text.

He did. The door swung open to reveal a sleepy-eyed Theo. He had a few pillow lines on his cheek, and his hair was ruffled. He was dressed, wearing some workout shorts and a tee . . . well, unless that's what he slept in, it was hard to tell.

"Hey," he said. "Come in." He was barefoot but holding a pair of socks.

"I didn't wake you, did I?"

"I look that bad, huh?"

I wasn't sure Theo could ever look bad. He actually looked

kind of adorable with sleep face. "No, you look good, I mean fine. I mean— Never mind."

He let out a low chuckle and led the way down the hall. "You look good and fine too."

I knew he was mocking me, so I rolled my eyes. "Is your mom okay with all this?"

"What's all this?" he asked, plopping onto a kitchen chair and pulling on his socks.

"Me. You. Not like . . . me and you . . . like me being here, you teaching me. Wow, what is wrong with me?" I didn't normally stumble on words, or I tried not to, but I seemed to be doing that a lot when it came to him.

"Not sure," he said, looking up at me through his lashes. "Sometimes I have that effect on people."

"You did not just say that."

"I only speak the truth." He stood and retrieved a pair of shoes by the island. "Did you bring your soccer cleats?"

"Should I have?" The shoes he was holding were regular running shoes. "I don't even know if I have them anymore." They were probably somewhere under a pile of clothes in my closet.

"Did Jensen never tell you that kickers usually wear soccer cleats?"

"No, he didn't."

"Huh. Maybe in the back of his mind he always knew you could steal this from him."

"Let's not get ahead of ourselves. I've kicked a football once. Not sure I'm stealing anything from anyone."

A scar ran down his kneecap, and I studied it as he tied his shoes. He brushed his hand once over his knee, catching me staring. I averted my gaze. "What happened?" I asked.

"Partially tore my ACL the practice before the last game."

"Oh, right." His injury. I didn't realize it had been so serious. "You had to have surgery?"

"Yep," he said, standing, his single-word answer and his body language telling me he didn't want to talk about it. He gestured toward the back door with his head. "Let's go see what you got before we hit the weights."

"Hit the weights?" I asked. "What does that mean?"

"You've lifted weights before. I've seen you in the weight room at school."

I hadn't been in the weight room since soccer season last year. He'd seen me? "I wasn't sure if it meant something else in kicker terminology."

His eyebrows popped up like he was trying to decide if I was as stupid as I seemed. "It means the same thing." He opened the back door, and soon we were out by the net and the shed with a football that he'd put on a small plastic stand on the grass. The ocean and its rhythmic waves made up the background noise.

"Don't I just drop-kick it?" I asked, looking at the ball.

He leveled me with a stare.

"I take it that's a no."

"Tell me you know how this game works."

I cringed. "I mean . . . mostly?"

"I have to teach you how to kick *and* all the rules and regulations of the game you want to play?"

86

"You don't *have* to do anything," I said. "This is probably the worst idea anyway. I can leave right now and save us both a lot of time."

"No need to overreact."

"I'm not overreacting. I'm just reacting."

He held up his hands. "Don't be mad."

I looked at his hands and his doe-eyed expression. "Does that usually work for you?"

"Girls aren't usually mad at me."

"I find that hard to believe."

He smiled.

"And I'm not mad at you," I said.

"See, it worked."

I shook my head and gave a reluctant smile. "I will research the rules and regulations of football on my own. But a few pointers would be nice."

He straightened his shoulders and proceeded to tell me the difference between a punter and a kicker and how Jensen wasn't a punter. How punting was more about power (which was apparently why a beefy guy named Greg did that) and kicking was more about accuracy. How the ball was normally held for a field goal, but we'd start by practicing with the plastic stand.

When he was done explaining, Theo picked up the ball and walked until he stood in front of me. "You ready?"

No. "I think."

He squatted down and ran a hand down the back of my right calf until he held the heel of my shoe in his palm.

I barely contained the shiver that went through me. "What are you doing?"

He placed the football on my instep. "Don't kick with this part of your foot. Wedge kicks aren't as accurate. Your boyfriend *loves* wedge kicks."

"He's very much *not* my boyfriend."

"Right. Jensen does a wedge kick. It's why he's not as accurate as he could be. He has gotten better, though, so you're not going to be able to walk into this position. Plus, he has experience."

"And he's a guy," I said.

He didn't try to pretend that wouldn't make a difference. "And he's a guy. But Coach is pretty cool. If you're better, you're better."

"Then let's make me better."

He stared up at me from where he was still squatting down, still holding my foot. He seemed to be taking this job very seriously.

"No wedge kicks. Got it," I said.

"Right. I want you to kick with this part of your foot." He stuck the ball on the big bone toward the inside of my foot but close to the shoelaces.

I swallowed and took my foot from him. "Okay."

He replaced the ball on the holder and then took about three steps back from it and two to the left. "Pretend there's an invisible line going from the center of my body to the left of the ball. That's the line I want you to drive along." He turned and looked at me. "You're a right-footed kicker, yes?"

"Yes."

"That's what I thought. You'll plant with your left foot to the left of the ball. Your right leg will swing through and strike just to the left of the seam there." He mimicked the motion without actually kicking the ball.

"Are you going to kick it?" I asked.

"No," he said shortly.

"Why?"

"This is your session," he said.

"And that means you can't kick it? I think it would be good for me to see how it's supposed to look. Wait . . . can you *not* kick anymore?" I pointed to his scar. It ran along his left kneecap, which I was just now noticing was his planting leg. If it was weak, it would probably affect his kicking a lot.

"I'm working on it," he said defensively. "It's only been four months."

"I'm not judging you. I just didn't realize. Does it throw off your balance?"

"We're not talking about me," he said. "Kick the ball."

"No need to overreact," I said, quoting his earlier line.

"You asked me to teach you. You don't think I can teach you because I can't kick a ball right now?"

"I *definitely* didn't say that."

"Then let me teach you."

"You don't want to actually talk or get to know each other at all. Got it," I said.

He sighed, like he'd run out of patience for me. This was going to be a long four weeks. "What do you want to know? That I got hit so hard in practice that I lost my college offer and that I'm trying to figure out what my future looks like without football?"

My breath caught in my throat, and his gaze went to the ground as if he immediately regretted saying that. "I'm sorry," I said. "I thought podcasting was my future, so I get it."

"And it's not anymore?"

"It will be harder," I said. "What about you? You don't think football can be your future anymore?"

"It will be harder," he mimicked.

"In the meantime, you'll help me with revenge?" I asked.

"Yeeesss," he said on an exaggerated sigh as if I was finally coming around to *his* plan instead of him being part of mine.

"Okay, okay, let's get started," I said, squaring my shoulders and facing the ball.

Chapter eleven

"AM I GETTING WORSE?" I ASKED AFTER A KICK LANDED me on my butt. I was ready to say *Never mind, this was a bad idea.* My face felt hot, and I knew it was probably red. "I feel worse."

"Surprisingly, no," Theo said. "You're getting the motion down. You don't have the right shoes either, so there's that. Bring your soccer cleats tomorrow; they'll help with traction."

"Tomorrow?" I asked, standing and wiping the grass off my hands and backside.

"Well, whenever you come next."

"Tomorrow will work." Between school and homework and responsibilities at home, really, we probably only had weekends. And there weren't very many of those left, so he was right, I needed to come tomorrow.

"Weights time." He led me back to the house, where I assumed a weight system must've been set up in the garage.

But it was more than that. Way more. He basically had a gym.

And not in his garage either. A dedicated room in the house. Mirrored walls, a stationary bike and elliptical, free weights but also machines with ropes and pulleys. A punching bag hung from the ceiling in the corner.

I hit the punching bag as I took a lap around the gym. "This is better equipped than the school weight room. Must be nice." I added that last sentence under my breath.

"It is," he answered. And I wasn't sure if that was a response to my first sentence or my second. I didn't ask him to clarify. "How often do you lift?" he asked.

I cleared my throat. "I used to lift a lot."

"I didn't ask how much you used to lift."

"I know! But that was the better answer."

He laughed. "So never?"

"Pretty much."

He gave a single nod. "Legs every other day until tryouts."

I widened my eyes. "Are you trying to give me Hulk legs?"

"You won't get Hulk legs."

"Have you been waiting all your life for the opportunity to torture someone? Is that why you agreed to this? Is that why you have a little gleam in your eye right now?"

He didn't deny it. "Grab that squat bar off the wall."

"UGH," I GROANED IN PAIN. I LAY ON THE BLACK RUBBER-tiled floor of Theo's gym, my legs twitching even though they weren't working anymore. He expected me to be able to kick tomorrow? I wasn't sure I'd be able to move. Sweat dripped down my temple, and I swiped at it with the back of my hand.

I held a fake microphone to my mouth. "How does it feel to have killed your trainee on day one?" I threw my hand in the air, pointing my fist toward him.

He walked over, pretended to tap it for a sound check, then leaned down and into my hand said, "Feels like my trainee needs to toughen up."

I froze, looking up at him from my place on the floor, his face upside down in my view.

"What?" he asked.

I dropped my hand to the side. "Nothing," I said, having a hard time shaking the surprise of him actually playing along.

"How are you with extreme cold?" Theo didn't seem dead at all even though he'd done a lot of the workout alongside me. He had definitely favored his left leg. I'd tried not to notice and I absolutely didn't point it out after how defensive he'd been about his injury, but he did.

"In what context?" I asked.

"In the context of being surrounded by floating chunks of ice." He pointed to a windowed door in the room that led outside.

I pushed myself up to sitting with a grunt. "I'm confused."

"There's an ice barrel out there."

"A what?"

"I'll show you."

He led the way out the door to a small patio on the side of the house. A black barrel with a three-step stool jutting off the side stood on one corner of the cement. Against the house was a full-on ice machine, like the ones at hotels. He lifted the door and began scooping ice into a bucket.

"Your whole house is set up like an NFL star lives here. Wait, is your dad an NFL star or something?"

He looked over his shoulder at me as he poured the first bucket of ice into the tall barrel. It made a sloshing noise as it hit the water. I should've stopped him. I really did not want an ice bath. I hadn't even brought a swimsuit.

"Pretty sure the whole school would know if my dad was an NFL star."

"Maybe a retired one?"

"No." He moved back to the machine to fill the bucket again. "My dad played in high school."

I turned a slow circle. From this side patio, I could see the shed and kicking net in the backyard. My circle finished with me looking back through the windows into the decked-out gym. His parents had put a lot of money into his football career. I wondered if they were just as upset as he was about his injury. This house, this setup, showed that they expected a lot of him.

He stepped back from the barrel and held his hand out to the side like an invitation.

I groaned again. "I don't have a suit."

He looked at my running shorts like he didn't understand what I was saying.

I sighed. "Fine."

I was wearing a sports bra under my tee. So what if my shorts got wet. I toed out of my shoes, peeled off my socks, and approached the three small steps that would end in more torture. I took a deep breath, took off my shirt, threw it on top of my shoes behind me, then went for it. It was cold . . . freezing . . . and I was only shin-deep. My arms were shaking from holding myself out of the water.

"It works better if you get all the way in," he said.

"Just hold your stupid horses. It's cold."

"My horses aren't stupid," he said. "They are very intelligent."

My toes were now numb as I lowered myself another inch. "Do you actually have horses?" I asked, not really surprised.

"No, I don't. But my figurative horses are smart."

My chin quivered with the cold, my teeth clicking together, making an actual sound.

"Once you get all the way in, I'll start the countdown." He held up his phone to show me the timer on his screen.

I lowered myself immediately with a hiss of air. The back of my legs bumped into something. "Is there a ledge in here? Is it this barrel's intention that I actually sit for a length of time, as if this is some sort of leisure activity?"

"Yes, it's a sitting ledge. But since your lips are purple, you will only stay in for one minute. That ledge will help you exit."

My skin felt like it was being pierced by a thousand needles. "I can't last one minute."

"Forty seconds now. You can last forty."

I shivered even harder now. "How long can you last in here?"

"I usually do three minutes. Sometimes five." His timer said thirty seconds.

"I can't, I can't. I need to get out," I said, my breath gone, the needles still stabbing my legs and chest now. I wasn't sure my numb legs were coordinated enough in their current state to exit the barrel, but I moved to the edge.

He seemed to sense my concern and said, "I'll help you."

I nodded, my teeth still clacking away, my skin on fire. I stepped onto the ledge and then swung one leg over the side. He put one foot on the bottom step, and I braced my hands on his shoulders as I pulled the other leg out. I now sat on the lip of the barrel, my hands on his shoulders, staring down at the step that seemed too low to reach from this position. Who designed this thing?

"Just slide down," he said. "I'll help."

"Am I going to hurt you?" I said through my shivering lips.

"You're not going to hurt me. I have you."

"I don't feel had."

He reached up, took me by the waist, and lifted me up and around until both my feet were on the patio next to the steps.

I gasped in a cold breath of air. Oh. I was had.

A cabinet of towels stood to the right of the door. He got one and tossed it to me.

"Thanks," I said. I felt stupid for not staying in for the full minute. But it had felt impossible while I was in there.

"No problem."

"Your turn." I wrapped the towel around my shoulders, then nodded to the barrel. "You need to prove this five-minute claim."

He smiled but was obviously competitive because he was shoeless and shirtless and in the barrel in less than ten seconds. "Ah," he

96

said, resting his chin on his crossed forearms, which were draped along the edge. "So relaxing."

I pulled out my phone and made a show of turning on my timer. His breathing didn't even sound strained as the seconds ticked away.

"You hide your pain face well," I said as he passed the two-minute mark.

"You do not."

"No, I don't. My grandma says my face is always giving me away. She says it's because I have such a pure heart that it shines out my eyes."

Theo scoffed. "Does she know your pure heart has turned evil for the next four weeks?"

The smile that had been on my face moments before wavered.

He threw a piece of ice in my direction. "Don't lose heart now. We both know he deserves it."

The timer passed three minutes. "I better go." It felt like I'd been here for hours even though it was only ten o'clock.

He vaulted out of the barrel. It was really unfair how good he looked doing it. I averted my eyes as he grabbed a towel.

I tugged my shirt back over my head and collected my shoes. I started to hand him the towel when he said, "You can bring it back tomorrow."

"Okay, thanks."

"You did good today, Soccer Star."

"Stop calling me that," I said.

He just chuckled. If he knew I played soccer, he must've known

I wasn't that great at it. That Deja was the actual soccer star. I wondered if that's why he found it so funny. That hit a nerve.

Was one session enough? Could my friends take over the job of training me now?

I closed my eyes and took a deep breath. Four weeks. Just four weeks. "See you tomorrow."

Chapter
twelve

MY EYES FLEW OPEN, AND EVEN THAT SMALL MOVE-
ment made me groan with pain. I rolled onto my side and groaned
again. Every muscle in my body was sore. My bones felt sore too.
Like my muscles were clinging on to them for dear life. I reached
for my phone ever so slowly and sent a text.

Need a recovery day. Can't move.

Theo texted back a few minutes later: *The best thing for sore
muscles is to work them out.*

I literally can't move.

*You're still in bed? Of course you can't move. Get them warmed up
and meet me in thirty minutes at the school. We'll lay off weights today.*

Fine. P.S. You're mean.

I rolled out of bed, literally, and landed on my hands and knees
on the floor. From there I crawled to the bathroom, barely able
to pull myself onto the toilet. After washing my hands, I crawled
down the hall.

"What are you doing?" Grandma asked from where she sat at the kitchen table.

"I'm warming up my muscles."

"Since when do you wake up early both weekend mornings?" Dad asked. I hadn't noticed him from floor height, but he sat next to Grandma.

"Since I enlisted the punisher as my trainer," I mumbled.

"What?" Dad asked.

"Nothing." I crawled to a chair and used its rungs to heave myself to standing. Then I walked to the cupboard where we kept the medicine and found a bottle of ibuprofen.

"Are you training for something?" Mom asked. She was at the table as well. It was a regular family reunion.

"Yes," I said. If I lived through today, I *would* need a good excuse for all the working out I'd be doing. And she just gave me that excuse. "One of those mini triathlons."

"Really?" she asked.

"When? Where?" Dad added.

"I'll send you the website later." As in, when I found one. There had to be someone hosting one of those things somewhere. "It will answer all your questions."

"Is Jensen competing with you?" Grandma asked. "He'd do wonderful at something like that."

I sucked in some air. "No, Grandma. Jensen and I broke up. Remember?" And he's not good at *everything*, I wanted to add but kept it to myself. His current track record proved that thought wrong anyway.

"Did you break his heart?" Grandma asked. "That poor boy."

"More like the other way around," I said.

"You still owe me that long story," Mom said, pointing her spoon at me.

He stole my dream. *Why couldn't I say that?* "I know, I know. When my bones don't hurt." I downed a couple pills with a glass of water.

"Well, I'm glad you're doing a triathlon," she said. "It's nice to see you trying something new."

"Right," I said, then, changing the subject, quickly asked, "Did you listen to the latest podcast I emailed you?"

"I did. It was so good. Why didn't you publish it?"

I waved my hand through the air. "Because you're the only one who listens. But that's not why I asked. Did Grandma ever tell you that she was friends with Andrew Lancaster? That he painted her a surfboard?"

"I'm sitting right here," Grandma said.

"Did you tell my mom?"

"I think so," Grandma said.

"You never told me that," Mom said, and she looked at me like she thought maybe it hadn't really happened. Like Grandma wasn't entirely in her right mind. Like she'd made the whole thing up. But that hadn't been my experience with her early memories. Most of those had been spot-on.

"I don't tell you everything," Grandma singsonged. "Andrew was a beautiful painter. He didn't know it at first. But I did."

"He didn't know it?" Dad asked, as if she'd told a joke.

"No, some people need to be told what they're good at," Grandma insisted. "And I told him. I'll show you a picture."

"We don't have any pictures, Mom."

"Why?" she asked.

"The fire. Remember?"

"Oh, right. What a shame." She stirred her oatmeal around in her bowl.

"Was it a wood board?" I asked, remembering what Andrew was famous for.

"Balsa wood with a waterproof finish over the painting," Grandma said. "You would've loved it."

"I'm sure I would've," I said.

"But Cheryl Millcreek borrowed it and I never saw it again," she said.

"Who's Cheryl Millcreek?" I looked at my mom.

"I'm not sure," Mom answered. "I've never heard that name before."

"Someone who doesn't return things, that's who," Grandma said.

"She sounds terrible," I said.

"Finley," Mom chastised.

"What? She does."

Mom shook her head.

The clock on my phone told me I didn't have much time left. "I have to go. Let's talk more about this Cheryl person later," I said, shuffling my way out of the kitchen, my muscles screaming again after the short break I'd given them.

"A mini triathlon is supposed to be fun!" Mom called after me.

"I'm having the time of my life!" I called back.

Chapter
thirteen

"OUCH, OUCH, OUCH, OUCH," I PROVIDED AS SOUND EF-fects for my walk from my car in the parking lot to where Theo was leaning against the back of his, watching my slow progression. I placed the folded towel I'd taken from his house the day before onto the trunk next to where he was leaning.

"Such a baby," he said, twisting toward me, like he wasn't in any pain whatsoever.

"Are you not sore at all?"

"Not at all."

I reached out and squeezed his triceps. He sucked in some air. I laughed. "That's what I thought."

"Fine. A little sore."

"So you *are* human."

He nodded toward my foot, then said, "Put your heel on the bumper for some hamstring stretches."

I obeyed, making more pained noises as I did.

"Why'd you park so far away from me?" he asked.

"In case anyone drives by. They can't see our cars together here at the school on a weekend."

"We don't want anyone to think our cars are involved in an inappropriate relationship?" he asked, his voice as sarcastic as his question.

I pointed in the general direction of the football field. "I told you, this arrangement cannot get back to Jensen or . . ." *I'll be made to look like an even bigger fool if I fail at this too.*

"Or what?" he asked when I didn't say my fear out loud.

"I don't know—he'll stop it, or he'll know what's coming, or he'll start training extra hard."

There was a smile in his eyes when he said, "I've seen that man train extra hard. I'm not worried."

"Theo."

"He won't find out," he said in an even voice.

"Great. We're on the same page."

"Great."

I pulled up a browser on my phone as I continued to stretch. "Do you know of any mini triathlons happening around here in the next couple months?"

"No. Part of your payback? Did Jensen hate triathlons or something?"

"No, it's what I told my parents I was doing, you know, instead of admitting what I'm really doing."

"Weren't they also pissed at Jensen for stealing your spot?"

"I haven't told them."

"Why?"

"I don't know. Maybe I'm still trying to pretend it didn't happen." Maybe I didn't want to tell them he'd so easily stolen the spot I'd worked incredibly hard for. Maybe they'd think that meant I wasn't good at the thing I wanted for my future if someone with zero experience could steal it that easily from me. They'd think I was a failure.

I found a mini tri taking place in Pismo Beach, only about thirty minutes from us. I turned my screen and showed Theo. "The second Saturday in April. Same weekend as football tryouts. It's serendipity."

He squinted at my phone, then read one of the captions under the picture of the ocean, "Swim with the sharks? Is that their selling point?"

"I assume the biking and running portions are not with the sharks," I said.

"Too bad." He gestured toward my foot. "Other leg."

I put my other foot on the bumper, screenshot the page, and forwarded it to my mom. My phone buzzed with what I assumed was my mom's response, but it was Deja in the group chat: *We still on for lunch at the diner today? I work till 1. But after that.*

Maxwell: *I need to hear all about training with the hottie.*

Lee: *I'm right here.*

Me: *I can hardly sit or stand. But yes!*

"Do your parents think a triathlon with the sharks is a bad idea?" He obviously thought that's who I was texting.

"Oh, no, just Deja and the guys confirming lunch today."

"We're going to lunch today?"

"Not you. Me," I said. "With my friends."

"Got it," he said.

"Wait, do you *want* to come?"

"Absolutely not," he said, straightening up and beginning to stretch beside me.

"Good, because after you pranked us into coming early to the party on Friday, you wouldn't be welcome anyway."

"Early? You were late."

"No, I mean the real party."

He laughed. "My grandma's birthday *was* the real party. I invited other people after you got there because I realized you were embarrassed."

I paused and reassessed that night. How he'd talked to his mom, probably asking if he could have friends over. How she'd argued with him for a couple minutes but then conceded. "Why did you invite me in the first place? You knew I'd be embarrassed to come to a family party."

"I didn't expect you to come. I had kind of thought you were kidding."

"Nice," I said.

"I know you don't think so, but I really am a nice guy."

I didn't know what to believe about Theo. My instincts were telling me to keep him at a distance. Between what I'd experienced with him and the stories I'd heard from Jensen, I was wary. "My muscles say otherwise."

"Your muscles are going to love me."

"Both my brain and body hate you right now," I said, meeting his eyes.

His mouth curved into a half smile, and he nodded toward the school. "Let's learn some football."

We headed through the halls toward the field.

"I didn't invite Jensen to the party, by the way," he said as we walked. "Someone else must've."

"I figured."

"But it was good, right? He saw you looking hot." He winked my way.

"Are you saying I don't always look hot?" I asked. Two could play at his ultra-confident game.

"Nope." But that's all he said. He didn't elaborate. Safe answer.

"Did you tell Jensen about his stuff, by the way?" I asked.

"His stuff?"

"The stuff I brought to your house that I wanted to burn?"

"I didn't talk to Jensen at all that night. I wanted to kick him out but got distracted with your revenge plan, and that sounded like a better idea."

Who else could've told Jensen about the bag? Had Theo's mom overheard me?

We arrived at a large chain-link gate that during the school week was open but was now very much closed, with a chain, a padlock and everything.

He let out a grunt. "Since when do they close the field?"

"Outside of football season? Almost always. We once got locked out of soccer practice."

"And you didn't think to say this on our walk over?"

I shrugged. "I thought you had popularity privileges. That you got the janitor to open it up or something."

"No privileges," he muttered. Then he looked up at the top of the gate as though assessing its scalability.

"I am way too sore to climb this," I said before the idea became too firmly planted in his mind.

"Here, step in my hands." He assumed position, hands clasped, legs braced, shoulder against the fence.

"I am not climbing this, Theo," I said, unmoving.

"Come on, you won't hurt me."

"I will hurt *me*," I said.

"I'm beginning to think you're stubborn," he said, dropping his hands to his sides.

"Maybe you're the stubborn one. Follow me." I walked along the fence line as he trailed behind.

"Do you know a secret way onto the field?"

"I might." If it hadn't been fixed since last year.

The football field and the soccer field were one and the same at our small beach-town school. And last year, the entire girls' soccer team had ended up here at midnight. It had been the day before Deja's birthday; someone started a group chat that we should all meet at midfield at midnight because she was turning sixteen, and apparently this was the way to show how special that was. When we couldn't get in, we found an opening on the far side of the field where the school fence shared a wall with the adjoining walking trail and neighborhood. We'd all squeezed through it and played a game of soccer in the dark.

I must've been wrapped up in the memory, because I didn't hear the voices until Theo grabbed me around the waist and pulled me behind the janitor's shed. The voices were on the far side of the fence, moving along the walking trail. Theo's arm was still around my waist, both our backs pushed against the building, listening intently. It sounded like a group of kids.

He clearly came to the same realization, because he said, "See, I'm a vault with your secret."

"Such a vault," I agreed. Our breaths were heavy with the panic of the moment. I knew this because my right shoulder was tucked into his left.

His fingers tightened on my waist before he dropped his arm, retrieving it from behind me. "I think we're safe now."

I nodded, but neither of us moved.

After several more breaths, I pushed myself off the wall and peered around the corner of the shed. Most of the fence was crawling with morning glory vines, its purple flowers and green leaves providing a thick cover. "We're good."

We reached the corner. I pushed on the fence, revealing how the sides were only connected to each other at the top and bottom.

His eyebrows popped up. "What kind of delinquent are you?"

I stepped through the opening. "The kind that really didn't want to have to climb today."

He laughed, following me through.

"And if this year's team is anything like last year's, then there should be . . ." I kicked aside some leaves that covered a hole revealing a soccer ball. I picked it up and bounced it several times from one knee to the other. It was a little dirty but aired up, which let me know that either Deja had carried on the midnight birthday tradition with others or someone else had. For a second I was hurt I hadn't been invited, but I'd done it to myself when I dropped out.

Moved on with my life. I gave one last bump with my knee, sending the ball flying toward Theo. He caught it.

"Not too sore to knee a soccer ball, I guess."

"I have put on my brave face," I said.

"That's what your brave face looks like?"

"What does yours look like?"

"No wincing is involved." He dropped the ball and tapped it to me. Without a word we passed it back and forth as we walked to the middle of the field.

"Does football start with a kickoff too?" I asked when we stopped.

"Yes," he said. "But that'll feel easy after you master this."

"If you say so," I responded.

"Then the opposite team returns it and game play starts. The driving toward the endzone."

"I thought you were going to make me learn the rules on my own," I said.

"Yeah, well, we're here." He backed away from me, putting space between us so he could kick the ball farther.

"You better watch out. If you keep helping people like this, they might take your School Jerk title away."

"Who awarded me that title? Jensen?"

"Among other people," I said.

"And you agree?"

"I . . ." I hesitated.

"It's time to start forming your own opinions, don't you think?"

My mouth opened and shut. I wanted to say that I had plenty of my own opinions, but I wasn't proving that very well. I was finally able to stutter out, "Jensen has taken over your spot in my book. But you still hold the cocky title. Walking around with your earbuds in all the time with that face and that body."

He raised his eyebrows. "I was born with two of those things. Can't really help it."

"But you think you're better than everyone."

"You must agree that I'm the best to some extent. You chose me to teach you, after all."

"I was desperate," I said.

He smirked. "Good to know."

Chapter
fourteen

WHEN I WALKED IN THE DINER WITH THEO, MAX'S SMILE turned big, Lee's curious, and Deja's slipped off her face. She must've just gotten off work because her hair was pulled up and she wore a green collared shirt. Even the uniforms at the Purple Starfish weren't purple. Now that I thought about it, maybe her parents were marketing geniuses.

After Theo and I had finished our training session and headed back to our cars, I'd said, *I mean, everyone has to eat.*

He'd responded, *I'll follow you over.*

I gave Max a small shake of my head now. He had the ability to make this weird with his revenge-dating and make-out talk, and I didn't want him to.

"*Now* how are we going to talk about him?" Maxwell asked when we got to the booth.

"Seriously," Deja agreed but for much different reasons.

"He doesn't mind being talked about in front of his face. He kind of likes it," I said.

"I do," Theo said. "It's how I feed my ego, right, Finley?"

"I never said your ego was fed by others. I think you do a good job feeding it yourself."

Lee's eyebrows popped up. "Two days in and you already have banter? That seems fast."

"We've had banter since arguing over pool lights," Theo said.

"When was that?" Lee asked.

I looked at Theo. I honestly didn't think he remembered that discussion from a year ago. He just stared back at me with an even expression.

"You're only calling it an argument because I disagreed with you," I said. "It was probably the first time that has ever happened."

"Second," he deadpanned.

"I'm liking this origin story," Maxwell said.

"An origin to what?" Theo asked, and that knowing smirk of his came onto his face. But I didn't know what he thought he knew because the only ending our story was going to have was us bringing Jensen down together.

Maxwell and Lee sat on one bench seat, and Deja sat across on the other. It really wasn't a booth for five, but Deja slid as close to the window as possible as though both Theo and I were going to be able to fit in the space left. Despite his wide frame, he seemed to think we would too, because he sat down, leaving a small end for me.

I was just about to drag a chair over when he grabbed my hand and pulled me down next to him.

"So how is our girl Finley doing in her training?" Max asked.

I put my hands under my chin. "Yes, how am I doing?"

"She whines a lot," he said. "Something about sore muscles."

I elbowed him. "Watch it, or I'll show you how well I can complain."

Deja's mom called a number, and Lee stood up. "Our fries. Don't talk about anything interesting while I'm gone."

"We won't," I said.

"Hurry, then," Maxwell said.

We were all silent, as if we really couldn't say anything at all without Lee present. Out the window to our right sailboats dotted the bay, most anchored in place, one moving slowly in the distance. Lee came back quickly and set down two big orders of fries. It's all we ever ordered here even though we always said we were meeting for lunch. Fries counted as lunch to us.

Theo wasn't having it, though. "Where is the real food?"

Deja gasped. "This is real food."

"Finley needs protein," he said.

I let out a breathy laugh. "Okay, Coach."

"No, I'm serious. You should order something else."

"I'll eat at home later."

"Let me out." He twisted his upper body toward me like I was going to move immediately.

"Why?" I asked.

"I'm going to order you a burger. Which one do you want?"

"I'm good with fries."

"No, you're not. You have to take care of your body if you want to maximize our training."

"I take care of my body. Like I said, I'll eat more when I get home. Fries are just our tradition."

"It's important to get protein within an hour after you work out. Stand up." He was attempting to move me by pushing his thigh against mine.

I held on to the table and dug my feet into the ground. "We hardly worked out. We kicked a ball around. You taught me about downs and positions and penalties."

"But you're still recovering from yesterday—you need to eat."

"You're not my boss."

"You really are stubborn," he said.

"*You* really are stubborn."

He must not have been trying before because after my statement he put real effort into his force and I slid down the bench, barely getting my feet under me, saving myself from falling.

"Ouch," I hissed, my muscles protesting the effort. I wanted to rush the register before he got there, but I'd only brought a few dollars to contribute to the fry haul. I hadn't brought burger money.

"Hey, Mrs. Patel! Don't serve him!" I yelled to Deja's mom behind the counter.

She thought I was kidding and just laughed in my direction.

I huffed and turned my attention back to my completely silent friends, who were all staring at me with wide-eyed expressions. "What?"

"Really?" Max said. "I didn't know *all* my dreams in our revenge plot were possible. You really are going to fall for your ex-boyfriend's nemesis, and it isn't even going to be that hard."

"No," Deja said. Then, under her breath, with a glance toward the register, added, "Is he always that controlling?"

"I wouldn't call it controlling," Lee said. "He was worried."

"And protective," Max agreed.

"What would you call it, Finley?" Deja asked.

"I . . ." My first thought was to defend him. Agree with the guys. But maybe I had let my guard down a little. I couldn't do that. Wouldn't. Not when I'd just been burned by someone so bad that I could still feel it in my chest. Someone who I thought was nice. Theo didn't even pretend to be nice. "He's stubborn. Probably too stubborn." Always thought he was right. Arrogant people weren't careful. I needed careful.

"Exactly," Deja said, as if that was all she needed to hear to back up her thoughts.

"He smells really good," Max said. "Would it be weird if I just stuck my nose on his shirt?"

"Even my grandma wouldn't do that, and she's gotten pretty bold lately."

"Oh, speaking of, I've been meaning to ask you," Deja said. "Did you stop posting your podcast for some reason?"

My head whipped in her direction. "Have you been listening?"

"Yes! I love your grandma. And the story was just getting good. Her family moving to California. Her hating its guts. What happens next?"

I scrunched my brows together. Was that where I had left off? "Get this," I said. "She met a surfer boy and claims that boy was Andrew Lancaster."

"The painter?" Lee asked.

"Yes! And apparently he taught her to surf and gifted her a

painted surfboard. Not only that, she's the one who convinced him he had talent. Hers was the first board he ever painted."

"What? Why haven't you posted *that*?" Maxwell asked.

"Because I thought my mom and my brother were the only ones listening, but apparently it's just my mom and you." I nudged Deja with my elbow. "My brother is getting a strongly worded text later."

"Don't tell him I tattled," Deja said. "But do you think it's true? Do you think your grandma really knew Andrew Lancaster? Was his muse or whatever?"

"I don't know. My mom doesn't think so. But Grandma has such a clear memory of her early years that I think it might be true."

"I need to listen to your podcast," Lee said.

"I want to see this painted surfboard," Maxwell said. "Is there a picture online somewhere?"

"That's the thing," I said. "She supposedly lent it to a friend one summer, never to see it again."

"What's it look like?" Lee asked.

"What's what look like?" Theo asked, coming back to the table and sliding in next to me. I tried to scoot as close as I could to Deja, but even so, his thigh and shoulder were pressed up against mine, distracting me for a moment.

"Her grandma's surfboard," Lee answered for me.

"Right, yes," I said.

"Your grandma surfs?"

"Well, not anymore, but she used to, I guess. The problem is that I don't know what the board looks like. We have no pictures."

"Ask her on your podcast so I can hear," Deja said.

117

"You have a podcast?" Theo asked.

"Not really," I answered, but Deja said, "Yes," at the same time.

"It has two listeners," I said.

"A podcast is only real with a certain number of listeners?" Lee asked.

"You know what I mean," I said.

They all pretended like they didn't.

"We should try to find the surfboard," Deja said.

"I don't have much to go on," I said.

"Try to get more, then," she said. "Like the name of this terrible person who borrowed and didn't return it."

"Oh! Cheryl Millcreek. She was the terrible friend."

"Did your grandma go to high school here?" Theo asked.

"Yes."

"So did mine. Maybe she can ask some of her friends if they knew her. I'll talk to her."

"You will?" I asked.

Mrs. Patel brought over the burger right at that moment. She set it in front of Theo with a smile.

"Thank you," he said, and slid it over to me.

Why was he here? Why did he want to help me? It couldn't just be that he saw me kick a ball and Jensen annoyed him. He was giving up too much of his time for such weak motives. And it was obvious he didn't do things out of the goodness of his heart. I'd add that to the list of things I was working on at the moment—find out why Theo Torres was really doing this.

Chapter fifteen

"DO YOU KEEP OLD YEARBOOKS HERE?" I ASKED THE librarian, Mrs. Hughs, the next day at school during lunch break. The night before, my mom and I had spent hours looking through family pictures. While it was fun to walk down memory lane, there were zero pictures featuring the surfboard. Not that we thought there would be, since the surfboard predated my mom, but we thought we'd at least try.

"Yes, we keep old yearbooks," she said. "What year are you looking for?"

"Sixties?"

"Follow me." She led me up the stairs and to the back corner, then presented the wall of yearbooks. "They're in order, so you'll find the sixties over here."

"Thanks," I said.

"You looking for grandparents?"

"Sort of."

"Good luck."

First, I went to last year's yearbook and pulled it down. I flipped through till I found Jensen. I pulled a sticky note out of my backpack and wrote the words *world's worst boyfriend* with an arrow and stuck it next to his picture. It was silly and immature, but it brought me a sense of satisfaction. Someone at some point in the future, maybe his grandkid, would see that and ask him about it. The thought that even in fifty years he might have to defend what he'd done to me made me smile. I shut the book and slid it back into place. The 1960s section was on the far left all the way on the bottom, so I sat down and pulled one out.

Where are you? The text from Deja buzzed through on my phone.

In the library. I'll be out in a minute.

What's in the library? she asked.

Your mom, I retorted.

Tell her to get back to work. The library is no place for people who want to make money.

She told me to tell you that you're grounded for that comment.

I knew Deja, and she probably rolled her eyes while reading my last couple joking texts. *Whatever secret mission you're on, hurry.*

I will.

The upstairs section of the library was a loft area that had a half wall overlooking the bottom floor. It allowed the noise from the lower level to drift up perfectly. That's how I heard a group of guys come in talking about the school's podcast.

"Does anyone even listen to it?" someone said.

"I only listen to comedy podcasts. And only when I'm driving."

"Nerd," someone else said, and they all laughed.

I slid the book onto the floor and inched my way to the wall. I wondered why someone had introduced the subject of the school's podcast if none of them listened to it. I moved to a crouch, held on to the edge, and pulled myself up until just my eyes were above the wall. I should've known. A group of football players now sat at a round table. I could only see half the group. They were probably talking about the podcast because Jensen had joined and was at the center of drama because of it.

"I listened to it once," one of them said. "So boring. Who comes up with the topics anyway? Some teacher who forgot what it was like to be in high school?"

They all laughed again.

"Nice," I muttered. Not that I'd been responsible for any topics yet, but I would be. So much for Nolen's plan to get football players to listen. They apparently thought that only *their* interests were worth listening to. I slid back down the wall.

"What brilliant ideas would you come up with?" I heard the calm voice of Theo ask. My heart and breath seemed to stop in order to listen better. "What would entertain you?"

"I don't know," someone said. "Sports recaps?"

A smattering of laughter sounded.

"Bad-date recaps," someone else said to even more laughter.

When nobody else offered any ideas, he said, "Not as easy as it seems, is it?"

"Chill, Theo. We didn't mean anything by it. What's your problem?"

"I don't have a problem," he said. "Never listened to the thing and definitely won't start listening now."

They all laughed.

My breath came back to me, and my heart started beating double time.

I grumbled about how we wouldn't want them to listen anyway and went back to my spot by the shelves, searching through the yearbooks until I found a small grainy picture of Cheryl Millcreek. I snapped a pic with my phone and flipped through the rest of the book to see if she was shown anywhere else. I found her in one other spot: the Surf Club. She stood with a striped board next to her and a serious expression on her face. I took another pic.

Downstairs the football guys had changed the subject to some pickup game they'd played over the weekend and were asking Theo why he wasn't there.

"I had other plans," he said.

His other plans were me. I'd sworn him to secrecy, though. Was that the only reason he wasn't saying he was with me?

They were getting so loud that I was surprised Mrs. Hughs hadn't shushed them. I put the yearbook back and took pictures of Cheryl's other years as well. I had ten minutes left of lunch, and I hadn't eaten anything. My still-sore muscles reminded me of what Theo said about feeding and taking care of my body. Hopefully my friends had some leftover food, because I didn't have time to get anything from the food trucks or cafeteria.

I pushed myself off the ground and stood at the top of the stairs for several breaths. If I kept my head down, maybe he wouldn't see me. And even if he did see me, he wouldn't say anything, surrounded by his friends like he was.

I scurried down the stairs and was heading to the door when Theo said, "Soccer Star!"

I turned, and the whole table was staring at me. All with varying degrees of smirks on their faces. I narrowed my eyes at him.

Theo's smirk was worst of all, like the world was a joke to him. "Tell the guys about the podcast."

"What about it?" I asked.

"How hard it is to come up with ideas."

"Why? It's not like any of you are listening to it," I said. "But ask Jensen—he's the expert now." I turned toward the door again.

"I would listen if there were interviews of other students!" Theo called after me. I immediately remembered how he'd called that idea boring before.

"Ugh," someone at the table said. "That's the worst idea yet."

"Not as easy as you thought," someone else said with a laugh.

There were other words I couldn't make out.

I kept walking. The library door was heavy, and my still-sore legs didn't help as I struggled for a moment to open it.

"I don't think it's working," one of the guys said.

"Lift weights tonight!" Theo called. "It will help flush out the lactic acid."

I shoved my way out into the hall in a mix of anger and embarrassment.

Once I found my friends, the first thing I said was "He's going to tell everyone, and Jensen will find out and ruin our revenge plans."

Half a sandwich was sitting in front of Deja, and I picked it up and took a bite, then sat down next to her.

"Who is going to do what now?" Maxwell said.

I summarized what happened in the library.

"And how is that going to ruin everything?" Lee asked.

"Don't you think people are going to wonder why he's telling me to work out? Realize he's probably training me to kick?"

"Probably," Deja agreed. "He's an idiot."

"Nobody will think twice about it. He's an athlete," Max said. "He was just trying to be funny."

"Well, it wasn't funny," I groaned, burying my head in my hands.

"You also have trust issues," Max observed, and I groaned again.

Deja said, "He doesn't deserve your trust."

Lee put his hand on my arm. "Your real trust issues are because you got screwed over not that long ago by someone you trusted with your whole heart. You're skeptical of anyone who's coming in the wake of that. It's totally understandable."

"Yes! I have a right to be screwed up," I said, and smiled gratefully his way.

"What secret project were you doing in the library anyway?" Deja asked.

"I was looking for a picture of Cheryl Millcreek that I can feed into the internet. The lady who borrowed my grandma's surfboard. If I find her, maybe she'll remember what happened to it." I didn't know why it was suddenly so important for me to find this surf-board. Maybe because it was a missing piece of my grandma's past that might bring her some joy. And making her happy was very important to me. It was the one spot of sunshine in my life right now. I needed that.

Chapter sixteen

"WHAT ARE YOU DOING?" THE VOICE OF MY GRANDMA pulled my head away from my laptop in surprise.

"Not much," I answered, closing my computer.

I couldn't tell her what I was really doing—a deep internet search for Cheryl. At least not until I had some solid leads. I didn't want to get her hopes up. And so far, my leads were anything but solid. I'd taken the picture of Cheryl I'd found in the yearbook the day before and reverse image searched it. It brought me to the Facebook page of a woman around my mom's age named Alice who had labeled the picture as *mom in high school*. Her last name was not Millcreek; it was Slater. I sent a DM that I knew would go to her "other" box and probably never get seen, telling her I thought her mom knew my grandma and that I'd love to ask her a few questions. I'd pressed enter, then stared at the chat screen like she was going to answer me back immediately.

So yes, Grandma scared me with her question. "What are *you* doing?" I asked.

"I am trying to decide what to wear for my date with your grandpa tomorrow."

Unless she was referring to his ghost, which I was 99 percent sure she wasn't, I knew grandma was having a bad memory day. Bad memory days were hard because if we tried to correct her, she would get confused and upset. Sometimes even angry. Usually, it was best to just go along with her.

"I'll help you find something in a minute. Can we have a chat first?" Because if her mind was in the past, maybe it was a good time to get her words out, to talk about it. I held out the headphones for her.

She sat down next to me. "You'll have to take me to my house before the date so he knows where to pick me up."

Even if I did take her to her house, which I couldn't because other people lived there, she wouldn't recognize it. After the fire, it had to be torn down and rebuilt. It was a completely different house.

"Yes, for sure," I said, helping her put on the earphones. "Tell me about your very first date with Grandpa." I'd cut this section about my grandpa and add it into a later interview when we'd reached this portion of her history.

"We were in the same math class together in college. I was better, by the way. I think Lawrence just talked to me because he was hoping he could get some free tutoring." I'd heard this story many times, but it made me smile every time.

"Not cool, Lawrence," I said.

"That's how I made my money, though. Even with his baby-blue eyes, he was not getting my brain for free."

"Way to be a feminist, Grandma."

"He had to take me to dinner first," she said, ruining my feminist comment.

"You gave him free tutoring after he bought you dinner?"

"It wasn't free if I got food out of it, now was it?"

"You have me there." I adjusted the headphones on my ears and reminded myself to watch my filler words. "What about your first date with Andrew Lancaster? Did you have one of those, or was he just your surfing instructor?"

"Andrew. I haven't heard his name in a long time."

I didn't remind her that she literally said his name a few days ago.

"He was teaching me to surf. We were sitting out there in the water on our boards waiting for a wave, and he said, *If I catch the next wave, will you go out with me?* And I said, *We are out.* He shook his head and said, *To dinner.* I said, *And if I catch the next wave, will you go out with me?* He gave a grunt and said, *And what if neither of us do?* Which was a real possibility, by the way, because the waves that day were terrible and I wasn't a great surfer. But then he said, *And if neither of us catch a wave, we should go out.*"

I controlled my laugh this time, kept it civilized. "That's so cute."

"He was pretty cute."

"Was this before or after you convinced him he could paint?"

"You knew he could paint?" she asked. "Have you seen his paintings?"

"Some of them."

"They're amazing."

"They're pretty cool. Which one of you caught the wave that day?" I asked.

"He did. I got tossed by it."

"Do you remember what the surfboard he painted for you looked like?"

Her brows came together in thought. "I don't remember, but it was really beautiful." That wasn't helpful at all.

"Did you know he turned into a really famous painter around here, Grandma? Did you ever go to any of his showings?"

"Probably. Ask Lawrence. His memory is better than mine."

Grandpa had been gone for a long time. *I* hardly remembered him. But it made me sad that she had to remember she missed him over and over again.

"YOUR GRANDMA TEXTED ME."

I had just walked into the conference room in the library and sat down when Jensen said that to me from across the table. We weren't the only two here. Ava sat beside him, and Nolen was at the whiteboard writing down our assignments for the day.

"What?" I asked. Did he not understand I never wanted to speak to him again?

"Your grandma texted me."

My curiosity got the better of me. "What did she say?"

"Asked me to come over. Had some old movies she wanted to show me."

"I told her we broke up," I said. "You know she has memory issues. Just ignore her or block her."

"You want me to block your grandma?" he asked, like that was the most hurtful thing anyone had ever suggested he do.

"Yes, it's super easy."

"You would know," he said, like I was going to deny I had blocked him.

I didn't. I said, "Yes, I *would*."

"Whatever," he muttered. "I'm not blocking your grandma."

"You responded to her, didn't you?" Jensen always had to play the nice guy even in the midst of screwing someone over.

"Why wouldn't I?"

"Because we broke up, Jensen."

"So I'm supposed to be mean to your grandma now? That's part of the breakup rules?"

"She won't remember if you don't respond." I made a mental note to take his number off her phone when I got home.

"I told her I'd come by."

"You did what?" I asked even though I heard him perfectly fine. "No."

"She invited me, Finley. I'd feel bad not going."

"*That's* what you feel bad about? That?"

He rolled his eyes, like me still mad over him sitting in this room was ridiculous. "I'll just say hi and tell her we broke up."

"You think it will be different coming from you? That you have this magic power to make her remember? Don't go to my house, Jensen."

"You don't have to be there."

"I'm serious." And I was getting more serious, more angry by the second. "Don't go to my house."

"Calm down, it's fine."

"*Excuse* me? Don't be an—"

"Hey, look what I found." The voice came from the chair to my right.

I swallowed down the end of my sentence and looked over to see Theo, an excited look on his face, holding out his phone.

"What?" I was so confused. First of all, seeing him here in my class, was disorienting. Second, I hadn't talked to him since the library incident two days ago and I was still kind of irritated with him. Plus, my irritation with Jensen was seeping out of my pores at the moment.

I had no idea where he'd come from or how long he'd been there. I'd obviously been so focused on my conversation with Jensen that I hadn't noticed him come in. I looked around the table; a lot more people had come in during our talk as well and they were all silent, pretending to look at phones or search through backpacks or write in notebooks, but it was obvious everyone had been listening to us.

"Look." Theo waved his phone under my nose, like he didn't care that the entire table was in our business. Had he heard the *whole* exchange with Jensen?

I glanced down at his phone. The Facebook page I'd found the night before of Cheryl Millcreek's daughter was pulled up.

"Should we message her?" he asked. His expression told me he was invested. Yet he wanted my permission before reaching out to her.

"I already did," I said.

"You already messaged her?"

I nodded. "I found that last night."

"And you didn't tell me?" he teased. "Gotta get to class. Talk to you later." He paused for a moment, meeting my eyes, his expression seeming to ask if I was okay. I was not okay, but I gave him a slight nod. With that, he got up and walked toward the door like that was the most natural interaction in the world.

The late bell rang out a sharp tone. When the room fell into silence again, Jensen said, "He's just doing that to bug me."

I leveled him with a stare. "Doing what?"

"Talking to you," he said. Someone on the other side of the room giggled. I could've sworn someone else said "I agree" under their breath.

Ava backhanded him on the arm. "Not everything is about you, dude."

"But this is. I guarantee it. You should be careful because he's not."

If only he knew just how careful I was being. But I wasn't about to tell him that. "You're the person I should've been warned about, Jensen. I think I'm good."

"Oh!" someone to my left said, as though that was the worst insult I could've given.

Jensen sighed like he was the one who should be frustrated over this interaction. "Do what you want, Finley."

I balled my fists near my thighs but did not respond how I wanted to. I'd already had too much of an audience for too much of my drama lately. I wasn't going to feed the gossip machine.

Nolen stood at the head of the table. "Okay, I know we're in the entertainment industry, but let's keep the drama to a minimum during class. Yeah?" He looked at me like I had somehow caused all the drama.

My clenched fists became tighter on my lap. *Do not make any comments, none at all,* I told myself. You will just end up looking like the bitter ex-girlfriend. I probably already did.

Chapter
seventeen

I RUSHED OUT OF THE CONFERENCE ROOM AND THEN the library it was connected to after class, still seething, glad lunch was our next period, because I wouldn't be able to concentrate on another class right now. I reached the hall, where I literally ran into the strong arm of Theo, stopping me in my tracks.

"Hey, whoa, slow down, you okay?"

"Why are you here?" I snapped, stunned by his appearance in front of me.

"Sometimes we sit in the library at lunch," he said. "But also, you seemed upset earlier."

"Did you hear what he said?" I looked over my shoulder, and when I saw the rest of the class, who hadn't been as quick to the door as me, now exiting, I clamped my mouth shut.

"Come here," he said, leading me out of the building and down the hall, then around a corner where he stopped. "What's going on?"

His look of concern, so different from his normal teasing smirk, was throwing me off.

"Jensen. My grandma texted him. He wants to visit her."

"Your grandma texted him?"

"She keeps forgetting we broke up. She has Alzheimer's."

"I'm sorry," he said.

"Yeah." My chest was tight and my eyes felt hot.

He put his hands on my shoulders but didn't say anything, just took a few breaths in and out. I found myself mimicking his actions until my chest loosened. "How did you do that?" I asked.

"I didn't do anything," he responded, but his hands still felt warm and steady on my shoulders. My hands, I realized, much to my surprise, were gripping the sides of his shirt.

I dropped them and cleared my throat, feeling emotions rise up my neck. "I'm okay," I said, nodding once, then twice, maybe three times.

"It's okay if you're not."

"I am. I'm good." I took a step back, out of his reach, swallowing hard as I looked around. This wasn't a populated area at lunch—most people ate in the courtyard or cafeteria—but it wasn't empty either.

"About the library the other day," he said. "Did I do something wrong?"

"You were being stupid," I said. "Annoying."

"I seem to accomplish that a lot."

"Yes, you do."

He chuckled a little, his smirk settling back into place. "You're mad at me."

"No, well, sort of. You don't have to pretend you'd listen to my podcast idea when you already told me it was boring."

"I never said that."

I shook my head in disagreement. "You especially shouldn't say it right after you told your friends you'd never listen to the podcast."

"Because Jensen is the host."

Oh.

"An-and also, I thought we were trying to keep our distance so people wouldn't talk. But then you tell me to work out in the library and you come to my class today." I pointed behind us.

"I didn't think you meant we couldn't talk *at all,* just that you didn't want anyone seeing us on the football field together." He whispered that last part. "We can't be seen together *anywhere*? You were at one of my parties. . . . People know we know each other now."

"But that was before we had a plan. And now we can't . . . we shouldn't talk."

He rolled his eyes. "You're pretty annoying too, you know."

"Yeah . . . well . . ." Everything he'd said was true. I had been fine talking to him before. Didn't think anything of it. I was overreacting. Nobody was going to make the jump that us hanging out together meant anything about Theo training me to kick unless they saw us in the act. And if they were going to make that jump, they would've made it already. Probably at his party.

He smiled. "No need to be so paranoid."

"It's just . . . I want this to work so bad. I need him to have some kind of consequence for what he did. And I don't want him to see it coming."

"I get it. But I'm not going to stop talking to you in public. At this point, I think *that* would be more suspicious. I *will* try to be more careful about the things I say if you're worried. I didn't mean to hurt your feelings, Soccer Star."

"Seriously, stop calling me that."

"Why does it bother you?"

"Because even when I played, I wasn't great. And you probably know that."

"I didn't know that."

"Plus, I quit."

"Huh."

"What?"

"You need to work on that."

"Getting better at soccer?"

"No, your confidence. If you don't believe in yourself, you're never going to get the position over him."

"Easier said than done. Oh," I said, pulling a twenty-dollar bill out of my pocket. I held it out for him.

"What's that for?"

"For the burger you bought the other day."

"Right." He took the bill without a fight and put it in his pocket. For some reason he didn't seem happy with this exchange. "What did Cheryl Millcreek's daughter say?"

"What?"

"You said you messaged her. What did she say?"

"She hasn't responded. I doubt she'll ever see my message. It's going to be in her spam folder, or wherever non-friend messages end up."

"You didn't request her as a friend?" he asked.

It hadn't even occurred to me. "Should I have?"

"Yes!" he said. "At least that will appear in her notifications. She'll look at your pic and think you're her niece she never remembers the name of or something."

"You've already characterized her as a terrible aunt?"

"We can only hope," he said with a smile.

I pulled out my phone to send the request, and he shifted so he was looking over my shoulder.

I clicked on the blue button. "Requested."

"Good," he said.

I looked up at him. He was still next to me and our noses nearly bumped. We both took a step back at the same time.

"I better go." He nodded toward the library, where his friends were probably waiting for him.

"Yes, of course. Thanks for . . ." I trailed off, not sure how to explain to him just how much he had calmed me down after the Jensen thing.

"Anytime," he said, seeming to know exactly what I was talking about. And then he was walking away. "Oh, Finley," he said, turning around and walking backward a few steps.

Maybe he needed to go back to calling me Soccer Star because my name on his lips set off a different kind of fire. "Yeah?"

"Publish another episode. It's an interesting story."

I THINK HE'S LISTENED TO MY PODCAST! I WROTE IN OUR group chat after school that day as I was setting up to record another episode with my grandma.

Who? Lee asked.

Theo! Why would he listen to my podcast?

Because it's good. Maxwell responded. *I've been listening to it too. Post the one where she talks about Andrew. You haven't posted it yet.*

I sat down in my chair and pulled up my stats bar on my computer. Sure enough, my last episode now had five hits. I moved the cursor over the publish button on the waiting episode but hesitated.

"You ready for me, Finley?" Grandma asked, and I released the mouse.

"Yes, come in."

She settled in quickly today, like she was ready to talk about Andrew. I was glad because I was ready to hear about him.

"Last I heard you lost the bet on the surfboard and so he got the privilege of taking you out. Where did he take you on your first date, and how was it?"

"We were young and neither of us had a job at the time, so he packed up a lunch and drove me down the coast to this beach with a series of caves. I'd never seen anything like it. We ate and talked, and he drew a picture in the sand with a stick that was so detailed, I didn't understand how he could've done it. *You're an artist,* I said. *No, just someone with lots of pictures in my head,* he responded. And, Finley, that was an understatement. Everywhere we went, he drew. On napkins and park benches and newspapers. Even on my hand sometimes."

"What did he draw?"

"People, mostly. Or parts of people. Eyes or lips or ears. Sometimes hair that looked like waves with another person surfing in the locks."

"Is that what he drew on your surfboard?" I asked.

"Something like that," she said hesitantly, obviously still not able to recall the details.

"If you can remember anything more specific, maybe our listeners can help us find it."

"What listeners? Are they listening right now?"

"No, I have to edit and work on the sound quality of our recording, and then I publish it. Then they listen to it." At least, that was what I used to do. Before I stopped the last step of that process several episodes ago.

"Kind of like a radio show," she said.

"Yes, true," I said. "The surfboard?" I added, trying to get her back on track.

"I remember it was beautiful. And I didn't understand how Andrew couldn't see that he was an artist."

"You're right," I said. "How couldn't he?"

"He thought a real artist was trained and had the right supplies and a specific amount of experience and was recognized by others."

"Oh," I said, understanding why he might feel that way. "So he drew you a picture in the sand on your first date and then what?"

"And then we took off our shoes and walked along the waterline, leaving footprints in the wet sand, until we came to the caves. The tide was coming in, so we couldn't explore them much, worried we would get trapped. As we stood inside that cave and the water lapped over my bare toes, he pulled me close and . . ."

She paused and didn't go on.

"He kissed you?" I asked, unable to wait for her to finish her sentence.

"He didn't," she said. "He was going to, but I turned and pointed out to the ocean and said, *Look at that otter.*"

"Why, Grandma?"

"Because I was scared. I'd never been kissed, and I wasn't sure I was ready for my first one to happen while I was worried about the tide and the caves and getting stuck."

"What did he do?"

"He looked out at the water too and said, *I think that's a sea lion.*"

I smiled. "Was it?"

"There was no otter *or* sea lion."

I gave a tempered laugh. "That was sweet of him."

"He didn't have to correct me," she said.

"But it was fake!"

"Exactly."

I reached out and squeezed her hand. My mom was wrong. "You *knew* Andrew Lancaster. That's so cool. You almost *kissed* Andrew Lancaster."

"Oh, we kissed. Just not that time."

My eyebrows popped up. "Oh, really? When did you finally kiss?"

"Wouldn't this be the time you leave the listeners wanting more?"

"Are you trying to steal my job?" I asked.

"Never." She slid the headphones off and set them on the desk.

Her eyes seemed distant tonight. Far away. Maybe even a bit sad. "I love you, baby girl. Thanks for that walk down memory lane."

I stood and gave her a hug. "Thanks for sharing it with me."

When she pulled the door shut, I relistened to the episode.

"He thought a real artist was trained and had the right supplies and a specific amount of experience and was recognized by others," my grandma's voice said over the speakers.

My stomach churned. It wasn't the same. Unlike Andrew, I'd already put myself out there. I wasn't picked for the school podcast. And the past podcast episodes I had published were still sitting there, not listened to, proof that I was obviously doing something wrong. The publish button stared back at me as my grandma's words continued over the speaker: "Wouldn't this be the time to leave your listeners wanting more?"

I sighed. At the very least, my friends wanted to listen to it. I could give them that. So after a thorough edit, I pushed publish.

Chapter eighteen

AS I WALKED THROUGH THE PARKING LOT AT SCHOOL Friday morning, a sea of pastels greeted me—pink potted flowers and light green balloons and lavender bouquets. It took me approximately fifteen strides to remember it was Bring on Spring. Every year, on the first day of spring, the student council sold flowers and candy and balloons to raise money for prom.

Last year, Jensen had bought me two dozen pink roses. I received four in every period, each with a handwritten note. I'd saved those notes, I remembered. Where were they now? Somewhere in some box in my closet or under my bed. Today seemed like a good day to destroy them. I never did get to burn his things at the party a week ago. He'd somehow walked away from that night in possession of all of them.

"Hey," Theo said, suddenly at my side. "Thoughts on the first day of spring?"

"I was just thinking that it felt like a good day to burn things."

He smiled. "Not a fan of flowers?"

"What about you?"

"I have received gifts every year. I'm hoping to get a few this year."

"You have?" I asked. "From who?" I had no idea what Theo's dating history was. As far as I knew, he hadn't had a girlfriend. At least not one that went to our school. But there were often girls hanging out with their group, so maybe I was wrong.

"From my many admirers. Be honest, are you sending me one this year?"

"Absolutely not."

"As your coach, I thought you would be more grateful. I see where I rank."

"I'm not burning any of your stuff, so you're not at the very bottom."

I stepped to the side of the hall, pulling him with me and turned to face him. "Be honest—am I wasting my time? And yours?"

"You're going to have to be more specific. Are you talking right now? If so, the answer is yes, a little. Or are you referring to the upcoming weekend activities?"

"You know what I'm talking about," I said.

He went quiet for a moment, as though taking my question to heart. So I believed him when he met my eyes again and in a sincere voice said, "It's only been a week. Technically only two days of training. But I would've never agreed to this in the first place if you didn't already have a natural ability. Muscle memory from your years of soccer, I'm guessing. And on top of that you're picking up the technique fast, Finley. You're driving the ball straight. That's a good sign. Do you want to add more practices?"

"More?" I already thought I was asking too much of him.

"I have time today, if you want."

As though someone couldn't wait a second longer, a small potted succulent was suddenly shoved between us. We both looked down. I reached for it without thinking, when the girl who held it said, "Theo, happy spring."

My hand dropped quickly to my side.

"Thanks," Theo said, turning a smile on the plant giver. "Is this from you?" Most of the time the gifts were delivered by the leadership students as we sat in class. But there was also an option to buy them and deliver them yourself.

"There's a note," she said, and then squeezed his biceps and scurried away.

"Nice," I said. "If this is your reality year after year, I'm suddenly seeing why your ego has grown to this size."

"It's not my fault people are drawn to me," he said.

I pushed myself off the wall where I had been leaning for our talk and continued walking. "I guess I'm covered in repellant."

He laughed. "Are you? I don't think you're using the right kind."

I sighed. "We're not practicing today. I'll feel too pathetic. And besides, one of those notes will probably be an invite to some date tonight. I wouldn't want you to miss that." I nodded toward the pot in his hand.

"So you *are* going to send me one of these and ask me out," he said.

"You wish."

"Maybe I do," he said.

My stupid stomach fluttered to life with his words, surprising me. We were not going there with him, I reminded it. He's too arrogant, too annoying, too risky. My body didn't get to forget that this soon. "Maybe it's your turn to *send* a gift for a change instead of always getting them," I said.

"Maybe it is."

Those were the words we parted on that morning, so when I was sitting in podcast class, brainstorming some topics I could research and the door swung open with a delivery, my heart skipped a beat. And that beat doubled in speed when a potted daisy was placed in front of me.

Across the way, Jensen's full attention was on me. He had the earphones that weren't plugged into anything on his head and the microphone pulled up close. He'd been doing another mock episode with Nolen watching on, but now he was quiet.

I unfolded the little attached card. My brain literally thought it was going to say: *Go out with me tonight. Life is about taking risks.* *—Theo*

Much to my relief, it did not say that. What it really said was *Smile big and try to blush. It will drive you-know-who crazy. —Deja*

I couldn't blush on command, so I quickly lowered my eyes to the table and forced a smile. Then I brought the flower to my nose and took a sniff. For whatever reason, that caused me to let out the loudest sneeze known to man. The class laughed. There was the blush I'd been instructed to produce earlier. I lifted my hand in a small wave, thanking my audience.

"Who is it from?" Ava asked from where she sat next to Jensen across the table.

"Um . . . Theo," I lied. Why did I lie? I could've just said I didn't know. I could've said a secret admirer. I could've said anyone else. But I knew Jensen was listening and I knew I did that for him, and I hated myself for it.

"Really?" she asked, as if she didn't believe me. "He's always the pursued and never seems interested. Until now, I guess."

"No, we're just friends," I said.

She lifted her eyebrows. "It seems like a little more than that."

I looked back down at my podcast topics notes, desperate to move past this.

My eyes couldn't stay focused for long, though. They traveled from the paper in front of me to where Jensen and Ava sat. She was laughing at something he said. They weren't even taking notes, or practicing anymore it seemed. They were literally just talking. Was this how all of next year was going to be? We would have to scramble around doing all the work while they worked on their chemistry and connection? The seniors overseeing us now would be gone, giving them even more freedom to do what they wanted.

As if sensing he was being watched, Jensen looked my way. "Can I see the podcast topics you've come up with?"

I almost said no but then noticed Nolen was watching. I'd already been on the wrong end of drama in here, so with a groan that could only be heard in my own head, I slid the notebook down the table. Jensen stopped it with a hand to the top. He read through the ideas I'd come up with and then narrowed his eyes a bit. "These are a good start," he said. "A little on the predictable side, though. I think our year should be more out of the box, entertaining for a larger audience." He slid the notebook back. "Keep trying."

Acid rose up my throat and I swallowed it down. Did he really think he was the leader in here now? How about this idea for a podcast: *How to get away with murdering your ex-boyfriend who is now a total jerk. Is that outside of the box enough? Relatable to a larger audience?*

The door opened again and another gift was brought in—a single rose. This one was delivered to Jensen. He smiled and blushed on cue.

Chapter
nineteen

I WAS STILL SEETHING WHEN I GOT HOME, READY TO find old notes to light up in flames. I must've been so in my head that I didn't notice an extra car out front because it wasn't until I walked into my house and saw Jensen sitting on the couch with my grandma that I knew he was there. Had I seen his car I could've prepared myself. But instead, I let out the loudest and crudest cuss word in my catalog.

My grandma gasped. "Finley!" She was holding one of the potted flowers from school that no doubt Jensen had brought for her.

"What are you doing here?" I asked. "Get out of my house."

"Finley," Grandma said. "What's gotten into you?"

Jensen didn't move. Didn't even pretend like he was going to stand and leave. "She texted me, Finley. I'm here for her, not you."

Grandma patted Jensen's arm like that was the sweetest thing he'd ever said. "You're here for both of us, dear."

"Grandma, we broke up. I don't want him here."

"When did you break up?"

"Jensen, I'm serious."

"You seem to be," he said. "Can we just talk?"

I wasn't sure if he meant him and my grandma or him and me, but either way, my answer was the same. "No."

"Finley," Grandma said, her voice shakier than before. "That's enough. Let's sit down and have a nice afternoon."

"You're upsetting her, Jensen. You need to leave."

"Only one of us is upsetting her," he said.

Mom came in at that moment from wherever she'd been at the back of the house. She took in the scene. I waited for her to tell Jensen to leave, but instead she nodded toward the kitchen, indicating I should follow her. I did.

"Grandma's having an off day" was how she started.

"So you let my ex-boyfriend in the house?"

"I thought maybe he told you he was coming?"

"He didn't."

"That maybe you guys made up," she said.

"We didn't. Not at all."

She clasped her hands together. "Can we just . . . Can you just . . . I don't know . . . play along for now? He seems to be helping her."

"Play along?" I asked.

Mom sighed. I saw the exhaustion behind her eyes.

"I'm just going to leave," I said. "Maybe that will be better for everyone."

"Maybe," she said, surprising me.

I clenched my teeth, keeping the bad words inside this time.

"I'll text you when he leaves," Mom said.

"Great plan," I said sarcastically, whirled around, and left. As I passed Jensen, my grandma's arm hooked in his, a memory flashed through my mind of this very scene from months ago. Only that time we were all together and laughing. Those happy feelings rushed through my body followed by a surge of sadness. I'd been so busy being angry at Jensen that the sadness shocked me. I pushed it down and left through the front door, pulling it shut behind me, trying to find my anger again.

In my car, I texted the group chat: *Jensen showed up at my house pretending to be concerned about my grandma.*

Deja responded first: *I shouldn't have sent you that flower today. My bad.*

Lee was next: *I almost sent you a flower too. Glad I didn't.*

And finally, Maxwell chimed in with *I did not almost send you a flower. I was hoping one of you losers would've sent me one. But noooo.*

I sent you one, Lee responded.

You're required. I meant my best friends.

I used my last ten bucks to make Jensen jealous, Deja said.

"Gah!" I threw my phone on the passenger seat. They were supposed to rage with me, not get in a fight over flowers. I pressed the ignition button in my car and drove to the only place that might help me right now.

I DIDN'T KNOCK ON THEO'S DOOR. I DIDN'T WANT TO ruin his day, but I didn't think he'd mind if I let myself in through the side gate to use the equipment. I hoped his parents weren't having some Spring Day dinner party or something.

The yard was full of its normal things, no decorated tables awaiting guests or party planners scurrying about setting up. The sun was heading toward the ocean, but it was still very much lighting the day as I stomped toward the shed. I pulled out some footballs and a plastic stand and got to work. I was obviously still in my school clothes—jeans and a sweater—having discovered Jensen immediately upon entering my house. The jeans were constricting and the sweater was hot and floppy, but neither of those things stopped me from kicking ball after ball, drawing on every ounce of anger.

Some hit the net, but most flew above it, off to far corners of the yard. I'd kicked through the pile, collected the balls, and started again when a voice behind me said, "I hope you're not imagining my face on those footballs, because I'd be very insulted."

"Jensen. It's his face," I said, kicking another ball. "His stupid, ugly, entitled face."

"What happened?" Theo asked.

"I'm just going to murder him, that's all." I kicked another ball.

"Finley, come on, you're going to hurt yourself."

"How exactly? By kicking the ball too hard? Is that a thing?" I drove my foot into another ball. Despite my snarky response, the top of my foot was actually starting to sting. I wasn't wearing the right shoes, just an old pair of Converse, but I didn't care. "Is this how you got hurt?"

"No," he said evenly. "It isn't."

I kicked the next ball, the last one in my second-round pile. I began to collect them again.

Theo followed me, gathering some as well. We both dropped our armload back at the starting point, and then I placed one on the plastic stand.

"Finley," he said.

I kicked. "You said we could work out today, right? I'm working out."

"Let me at least loan you the right clothes for this."

The next ball I kicked went off the side of my foot and careened to the left, landing in a patch of wildflowers. I stomped my foot in a fit of frustration. "You lied to me. You said I was doing well, wasn't wasting your time, but I'm not and I am. Why am I still doing this? I'm not going to be able to beat him, am I? He's going to win it all. The place on the podcast, the football spot. He even got a stupid flower today."

"Didn't everyone?"

I picked up a ball, then paused. "Who is giving him a flower after what he did to me? They think he's a catch? He's already moved on?"

"Would that bother you?" Theo asked.

"No . . . I don't know. I told someone you gave me a flower when you didn't. I don't think she believed me, but I told myself I was never going to do that."

"Do what?"

"Use someone to get back at someone else."

"Are you using me?"

"No . . ." I looked at the net and nodded toward it. "Maybe I have been all along. I didn't mean to. I . . . I'm sorry."

"You're not. I knew what I was getting into and why. You know I'm not his fan either. I volunteered." His eyes traveled to the ground, then back up to me. "You got a gift today?"

I nodded, and repeated what he'd said. "Didn't everyone?"

"From who?"

"Deja. She did it to make Jensen mad."

"And did it?"

"He showed up at my house when he knew I didn't want him there. So maybe."

"He showed up at your house?"

"Yes, and instead of kicking him out, my mom told me I was upsetting everyone and that I should leave."

"That's messed up."

"Thank you!"

He stared at the ball I held. "I wish I could kick Jensen's face too."

"You can," I said, extending it toward him. "I've seen you working out. You're strong."

He looked down at his knee and shook his head. "I need more time." He let out a sigh. "I should've gotten you a gift today. Candy or something."

My heart stuttered in my chest. "What?"

"I wanted to."

"You did?"

"I thought about how it would make Jensen mad too."

"Right." I placed another ball and kicked it hard. That one was Theo's face.

When I turned around to get another, Theo was there, right in front of me. Close.

"No more," he said. "Not like this, in the wrong clothes and the wrong shoes with the wrong mindset."

"Oh, please, just turn off your coach mode for a minute and let me vent," I said, trying to step around him.

He stepped in front of me.

"Stop, Theo. I need to do this. I need to practice."

"You don't need to do this today. We'll practice tomorrow."

"No, I need to today."

"Why?"

"Because I do."

"Why?" he pressed.

"Because I'm running out of time," I said. "We only have three weeks."

He shook his head, not buying that excuse. "Why?"

"Because he's in my house, with my grandma to make me sad or something, and it's working. I don't want to be sad! I'm angry! I was with him for an entire year. I listened when he complained; I helped him with homework and sat through all his comic book explanations. I brought him breakfast burritos to school once a week! I woke up early to make those. And all he did was take my future from me. I'm mad at myself for feeling even an ounce of sadness."

It wasn't until Theo pulled me into a hug that I realized I was crying. I thought about pushing away to get myself under control and wipe my face, but he held me tight. It felt good in his arms, so I melted against him.

He didn't say anything for a long time, just rubbed my back

and breathed in when I breathed out, his heartbeat steady against mine. His mouth rested ever so lightly against my forehead.

After what felt like an eternity and my tears had dried and the only feeling left was exhaustion, Theo said against my head, "You're allowed to be sad over the loss, Finley."

"I'm not anymore. I'm over it." I mean, really, I was. Not over what he'd done but definitely over him. That's why the feeling surprised me so much. Maybe Theo was right, I had been holding on to so much anger that I hadn't quite processed the loss yet. I had now. This was all I was giving myself.

He hummed thoughtfully, the noise vibrating through my chest. "You made that jerk weekly breakfast burritos?"

I let out a breathy laugh. "I know, right? I was more pathetic than I realized."

He held on to my upper arms and created some space between us, studying my face. For what, I wasn't sure. "He didn't take your future." He met my eyes with the statement, making it even more sincere.

I shrugged. Between the hosting spot and the internship that went with it, he pretty much had.

"You have more talent than he'll ever have. He didn't deserve you."

My heart raced with his words but also with the intensity in his eyes as he stared at me. "You don't know that," I said.

"I do."

I pushed his chest, finally breaking our connection. "Thanks . . . friend." The word tasted wrong in my mouth, and I hated that. I *wanted* to be his friend and forget that my body was suddenly trying

156

to tell me it wanted more. I couldn't have more. Not with him. Not when I didn't fully trust him. I didn't even fully trust myself.

And yet, I didn't stop him when he pulled me back into his arms again. In fact, I leaned in. And when he whispered, "You're not wasting my time," I let myself believe it.

Chapter
twenty

MEET ME HERE AT 9.

The text was followed by an address in Atascadero, a town about twenty minutes east of us. It was eight now.

When I'd left his house the day before after being comforted through my breakdown (something a good night's rest hadn't erased the embarrassment of), he'd said to be at his house at eight-thirty. This was a change of plans.

I thought we were training today, I responded. I needed to kick. Watching more than half the footballs I'd kicked the day before land far from the net, I knew I needed every second of practice I could get.

We are. See you at 9.

"Bossy," I said to my room. An image of yesterday, our chests pressed together, my forehead against his lips, flashed through my mind, and I had to brace myself on the edge of my bed.

My phone buzzed again and I thought Theo was adding some

sort of instruction to the morning, but the text was from Lee in our group chat.

Congrats on the views, Fin. Your last episode was fire.

What are you talking about?

Your podcast.

My brows shot down, and I went to my laptop at my desk, where I pulled up my stats bar. It told me forty-five people had listened to the installment I had published three days ago. "The Almost Kiss" was what I had labeled the episode. I was confused. Sure, forty-five wasn't that many, but it was more listeners than all the previous episodes combined.

That's weird, I texted back.

Why is that weird?

To go from five to forty-five from one episode to the next is odd.

It was a good episode. Maybe it got shared.

Did you share it? I texted.

No.

That leaves my mom and Deja. Not sure they have that kind of social media power.

Thanks, Deja chimed in. *Waking up to an insult is refreshing. But you're right, I didn't share it. Didn't you say Theo was listening to it. Would he have shared it?*

Theo hugged me yesterday. Deja saying his name easily pulled the confession out of me. I obviously needed to talk it through. *For a long time.*

What?! she responded. *No!*

Followed by a *Really?* from Lee.

And then I reiterated that we were friends, I texted.

Why would you say that after he did that? Lee replied. I could hear the confusion in the text.

I don't know why I said it . . . it felt right?

Deja was first to respond with *Like how when someone says* I love you *and the other person says* thank you? *That kind of right?*

No, it was more like I was having a breakdown after the Jensen at my house thing and he was comforting me and I didn't want him to get the wrong idea or for him to think I was getting the wrong idea. That kind of right.

Lee texted: *I think you mean you didn't want him to get the right idea.*

Wait, do you like him?! Deja asked. *Is that why you're analyzing this so much?*

No! I insisted.

Good, she texted. *Don't let him charm you into letting your guard down. He has a reputation for a reason. Stay focused on your goal. No more jerks.*

Max was the last to the group chat, and he must've caught up on all the texts because all he said was *I have given up my beauty sleep for your denial? Disappointing.*

You guys have been entirely unhelpful lately. I have to go.

"WHAT IS THIS?" I ASKED STARING AT THE RED BARN Theo and I stood in front of. Bleating sounds rang out in the distance and Theo had his signature teasing grin on his face, so I knew he was up to something. "A goat farm? Why are we at a goat farm?"

Even just twenty minutes inland, the March weather was much colder without the Pacific Ocean tempering it. I hadn't prepared well enough. I was in my workout clothes—shorts, a sports bra, and a tank top. I rubbed my arms.

Theo took off his sweatshirt and handed it to me.

"No, it's fine. I'm fine," I said.

"I know you are. Take it anyway."

I let an indignant breath out of my nose but pulled on his sweatshirt. Immediately his scent enveloped me. The soapy vanilla warmth I'd come to associate with him.

"Let's go—it starts in five minutes," he said, walking toward the barn.

"What starts in five minutes?" I asked, following him. Before he answered, I saw the chalkboard sign attached to the wall beside the open door of the barn. It read: *Goat Yoga.* I turned my stare on him. "I thought we were training today."

A couple brushed by us and into the barn. Now that we were closer, I could see the back doors were open as well. They led out to a fenced-in field where yoga mats were set up. Walking around and through and over those mats were . . . goats.

"This *is* for training," Theo said, turning back when he realized I had stopped. "Focus is important. This will help you focus."

I narrowed my eyes. "Is this about yesterday?" As if I already wasn't embarrassed enough about what had happened the day before, now he changed our whole training session to take care of the issues he obviously thought I had? "You think I'm too distracted? Too sad? Too preoccupied with Jensen?" Which was ironic, considering Deja thought I was too preoccupied with him.

"No, well . . . yes. But there are so many other distractions you'll have to shut out when kicking. The sounds of the crowd in the stands, the coach, the pressure of your teammates counting on you. Everything. You have to learn to shut out the world when you're staring down the line and driving toward that ball. It's just you and the uprights. This—" He pointed toward the people that were settling onto mats. "This will help you learn to shut things out and find your focus."

"You're annoying," I said, crossing my arms. But I walked through the barn anyway, toward the class because he was right—I did need to learn to shut out the world. Maybe this would help.

Soft music played through a portable speaker near the instructor. "Find your mats, everyone, and we'll get started."

Pellets of goat poop littered the ground as we walked toward two open mats in the back corner of the space. Theo stepped out of his shoes and onto his mat, where he sat cross-legged facing the instructor.

"Have you done this before?" I asked, following suit.

"I have," he said.

"You have?"

"I told you, kicking takes focus. All of us have distractions, Finley. Not just you."

I sat down and pulled my hair back into the holder I'd brought. "What are your distractions?" I whispered this because aside from the music and the bleating goats, it was very quiet.

"Right now?" he asked with a smirk. "You."

My heart thumped heavy in my chest seeming to think he was admitting to something. It took me too long to realize he just meant that I was literally distracting him from yoga in this moment. A goat approached me, pushing its head into my shoulder before bounding off to someone else.

"Can everyone assume Easy Seat," the instructor said.

I'd never done yoga before, so I watched closely, bending my body into the shapes demonstrated, most seemed to have animal names. I felt clumsy and wobbly as I tried to assume one-legged positions or wide stances. My discomfort came out in breathy laughs and mistakes that turned my cheeks pink. I concentrated hard on each pose, trying to get it right, do it exactly like the instructor showed us. Half an hour of various poses later and I wasn't succeeding.

Theo, on the other hand, was perfectly focused, his movements confident and strong, even when a goat had bounced off his leg.

"Slowly transition to Warrior Two," the instructor said.

I copied her position, lunging with my right and turning my back foot, my upper body and arms turned as well. Theo lunged with his opposite leg, probably the correct one, which resulted in us facing each other. He met my stare. His expression was both relaxed and steady, like his body was. He seemed so comfortable here, so comfortable in his own skin doing this. I felt the opposite—out of place and unsure of myself. Ready to abandon the rest of class and go sit in the car. I knew I looked ridiculous, wobbling every couple seconds, trying to ground my feet like the instructor was saying, tighten my core. Nothing was helping. And Theo was still staring.

Stop distracting me, I mouthed.

One side of his lips formed a half smile. And then a goat walked beneath me, between my legs, throwing me off-balance. My arms made wide circles to try to save me, but all they seemed to do was propel me to the ground. I landed straight on my butt, letting out a yelp as I did.

"Sorry," I said, clamping my mouth shut and scrambling to untangle myself from the goat that was now straddling one of my legs.

Theo rushed to my side to aid me in the process. After what seemed like minutes but was probably seconds, the goat was free and jumping to his next victim.

"You okay?" Theo asked, giving me a hand up.

"I'm unharmed," I said, hoping all eyes weren't on me. I refused to look around to find out.

Then the instructor was speaking again. "It's time to start our cooldown. Can everyone take child's pose?"

This was a face down position on the mat, knees tucked into chest, arms above the head relaxed.

"I'd like everyone to focus on their breathing," she continued. "Breathe in all the good energy and happy feelings and positive thoughts. Breathe out negativity and self-doubt and bad energy. Relax each muscle group starting at the tips of your fingers and then your hands and arms, the tops of your heads, your brows, your eyes, your cheeks. Let go. Loosen your neck and shoulders. . . ."

I listened and breathed and relaxed. Let myself feel the weight of my body and how it connected with the earth. A goat climbed onto my back, its hooves digging into my shoulder blades. I tried to shut it out, focus. I was vaguely aware of the instructor thanking everyone for coming. The goat settled in on my back, lying down. Now I could feel its little heartbeat, its warm solid body. My forehead on the mat felt heavy, like it would take a lot of effort to lift my head. And why would I when I could just stay here with a goat on my back and forget everything else? All I let my mind think about was my breathing. In and out, my chest rising and falling.

The sound of metal hitting metal, probably the gate banging closed, startled me and the goat and it jumped off. I sat up. Theo was pulling on his shoes.

He smiled at me.

"Did you share my podcast?" I asked, pushing the hair that had come loose from my ponytail out of my face.

"What?"

"My podcast. It had a bunch of views this week. I was just wondering if you shared it."

"Did you post another episode?"

I sat back and picked up my shoes from the corner of the mat. "I did."

"And you don't think it can have a lot of views because it's good and people just naturally wanted to share it?"

"Who would've been the first one to naturally share it, if not one of my friends, though? Some stranger?"

"Why not?"

"I don't know. I guess it's possible. My grandma is a natural storyteller."

"You are good at helping people tell a story naturally," he said.

I loosened the laces on my shoes so I could pull them on, not sure that was true.

"I'll have to listen to it," he said.

"You don't have to."

"Let me rephrase that: I want to listen to it."

I glanced around. The instructor was filling a trough with food for the goats, and they had all gathered around her, bleating and jumping. "This was cool. Thanks for bringing me."

"I started yoga after . . ." He brushed his hand over his knee, as if that action said it all, and stood up. "I don't usually come to the goat class, but I thought you'd like it."

"I would totally come again if I hadn't been so terrible at it."

He shook his head. "You didn't get graded."

"I graded myself."

"You need to stop doing that," he said.

"Doing what?"

"Being so hard on yourself."

"I'm just being honest. Realistic."

"Or you give up if you're not immediately perfect, to save yourself from . . ." He tilted his head as if assessing the many ways that sentence could end. "Embarrassment? Disappointment? I don't know—I'm still trying to figure that part out."

"You can stop analyzing me now." I tied my laces and stood.

"I'm trying to help you succeed."

"You think I'm going to quit the whole kicking thing?"

"It crossed my mind. Especially after you've said you might multiple times now."

"I'm not the only one who quits things." I nodded toward his knee.

"That's different and you know it."

166

"Is it?" Our eyes were locked on one another, and mine moved back and forth between his, a tension that wasn't all negative building. Maybe it wasn't negative at all. My body felt tight but also alive. I was the first to break the standoff. "I'm not going to quit."

"Good."

"And stop analyzing me," I huffed.

He smiled. "But I'm really good at it."

"You're not."

"Fine, I'll stop."

"Good."

We headed toward the exit, waving and thanking the instructor as we did. My phone buzzed in my pocket with a notification. I pulled it out as we walked through the barn toward the gravel parking lot and our cars.

"Oh," I said in surprise.

"What?" Theo asked.

"It's Alice, Cheryl Millcreek's daughter. She sent me a message."

Chapter
twenty-one

"ASK YOUR THIEF OF A MOTHER WHAT SHE DID WITH MY grandma's surfboard," Max said, waving his hand at my phone. "That's what you should say."

"I'm obviously not going to say that," I said. It was the following day. Theo and I had just finished an evening workout at his house because his mom had hosted a brunch that morning and didn't want us there working out. We now sat on the boardwalk behind the diner, waiting for Deja, who was closing up inside. "I actually want her help."

"I thought it was good," Theo said.

Max gave him a high five. It was just the three of us. Lee was at some family dinner.

A pelican was trying to land on the rounded top of a post at the edge of the boardwalk, its feet slipping and its wings flapping with each failure. The sun sat atop Morro Rock, about to sink behind it.

I should've answered Alice back the day before, but I didn't want to sound accusatory, and every message I'd composed and erased over the last twenty-four hours had sounded exactly that. Maybe not as bad as Max's suggestion, but still.

I pursed my lips and said, "How about just *I heard your mom was a surfer. So was my grandma. I'm looking for a board they might have shared?*"

"That's good," Max said.

"It is," Theo agreed. "She might actually be willing to respond to a message like that."

I typed in the words and pressed send. My back was leaned up against the railing running along the edge of the wooden walk that separated the restaurants from the bay. I could see Deja sweeping through the windows of the Purple Starfish.

Max must've seen her as well because he said, "I'm going to hurry her along."

"You just want to score leftovers," I said as he walked toward the door.

"Is that a possibility?" Theo asked, ready to follow him.

"I'll report back," Max said, and pushed the heavy side door open.

Theo watched him go, then settled onto the ground beside me, his shoulder bumping mine.

"I watched some videos this morning of you kicking a football," I said. I'd been to all the football games earlier this year even though Jensen rode the bench. But the truth was, I hardly watched the games. I mostly talked to my friends. Or we'd buy food or make fun of the uniforms. I'd only gone to support Jensen. And I'd never seen Theo kick a ball before finding the videos that morning.

169

His head turned toward me. "What? Why?"

"I used to watch tape all the time for soccer to improve my form and identify mistakes. You never did that?"

"Of course I did. I just . . . Where did you find tape of me? You asked Coach?"

"No way. I found some online. People post football games to YouTube all the time. I just had to dig through the footage to find you." And I had found him. I'd even found some clips where the poster had zoomed in nice and tight on his kick. His form was beautiful—smooth and strong and almost graceful. "You looked . . ."

Our legs were stretched out in front of us, my right running alongside his left. He was still in his shorts from our workout, and my eyes studied his scar. It seemed so innocent there, like it wasn't big enough or dark enough to represent what it had taken from him.

"I looked what?" he asked, his hand brushing over his knee.

I captured his hand in mine to stop his mindless habit. Or maybe to let him know that I hadn't meant to stare. "You looked beautiful." My throat felt tight with the word.

"Are you mocking me?" he asked, squeezing my hand. His lips twitched into a smirk.

"No, I'm not. I promise. I want to kick like that." I started to pull my hand away, but he held on, bringing it over to his lap and running a finger along each of my knuckles. A shiver went through me.

"I want to kick like that again too," he said, his voice low.

Despite the fact that his finger was gliding over my skin, causing goose bumps to form over every inch of me, I wasn't sure if he was feeling anything. He seemed to be lost in his thoughts, absent-mindedly moving his body.

"You don't think you will?" I asked.

"Do you know what happens when you're an only child? All your parents' unfulfilled potential rests on your shoulders, and even when it's something you want for yourself, you feel triple the pressure to achieve it."

"That's hard," I said.

His shoulder was getting heavier against mine. I looked over at him, and his eyes locked with mine.

I was very aware that my hair was greasy, and my skin sticky from our workout. I gently took my hand from him and shifted sideways, tucking my legs beneath me and looking out at the water. It was choppy and a dark blue with the setting sun. A dinner-cruise boat was slowly moving in the distance.

"Is it an otter?" Theo asked, bringing my gaze sharply back to him.

"What?" I asked.

"An otter," he said again, not looking at the water at all, instead, his eyes still on me. Had he listened to the podcast? Was he referencing the words my grandma had said to avoid a kiss? And did that mean he had been about to kiss me and I had stopped it with my sideways shift away from him? My stomach fluttered with that thought.

"I thought it looked more like a sea lion," I said back.

He gave a breathy laugh. "That was a really good episode. I can see why it has so many views."

He *had* been referencing the podcast, then. But was it just that? A reference? And what did I want it to be? I felt like anything, even a kiss, with Theo was complicated. There was too much baggage surrounding us. Too many people would think we had ulterior motives. Even my best friend didn't support it, saw the complications, thought he wasn't right for me. And maybe I still didn't fully trust him either.

"Yeah, um . . . thanks. My grandma is pretty cool." I was facing Theo, my legs crossed in front of me and my elbows resting on my knees. He still sat with his back against the railing and his legs stretched out in front of him.

"Hopefully Alice gets back to you soon," he said. Again, his finger found my skin. This time gliding over my kneecap. But this time, instead of seeming to be in another world, his eyes didn't leave mine.

I swallowed. "Yeah, hopefully." My voice sounded breathy.

"When's your next interview with your grandma?"

I trapped his finger in my fist, mainly so he'd stop causing jolts of electricity to shoot up my leg, but also because despite everything I'd said about how complicated we were, I wanted to touch him too. "I can't really plan them. It just depends on if she's up to it or not. Some days are better than others."

"I hope you get to it soon," he said. "I need the kiss." His smirk was back. The little punk knew exactly what he was doing.

I dropped his finger and playfully shoved his shoulder.

He chuckled. "What?"

"You know what," I said with a laugh.

"*That's* your real laugh," he said.

"What?"

"Why do you fake laugh on your podcast?"

"For the general good of the listeners," I said. "To save their ears."

"Your real laugh is better," he said.

I reached out to shove his shoulder again, and he captured my wrist, tugging me forward in the process. I caught myself on his knee, and he sucked in some air. I immediately recoiled. "I'm so sorry."

"No, it's okay."

"I didn't mean to." My eyes zeroed in on his leg, my hands hovering above his scar, as if I could feel from an inch away if I had somehow caused an injury. "Are you okay? Did I hurt you?"

"I'm fine. It was just reflex. You didn't hurt me."

"I'm so sorry."

"Finley," he said, and I raised my gaze to his. "I'm not that fragile."

"You're fine?"

"I'm fine. And it wasn't your fault. I'm the one that pulled you closer."

My heart beat heavily in my ears. My hands, no longer hovering over his knee, had instead come to rest on it. We were close. His eyes were bouncing from my eyes to my lips, which suddenly felt dry. I sucked my bottom one into my mouth.

"Good news!" Max's voice broke through the silence, and my body practically flung itself into the ocean, startled by the words. "There were leftovers, and I have decided to share them."

Theo pushed himself off the ground and joined Max on the bench, where he'd set a basket of fries and a couple burgers. "You are a saint."

"Have never been called that before, but I'll take it."

Deja emerged from the side door looking harried. "I wish I could hang, but I'm going to play soccer."

"Play soccer?" I asked.

"Some of us are getting together to stay conditioned for summer league."

"Oh."

"You wrote Alice back, right?" she asked.

"Yes, I did."

"Good," she said with a smile. "I hope we find the board. I can't wait to see it."

"Me too."

She gave a double-handed wave and disappeared down the walk.

Max took another bite of burger, then stood. "I didn't realize she wasn't going to hang with us. This third wheel is leaving now."

"You're not a third wheel," I said. "We're just—"

"Friends?" Max said. "Yeah, yeah. I know. I'll see you at school tomorrow."

He left, and Theo picked up the rest of the remaining burger and came to sit on the ground next to me again. He handed me the food.

I took a bite without arguing this time. I was pretty hungry after our workout.

"Deja hates me," he said.

I practically choked on the bite I'd just taken, but managed to chew and swallow without incident. "*Hate* is a strong word."

"So I'm not wrong," he returned.

"She doesn't know you. Doesn't trust you."

He narrowed his eyes and then gave a slow nod.

"What?" I asked.

"You haven't been talking about me with your friends. Telling them . . . anything."

"No, I have . . ." Hadn't I? In my haste to prove him wrong, I blurted out, "I told them we hugged for a long time on the first day of spring!"

His brows popped up.

That was the wrong thing to say. "I mean, just because I was trying to . . . I was embar— I didn't want you to . . . See, I talked about you," I finished in an unspectacular fashion.

"So based on what they now know, they think I'm the cocky jerk who hugs you?"

I smiled. "Yes."

He shook his head but gave a breathy laugh. "Great."

"They know you're helping me. That's gone a long way with Max and Lee."

"But not with Deja."

"She's wary. Doesn't understand why you'd want to help me."

"She doesn't . . . or *you* don't?" His question was accompanied by a hurt expression.

I hesitated before I said, "Her?"

"Ouch," he said.

"I have trust issues. Big ones. I'm sorry. I'm really trying to work through them. I want to work through them. I like you. I mean, not like . . . It's not that . . . As a friend."

"I'm helping you because I like to right wrongs," he said. "And Jensen has racked up a lot of wrongs."

"Do you go around righting all the wrongs at school or just this one?"

"Just this one . . . for now."

Chapter
twenty-two

"IT'S TIME TO TALK ABOUT DATE TWO WITH ANDREW, Grandma. The people want to hear it," I said a couple days later. The last episode was now at two hundred views, and I was getting daily messages on my social media asking for the next part. People loved my grandma. I understood. She was lovable.

"They're going to be disappointed with how underwhelming it was," she said.

"I doubt it."

The blinds on the window in my room were open today, and she was distracted by some kids who were riding scooters on the street outside. But she wasn't playing with the cord to her headphones, so that was good.

Despite her distraction, she answered my question. "In the summer, on the first weekend of the month, a band would come to the beach and perform. It was free and I went a lot, but this time,

Andrew asked me to go with him. He picked me up in a convertible he'd borrowed from his grandpa, and we drove it to the packed parking lot by the rock."

"Do you remember which band was playing that night?"

"I wish I did. It would make for a better story," she said.

"Either way it's a good story."

"They were usually local bands who mostly played cover songs. They'd get together one summer and were broken up by the next. Moved on with their lives to things that actually paid money."

"Sounds like some things never change," I said.

"And so many other things do," she said, her eyes still on the window.

"Was it a fun date?"

"It was loud and crowded and, yes, very fun. He bought me a hot dog and a lemonade, and we sang and laughed. That was the night he told me he was working on a painting for me."

"Did you know it would be on a surfboard?"

"I had no idea. I asked him if I could see it, and he told me to have patience. Then a slow song came on and he looked at me and said, *Do you know how to slow dance or do you need to stand on my feet?*"

I smiled. "He didn't give you the option to say no."

"I didn't want to say no."

"So did you dance or stand on his feet?"

"A little of both," she said with a smile. "I coiled my arms around his neck. He had long hair that came past his shoulders, and it was wavy and soft. I played with it as we swayed back and forth.

After I'd rejected his last attempt at a kiss, I could tell he was waiting this time, even though we were close, staring into each other's eyes. If I wanted a kiss, I was going to have to initiate."

"Did you?"

"It was romantic, but I didn't want my first kiss to be in the middle of a crowd. So no, we danced and held each other, sand pressing between our toes, the moon bright overhead, but we didn't kiss."

"Sounds like a lot of excuses, Grandma," I teased. "When you were really just scared."

"I was," she admitted. "I liked him at this point, but I didn't quite trust him. He was the type who could have any girl he wanted. Why me?"

"What did he say to change your mind?" I asked, hoping she had some insight because I completely understood where she was coming from. "To convince you."

"He didn't say anything. He just kept being him."

"I LIKED YOUR LATEST EPISODE," JENSEN SAID. "SEEMS like everyone else did as well."

We were outside, heading toward the cafeteria for some reason. Nolen had been intentionally vague when we got to class, saying we were going on a field trip of sorts. And now we were walking across campus. The seagulls sounded louder when the hallways were empty like they were now, and their squawks echoed around

179

us. I was just about to jog ahead, ignore him, catch up with Ava, when Nolen turned around.

"You have a podcast?" He walked backward with the question. He had obviously overheard Jensen's words.

"I do," I said. "It's about my grandma's life."

He slowed down until I'd caught up, then started walking beside me, on the opposite side as Jensen. "What was significant about her life?" It was a rude question, but I knew what he meant.

"Nothing," I said. "And everything. She was just a normal person, but the way she tells her story makes it interesting."

Jensen could've said that I helped her tell an interesting story, like Theo had, but instead he contradicted me and said, "She dated Andrew Lancaster." As if that was the only thing that made her story worth telling.

"The painter?" Nolen asked. "That's really cool."

"I think it's less about the fact that he was a famous painter and more about the fact that he was just a regular guy, falling in love."

Jensen and Nolen shared a glance as if that wasn't true at all.

"It has over a thousand listens now, and we have talked very little about his painting life," I insisted. I still couldn't believe a thousand people had listened. I'd only recorded and posted the latest episode two days ago.

"Wow, that's impressive," Nolen said. "Good job. That's hard to do as an indie podcast."

"Thanks," I said.

Jensen mumbled something under his breath.

"What?" I asked.

"I shared it on my Insta last week."

"What?" I asked again.

"Your podcast. I told people to listen to it." *He* was the one who had shared it?

Nolen let out a surprised hum. "That was good of you. Hopefully your support of our podcast will drive some numbers our way as well."

We were approaching the cafeteria, and Nolen, who had fallen to the middle of the pack while talking to us, seemed to realize he was the leader here. He gave us a nod before rushing to the front.

"You're something else," I said. Jensen shouldn't have been able to surprise me with his actions anymore, but he still managed to.

He seemed to think that was a compliment instead of the sarcastic insult it obviously was because he said, "You're welcome." And not in a snarky way.

"Ugh," I groaned. "Don't talk to me." With those words, I really left to find Ava.

"What are we doing here?" she asked as we walked through the doors of the cafeteria.

It had been a while since I'd eaten in the cafeteria, but I suddenly remembered a time last year when it was raining out and nearly everyone had piled into the building from where they normally sat in the courtyard or front lawn. It was packed, and there were no seats as I looked for Jensen or my friends. I wasn't watching where I was going in my search and nearly ran into Theo. He'd prevented the crash with a quick hand to my elbow, and then he kept walking. That memory immediately washed out the bad taste in my mouth left by the conversation with Jensen.

It wasn't raining now, and the cafeteria was empty. It was Thursday and I hadn't seen Theo much this week. Just a couple times while passing in the halls. His earbuds in, his hands in his pockets. He'd give me a nod and a smile, but didn't try to catch up with me or walk me to first period like he'd been doing the week before. After seeing him so much last weekend, it felt a bit like withdrawal. I wondered if I'd hurt him more than I realized on Sunday when I said I didn't trust him. The acidic taste was back in my mouth.

"I'm not sure why we're here," I said to Ava.

"Okay!" Nolen called as we stopped in front of a table with two cafeteria trays. "Features are short side stories that can be told in regular reports as part of the bigger podcast. For example, Jensen thought a fun feature could be a weekly review of the cafeteria food. He also thought this would be a way for more people to have a voice on the podcast."

"Jensen?" I said with a scoff, not able to keep it in. "Features were literally something I wrote in my topics notebook that he looked at."

"I didn't know what *features* meant when I saw it in your notebook," he said.

I pursed my lips together, forcing myself to shut up because the look on Nolen's face said that he thought I was acting immature.

He continued as if I hadn't interrupted. "I would like you each to put in a bid. As to why you'd be good for the job as feature reporter. I'd also like to hear a few other ideas for features. It will be great on-mic practice and could lead to a bigger role on the podcast if they're well received." His gaze fell on me with those words.

Maybe I was being ungrateful, but this felt like a consolation prize. A pat on the head. Or maybe Nolen was looking at me because he wished he'd picked me instead of Jensen, who knew next to nothing about podcasting.

"Thanks, once again, Jensen," Nolen said. "For this great idea. This is what happens, people, when you bring in an outsider. It might seem threatening at first, but there is something to be said about fresh blood."

I almost rolled my eyes but held back. He talked a little bit more about features, and when he was done people asked if they could actually try the food on the table. That's how class ended. I held back as everyone quickly left the cafeteria, then approached Nolen and Susie, who were cleaning up the trays from the table.

"Hey, guys, can I . . . ?" How did I even start this? I really didn't want them to think I was a sore loser, but Jensen taking credit for my ideas again today was simmering in my chest. "I had that feature idea written in the notebook he looked at."

Nolen nodded. "You have good ideas. We're glad to have you on the team."

Susie just gave me a sympathetic look.

Right. They didn't care. I turned toward the door.

"Finley," Nolen said.

"Yeah?"

"We almost picked you," he said. "We did. And had Jensen not tried out, we would've. But your main problem is that you're in your head too much. We can see you thinking. Trying to get it just right.

183

You need to relax behind the mic. Let yourself make mistakes. Mistakes make you more relatable."

"I have a feeling Jensen will be very relatable, then," I said. I couldn't help myself. I understood what Nolen was trying to say, but too many mistakes were just messy.

Chapter
twenty-three

I'LL SHOW HIM FRESH BLOOD, I TEXTED THAT DAY AFTER school as I headed through campus to my car, recounting what had happened during podcast class in a string of long, ranty texts. I hadn't told them at lunch. I had still been seething, and we had been surrounded by people I hadn't wanted to overhear my rage-filled monologue.

What does that mean? Max responded. *Are you going to stab him?*

I let out a laugh, then typed: *I want to.*

Let's stay out of jail, Lee responded.

Fresh blood, I typed again. *Nolen acts like it's an original idea. Features are basic.*

Deja said nothing. I wondered if she was driving, on her way to work. I realized I didn't know her schedule. Usually, I asked her every Sunday. I hadn't asked her this week. *How did soccer conditioning go on Sunday, Deja?*

Again, there was no response. She was definitely on her way to work. It was Thursday. She normally worked on Thursdays.

I reached the parking lot, and as I tucked my phone away and stepped onto the asphalt, I saw Theo across the way, heading for his car. I looked both ways to make sure there was no traffic and rushed to catch him. He had his earbuds in, so it was pointless to call out his name. I got to him right before he reached his car, though, and I plucked one of them out.

His head whipped in my direction, a look of confusion or irritation on his face. When he saw it was me, that look transformed into a smile.

"Hi," I said. "What are you doing?"

He pointed to his car. "Going home. What are *you* doing?"

"Trying to channel yoga teachings because Nolen is driving me insane. He's a Jensen fanboy, I think." I was trying to forget the other things he said. Because the bottom line was that he'd admitted I would've made the host spot had Jensen not tried out.

"I think there's a club," Theo said.

I held up his earbud. "Why do you always walk around with these? You don't like to talk to anyone?"

"I talk to you a lot."

I shouldn't have let myself be flattered by that, but I did. "Your friends annoy you?"

"I like music."

"Well . . ." I held out his earbud for him, and he took it. "This is one of the reasons people think you're a snob."

He smirked. "So I've heard."

I remembered that first night I'd met him, how he knew the order of the pool lights. "You spend a lot of time in your head."

He shrugged. "I have a lot to think about."

"What are you thinking about now?" I asked.

"I was wondering what you were doing tonight?"

"Tonight?"

"Yes, that thing that comes after today."

"Funny. Nothing. Why?" *Was he about to ask me out?*

"Meet me at the elementary school at seven?"

"For training?" I shouldn't have been disappointed. I needed to train.

"Yes."

"On a Thursday night?"

"Yes."

I nodded, and his smile grew.

"Good. I'll see you there." He pointedly put his earbud back in while staring at me.

I laughed, and he climbed in his car. I turned and walked to mine. It was then I realized that I *wanted* to trust Theo. He was making it easy.

I HEADED TOWARD THE FIELD BEHIND THE ELEMENTARY school slowly, a mass of kids occupying the space. My soccer cleats dangled over my shoulder by their laces. I looked at my phone again.

Meet me on the soccer field, the text from Theo read.

Did he not realize there would be some sort of game going on? His car had been in the parking lot, but I didn't see him.

The school sat on a hill, and from here I could see the ocean and giant Morro Rock in the distance. The wind kicked up, sweeping hair across my face. I pulled it back into a ponytail and secured it with the holder I'd brought. Next to the school was a park and an older couple was playing pickleball on the courts. The sounds of the ball hitting the racket and the kids screaming mingled in the air.

As I got closer to the field, I could see long strips of colorful material dangling off white belts strapped around the waist of each child. A couple footballs were being tossed as well. My eyes scanned the bleachers, where a few parents sat watching.

"Finley!" Theo was waving at me from the middle of the field.

I finished the walk to him. "Hi," I said. "What are you doing?"

"I help coach flag football on Thursdays."

"Oh."

"Coach T, my shoe's untied," a little boy said, stopping in front of him and lifting his foot.

"It sure is." Theo took a knee and tied the boy's shoe; then he ran off with his friends.

When Theo stood, a slight wince colored his expression. I found myself wincing right along with him. I relaxed my expression before he noticed.

"Everyone, gather round!" he called, and as he did he pulled something out of his pocket. It wasn't until he was slinging it around my waist that I realized it was one of the belts that all the kids were wearing. "Finley has never played flag football before!"

What? How? Oh no! were some of the words I was able to decipher through the collective shout of the kids around us.

"You think we can teach her?" he asked.

"Yes!" they all screamed at once.

He tugged on both ends of the belt, which forced me closer to him. Then he was threading one end into the metal buckle piece of the other end. He was bent over for the task, his hair brushing my cheek in the process. "I know what you're thinking," he said quietly. *"Someone will suspect.* But if this somehow gets out, you can say volunteering looks good on résumés. You're here for volunteer work."

I hadn't been thinking much of anything with his hands brushing against my waist and his hair tickling my cheek, but it was obvious he had thought it through. "Are you going to play too?" I asked, noticing he wasn't wearing a belt.

"Yes, Coach, play!" one of the girls said.

"I'll play," he said, freeing another belt from his pocket.

"Yay!" The cheer was loud.

He buckled on his belt.

"Oh, look what I finally found." I lifted my cleats off my shoulder.

"Nice." He took them from me and flung them toward the sidelines. "We'll use them later."

The next five minutes were spent teaching me the rules, which were mostly the same as regular football, except no tackling was involved. By the time the ball was placed on the scrimmage line, I thought I had it down, despite the fact that twenty kids were yelling different things at me the whole time. Theo had assigned me to the yellow team and himself to the red, so we stood on opposite sides of that invisible line, staring at each other. He'd made me the quarterback, which I thought was really rude, but my plan was to get rid of the ball as quickly as possible after each snap.

That plan was harder said than done. The kids were fast. My yellow ribbons were torn from my belt after each snap three separate times. On the fourth down, Theo whispered to the line of kids something that I suspected went, *Let her throw the ball.*

"Don't go easy on me!" I called.

He laughed. "Fine, don't go easy on her, team."

This time when the ball was snapped, I backed up more, and my pocket of protectors actually protected me as I looked down the field for someone to throw it to. A dark-haired little girl was open on the right, and our eyes met. I chucked the ball, very poorly, but she managed to catch it. Just as I released the ball, Theo was by my side, tugging one of the ribbons on my belt. The Velcro must've been super strength because the action threw me off-balance and I careened into his chest. His arm wrapped around me, possibly to keep me from falling.

"Too late," I said, with a smile, against his chest.

"Lucky pass," he said.

"Talent," I assured him.

"Maybe you're trying out for the wrong position."

I laughed. "You're right—I should just try out for all the positions."

Shouts upfield drew our attention away from each other, and he released his hold on me. Down the way, my little teammate had made it all the way to the endzone. I let out a whoop and high-fived the kid next to me.

I held my fake microphone up to my mouth. "Coach Theo, you

have now witnessed the person you literally just taught the game to throw a touchdown pass to take the lead. How does that make you feel?"

He took my hand in his and brought it up to his mouth. "I feel like I need to show you how it's done." With those words, he went to collect the ball.

Kids trailed after him, like shadows, mimicking his every move, it seemed. Once he had the ball, he turned and said something that made his shadows laugh. My heart gave a lurch.

Then we were back to the game, him playing quarterback this time and, apparently, me making it my one and only goal to relieve him of a ribbon. I would race around and through and past players, reaching for the red material.

On his third completed pass, he narrowed his eyes at me after my failed attempt, playfully swatting my hand away from his waist. "I'm not even who you're supposed to be after."

"Oh, you are," I said. "You are."

He laughed. A laugh that lit up his whole face. "Get back to your side."

The little boy next to me looked up when I was standing in my place. "You go that way and block Micah from catching the ball." He pointed behind me.

"Or we can all go after Coach," I said, whispering to the kids around me. "Do you all want to go after Coach?"

They nodded in unison, and that time on the snap, we rushed Theo. I got behind him and wrapped my arms around his, pinning them to his sides as a gaggle of kids ripped the ribbons from his belt.

"Cheaters!" he yelled. "All of you are cheaters."

The kids howled with laughter as I released him, and he turned to face me. "Especially you," he said. "The biggest cheater of all." He scooped me into his arms and lifted me off the ground, spinning once. I tensed, worried about his knee, but he just set me back down and shouted, "Ten-yard penalty!"

"Worth it!" I said.

"You're a bad influence," he said.

"Thank you," I called over my shoulder as I headed to my team.

The rest of the hour was more straightforward; we followed the rules and both teams scored a couple more touchdowns. And then it was over. Parents were collecting their kids, and kids were saying goodbye as the lights on the field clicked on. Then it was just Theo and me standing midfield with a pile of belts and a couple of footballs.

"That was fun," I said.

"You were good with them."

"*You* were good with them." I sat next to the pile of belts and began reattaching some ribbons that had come loose. "How long have you been doing this?"

"I've been helping out during off season since"—he shrugged like it was no big deal, sitting down next to me—"freshman year."

"You really are a nice guy."

He let out a single laugh. "You're still not convinced, are you?"

"I am!" I said. "You are."

"I don't know how to respond to that."

"Thank you?" I suggested.

"Thank you?" he said, keeping the question in his inflection and everything.

"I'm sorry it took me this long to truly believe it. It's my issues, not yours."

"Oh, I know."

This time I laughed, then picked up a handful of belts. "What do we do with all this stuff?"

"There's a mesh bag by the bleachers." He stood, and again I saw the wince as he did.

I couldn't help myself and asked, "Is your knee bothering you more than normal?"

"Just a little stiff. It's fine." He scooped up the rest of the belts.

"I'm sorry," I said.

"Don't be."

"Is it because of all the extra practices you're putting in with me?"

"They're good for me." He deposited the belts into the bag, then picked up a ball. "Do you have time to stick around for a bit longer? Practice kicking?"

I looked at his knee. "Are you sure?"

"You'll be the one kicking, not me." He handed me my cleats that I hadn't noticed on the ground near us.

"Thanks." I squatted down to change out the shoes I was wearing for my cleats. I hadn't put them on in a year, and they felt tight . . . snug. I stared out over the field, little white bugs floated above the grass, beating their wings.

"You miss soccer?" he asked.

"I miss bonding with a team, hanging out with Deja more," I confided. "But I honestly don't miss soccer. I'll miss podcasting."

I met his eyes. They were a golden brown and seemed to want to say something.

"You're analyzing me again."

He smiled. "I don't understand. Why do you have to miss it?"

"Well, for one, my grandma's story will be done or she won't be able to tell it anymore."

He nodded in sympathy.

"And for two, I need more than a personal podcast. I need better equipment and more training. And at the school I'm planning to go to, there is one path into their podcast program and it will be taken by Jensen and Ava." And I couldn't move away. Not anytime soon. Not only could I not afford it right now, but I wanted as much time as possible with my grandma.

"The internship?" he asked.

"Yeah," I said.

"Maybe you need to make another path. Submit your personal podcast to them. Show them there shouldn't only be one path."

"Maybe," I said.

"You're scared to do that?"

"It's more that I don't think it will work. So yeah, I guess I'm scared. These past few weeks have shown me I'm more of a coward than I ever realized."

"You're not a coward." He spun the football on his palm. "What you're doing right now, with this, is beyond brave."

I laughed. "Revenge?"

A half smile crept onto his face. "Well, that too."

I snatched the ball from him. "I appreciate the pep talk, Coach, but we have to turn me into the best kicker in the land."

"In the land?" he asked.

"Fine, I'll settle for top ten."

He smiled. "Stop grading yourself. All you need to be is better than one particular kicker."

I gave a single nod. "I can do that."

"Yes, you can."

My phone buzzed in my pocket, and I pulled it out. It was a Facebook notification. When I opened it, I found a message from Alice waiting.

"What?" Theo asked. I must've gone still.

I turned the phone toward him, and we read it together.

There's a shed in the back of my mom's house if you want to come look through it for the surfboard this weekend. You're welcome to.

"Tell her yes!" he said in excitement. "Let's do it."

Chapter
twenty-four

"SO YOU DIDN'T KISS THE BOY ON THE FIRST DATE OR the second. What about the third, Grandma?" I asked her the next night at our setup in my bedroom.

The comment section on the Instagram posts I was linking the podcast to were blowing up just as much as the podcast itself. People I didn't know from all over were leaving comments asking for the next episode or talking about how cute my grandma was. They were also giving me suggestions on where to search for the surfboard. I'd followed a few promising leads but had found nothing yet. I was excited for the following day, when Theo and I would search Cheryl's shed. That felt like the most solid lead yet.

"Our third date was in Paso Robles," Grandma said. "The summer had just ended, and the county fair was in town. We went on a few rides, and then he tried to win me a stuffed animal at the balloon dart game. He had many theories on why he was unsuccessful."

"Oh yeah? What were his theories?"

"The darts weren't sharp enough, the balloons were under-inflated. You know, typical excuses."

"Tell me that you took over and popped a couple balloons."

"Of course I didn't. The darts weren't sharp enough and the balloons were underinflated," she said with a wink.

I laughed.

"I did win ring toss, though, and got a little goldfish in a bag."

"An actual goldfish?"

"Yes, I ended up having her for three years. She was a hardy thing. I cried when she died."

"I'm sorry."

"Me too. You think I can convince your mom to let me have a goldfish?"

"Ask her for a cat," I said, as if Mom didn't listen to this podcast and would realize I was trying to use my grandma to get the cat I always wanted.

"I'll try." She smirked, seeming to know my motivation.

"So you won a goldfish and had to carry it around the rest of the night?"

"They gave me a ticket, and I collected the goldfish at the end of the date."

"Smart. That way you had two free hands for all the hand-holding I assume was happening."

"There was some hand-holding," she said.

"Did he make his move at the top of the Ferris wheel?"

"He was still waiting for me to make the move after my rejection.

And the top of the Ferris wheel should've been my number one choice. But instead, it happened more unexpectedly."

"I like unexpected."

"We were walking through the big tent where all the FFA kids had their animals on display in pens. The whole tent smelled like . . . well, it smelled like a place where a hundred farm animals were being housed."

"Romantic," I teased.

"In the far back corner was a petting zoo. Three or four lambs and three or four goats comingled with a handful of kids."

"I recently did goat yoga. Goats can be both adorable and big jerks at the same time."

"Goat yoga? What's that?"

"It's yoga in a field while goats use you as their playground."

"Sounds . . . counterintuitive."

"It was actually surprisingly relaxing," I said. "I take it your petting zoo didn't involve yoga poses."

"No yoga poses, but a goat did use me as his playground. I was standing there minding my own business trying to pet one of the lambs when a goat headbutted me from the side, knocking me right into Andrew's arms."

"Do you think Andrew bribed that goat with feed?"

"I wouldn't rule it out. Because there I was, wrapped up in Andrew, saved from landing on the urine-soaked ground. He pulled me up to my feet, and I think he was about to ask me if I was okay when I pushed onto my toes and kissed him."

"What did he do?"

"He was surprised at first. He went still, but then his hands went around my waist and he kissed me back."

"Did all the children in the petting zoo yell *Gross!* at the top of their lungs?"

"I'm not sure what anyone else did. I was in the moment. Everything else vanished, the noise, the people, the animals. It was just him and me, kissing like we were alone."

I smiled, imagining it. "As far as first kisses go, how was it?"

"He was an excellent kisser," she said. "And it was even better for having waited."

THEO CLIMBED IN MY CAR SATURDAY MORNING AFTER we finished our workout. I was still a little sweaty from all the lunges we did at the end of our session.

"Are you sure we shouldn't take my car?" he asked.

"Are you a car snob?"

"Yes." He smiled to let me know he was at least partially joking.

"We're taking my car, and you aren't going to judge the trash."

"I don't see any trash," he said, looking around.

I kept my car relatively clean, but there was an empty Taco Bell cup in the drink holder. I pointed to it.

"I'm judging you," he said.

"Fair."

"What's the plan?" he asked, buckling his seat belt. "Are we meeting your friends there for the surfboard search, or are we picking them up?"

"Oh . . . neither." I actually hadn't told them. It hadn't even crossed my mind. Deja probably worked today anyway.

"Just us, then?" he asked.

"Just us." I pulled away from the curb.

"Are you nervous?" he asked.

"About it just being us? Yes, very."

"Funny," he said. "No about this visit."

"Yes. I'm worried that the board isn't going to be in the shed. That I'm getting my hopes up. I really want to find it for my grandma while she still has good days." There was a hair tie around the gear shift, and I twisted it several times while I drove.

"I'm sure it's hard to watch her slowly lose more of herself."

"It is. That's why I'm on this mission, I guess. It feels like something I can control in the whole process because so much of it I can't."

"You like to control things? I hadn't noticed."

I playfully smacked his arm. "I'll have you know that I barely edited my most recent episode." Which was true. I'd kept my loud laugh and even a few filler words, telling myself I needed to worry less about how other people saw me and more about being authentic.

"It was a really good episode."

"You listened?" I asked, glancing his way. Was he going to mention the kiss?

"I did." He turned his attention out the window. "Thanks for letting me come today."

"Can I ask you a question?" It was something I'd been wondering since reading the Facebook message from Alice with him on Thursday after flag football.

"You sound serious. Should I be scared?"

"No, it's just . . . why did you want to come? Why are you interested in finding the surfboard?"

"You're always questioning my motives," he said. "I wanted to come because your grandma's story is super interesting and I want to see this surfboard."

Of course, I thought. The same reason over a thousand people had listened to the podcast. Why else did I think he'd want to come?

"Was that the wrong answer?" he asked when I didn't say anything.

"No, it's a very solid reason." I smiled at him to sell it. "I'm glad so many people care about my grandma."

"She's a cool lady."

"She is."

Chapter
twenty-five

WE PARKED IN FRONT OF A BRIGHT BLUE HOUSE. ITS lawn was a collection of wildflowers. Metal formations that could've been trash but also could've been art littered the yard. The front porch was full of mismatched pots that all housed dead or dying plants.

We stopped on the porch, and Theo turned to me with an encouraging look, making it obvious that he believed I should be the one to knock.

I did just that—gave three short knocks.

The door swung open, and a woman appeared. She had salt-and-pepper curly hair that was pulled into a ponytail on top of her head. She had the kind of tan leathery skin that told me she was probably a surfer herself or at least spent a lot of time on the beach. She wore coveralls splattered in paint. Was she a painter too?

"Hi," I said. "I'm Finley Lucas. Charlotte Fox's granddaughter."

"Yes, hi. Let me show you out back to the shed. It's a mess, but you're welcome to take any surfboards you find in there."

I wondered if she would be as willing to give up a surfboard if she knew that it was painted by Andrew Lancaster. I was probably supposed to tell her that was a possibility now, but my mouth wouldn't open. I'd tell her if I actually found it. "Is your mom here? Can I ask her some questions?"

"My mom passed away last year. I'm still going through all her stuff. That's why I'm here this weekend."

My mouth opened, then shut, then opened again. "Oh. I'm so sorry. I didn't know."

"It's been hard. But life is like that, isn't it?"

I nodded, a knot forming in my stomach at the news.

"Follow me," she said.

The storage shed was more of a large workshop. It was huge. One of those metal structures that could've easily fit two or three cars. When we reached the door, Alice turned to us with a cringe and said, "I'm afraid you're going to have to wade through a lot of junk to see if there is anything real."

"That's okay," I said. "We appreciate you letting us look at all."

When she left, Theo faced me. "You okay?"

"What? Yeah, of course, this is exciting."

He tilted his head like he didn't believe me.

I did not want to discuss what the news of Cheryl's death did to my insides. It wasn't that Cheryl had died. It was sad, but I didn't know her. It was that she was my grandma's age. And now she no longer existed. Like Andrew. I didn't want to think about that at all.

"Let's go in," I said.

He turned the handle to reveal the contents of the shed. There was furniture and boxes and tools and canvases and books all stacked haphazardly on top of each other nearly ceiling high.

"What are the odds we'll find a surfboard in here?" I asked.

"Very low but not zero?" he said.

"What are the odds you're going to want to help me at all in the future?"

"Higher." He took a single step inside. That was about as far as he could go. "Let's move things outside so we can create some sort of path through the mess."

"Sounds good."

About an hour passed and we'd finally gained some ground. We had moved bigger pieces of furniture outside the shed, and I was winding my way through others.

"Everything is seconds away from crashing to the ground in here," he said. Boxes were stacked precariously high, the piles leaning against one another at odd angles. It was all coated in dust and spiderwebs, and I could feel a layer of both on my skin and hair.

"Yeah, it's crazy. Be careful," I said. I wouldn't be able to live with myself if he got injured while helping me.

Theo was unstacking a tower of boxes, moving them one by one outside. When the stack was low enough, I climbed over it, deeper into the building. That's when I saw the unmistakable shape of a surfboard against the far wall. It was covered with some sort of drape. I pointed, and Theo nodded, a smile spreading across his face.

"Do you think that's it?" he asked.

"Maybe." My heart was racing. The path to reach that surfboard was not clear and it took a lot of maneuvering, but finally, I reached the stack of boxes that covered the bottom half of the board. I assessed them, giving them a little shake, and then began climbing.

"What are you doing?" Theo asked, from right behind me.

"I just want to take off the cloth and see if it's even the board before we try to move these boxes through that maze we barely squeezed through."

Worry colored his features. I couldn't decide if he was worried that this wasn't the board or that the boxes were wobbling a bit beneath me.

He answered my question when I slowly stood and he said, "Please, Finley, be careful. Maybe I should climb up there."

"You absolutely should not. This is all me," I said.

One of his hands reached up and wrapped around my ankle, holding me steady.

"Will you catch me if I fall?" I teased.

"If you fall, I will be buried beneath this pile of boxes."

"I better not fall, then."

He mumbled something under his breath that I didn't understand as I reached for the yellowing fabric.

"Cross your fingers," I said, and pulled it off. Beneath the drape was just a basic foam surfboard. My hopes crashed to the ground. "No."

"That sucks," he said. "I'm sorry."

"It's whatever," I answered, trying not to let the disappointment settle in.

"Will you sit now . . . please?" he said, his hand still on my ankle.

"Am I stressing you out?" I asked, pretending to lose my balance.

"Finley, I swear," he said.

I laughed and lowered myself to sitting before he took me by the waist and lifted me off the box.

"My hero," I said.

"Do you want it?" he asked.

"Uh . . . what?"

"The board. Alice said if we found one, we could have it. Do you have a surfboard?"

"I don't."

"Do you want it?"

It wasn't the one I wanted, but why not? It could be fun to try. "Do you think we can get it out of here?"

"Yes, I just need to move the boxes you didn't let me move before climbing them."

"I was too excited."

He shook his head, but a small smile snuck onto his face as we began shifting things. The second box I attempted to move was heavier than I anticipated, and it fell to the floor, its contents spilling onto the cement.

"Ugh," I said, squatting down.

"They're pictures," Theo said, joining me in the cleanup.

I collected a stack and flipped through them. They were old pictures, some warped and yellowed but many well preserved. I flipped through them, changing from a squat to a sit on the ground. I had just planned on depositing them back into the box, but when they looked like they were from the same time period as the ones I saw in the yearbook, I kept flipping.

"What did your grandma look like when she was a teenager?"

"I don't know if we'll find my grandma in these, but maybe a picture of the board?"

I was wrong; after going through several piles of pictures, I found something that made my heart jump to my throat—my grandma with what I could only assume was the painted board. She was standing on the beach in the cutest bikini, the board upright, it's bottom stuck in the sand and her practically hugging it, a big smile on her face. Tears pricked my eyes and warmth spread throughout my body.

"Did you find something?" Theo asked.

I passed him the picture.

"This is amazing," he said. "Your grandma was a babe."

"I know."

"You look like her."

My cheeks went hot because Theo basically just called me a babe. "Not really," I said.

"You do," he assured me. "And this board. It's awesome. Now I want to find it even more." He passed the picture back to me.

The board was an eye. A huge sideways eye running the entire length of it. Not just any eye, my grandma's. The color on the picture was faded, but I knew if we found the board, it would be the vibrant greens and browns that made up her eyes. I swiped at a tear that had escaped down my cheek.

"What's wrong?" Theo asked.

"Her friend is dead, and she's going to fade and seeing her like this"—I held up the picture—"it's hard. Amazing, but hard."

"I get it," he said.

"I can't wait to show her this picture."

"Should we look for more?"

"Do you have time?" I asked.

"I came here for you," Theo said suddenly, an intensity in his voice. He pointed to the picture. "Your grandma's story is interesting and I know how much it means to you, but . . . I came here for you."

Chapter
twenty-six

WE HEADED THROUGH THE YARD BACK TOWARD MY car. Theo held the surfboard. I had the pictures tucked into my bag. Before we reached the gate, Theo pointed to a hose snaking through an extra-long patch of weeds against the side of the house. I immediately felt the dirt on my skin again at the thought of being able to wash it away.

After Theo's confession earlier, I had met his stare with what I could only assume was a terrified expression. It was really just a reflection of feeling my heart explode in my chest. I'd nodded and said thank you or something equally stupid, and we finished looking through the pictures. I'd found a couple more. Then we'd freed the surfboard, and now we were heading to the front of the house to talk to Alice. But not before using the hose.

I set my bag down by the house, and he propped the surfboard against the wall. Then he twisted on the spigot and followed the tangled line until he found the end.

"Here," I said. "I'll hold it so you have two hands to wash."

He narrowed his eyes at me. "Why don't I trust you?"

I gasped. "I'm so trustworthy."

He didn't seem to believe me but handed over control of the hose. I held it extra still while he scrubbed his hands and forearms. He had really nice forearms, all corded and strong. Then he cupped his hands and splashed water onto his face. Dirt dripped down his temples and chin.

"Not even close to clean," I said.

He tried again, this time running his hands up and down his face. A few streaks remained on his forehead, and I motioned him forward. He leaned closer, and I dipped my hand in the stream of water and then ran it across his forehead and by his ear. I studied his skin closely, making sure I got it all. When I finished, he was staring at me.

I gulped. "All done."

"Your turn." He gestured for the hose, and I handed it over.

I replicated his cleanup, scrubbing my hands and arms, then my face. And in turn, he helped me with the remaining streaks I couldn't see, his hand running gently over my cheek and then right below my bottom lip. His eyes carefully traveled my face until my insides were hot and melty.

We must've drifted closer together at some point because suddenly the stream of water from the hose he held was pouring down the front of my body.

I yelped and jumped back. "You did not!" I scream-laughed. "That is so cold!"

"It was an accident!"

"I trusted you!"

He laughed. "I'm *so* trustworthy!"

"Obviously not!" I wrestled for the hose.

He held on tight. "I don't deserve reciprocation!"

"You more than deserve it."

"I was distracted!"

"I was distracted too, but did you see me pour water down your fully clothed body?"

He laughed, then somehow managed in one swift motion to grab me by the arm and twist me around, pinning my back and arms against his chest. The hose in his other hand was still pouring water off to our left.

"No fair," I said, kicking my feet.

His cheek was against mine, and I could feel him smiling. "Truce?"

"Truce?" I asked. "Nothing has happened to you. A truce can only be called when both people have been victims."

"Is that so?"

"That is very so."

"Okay, if you insist."

Before I realized what that meant, he sprayed water into the air so it was raining down on both of us. He loosened his grip on me, and I turned in his arm so I could look him in the eyes and say, "You are so annoying."

"But you still like me."

Water dripped down his face and onto mine, and his smile turned serious. His hand holding the hose fell to his side, dropping it so water now flowed through the weeds and wildflowers at our feet. My wet hair continued to drip onto my forehead and shoulders and arms. His now-free arm joined his other one around my waist, pulling me closer. He paused for a moment, searching my eyes. I wondered if he was waiting for me to make a move because I had rejected a kiss on the boardwalk. But before I had even finished that thought, his mouth was on mine, hot against my cold lips. I sucked in some air, but then my hands traveled up his chest and around his neck, into his wet hair. My tongue brushed past his lips and tasted his mouth. His hands moved from my waist, up my back until they gently cupped my face.

He felt amazing against me, warm and steady. He tasted good too, like mint and cool air. My entire body felt like it was being dipped in that barrel on his back porch. Both hot and cold tingles all over.

"Did you find it?" a voice called from behind me, and Theo pulled away. I wanted to pull him right back. I was breathless and lightheaded when I turned to see Alice walking toward us.

Theo shut off the hose and pointed to the board. "No, this isn't the one we were looking for, but we thought we'd take it for a spin."

I smiled at his words, the same ones Andrew had said to my grandma all those years ago.

"Please do," Alice said, finally reaching us. "It probably misses the ocean." She looked over Theo's shoulder at my car. "You're going to put it in there?"

"We are going to attempt," he said, his brain obviously much more functional than mine, because as I was trying to think of responses to each of her questions, he was already answering them.

"We found some pictures," I finally spit out. "Of my grandma and the board we're looking for."

"Oh?" she said.

I pulled the photos out of my bag and handed them to her. "Have you seen this board?"

Alice squinted. "You know, it does look vaguely familiar. I'll ask my sister about it—maybe she's seen it."

"Can I . . . ?" I gestured to the pictures. "Can I have those?"

"Yes, you can." She placed them gently back in my hands.

"Thanks," I said. "We didn't quite make it all the way through the shed. Is there any way we can come back, maybe when you've emptied it out more?"

"Of course. I'll keep you updated. It might take a while."

"Thank you."

"You're welcome," she replied, and then she was heading back to the house. Theo picked up the board, tucked it under his arm, and made his way to my car. I straightened my shirt, slid the pictures back into my bag, took a deep breath, and followed after him.

He was studying the trunk. "This board is longer than your car."

"My back seats fold down," I said, opening the trunk, then walking around to the side door to release the seat latch. "It's definitely going to hang out, but I've seen people do worse." It was a beach town; the roads were full of surfboards being transported in various ways. I once saw a guy riding a bike holding a board.

"True," he agreed as he slid the board into my trunk.

I joined him to help with the task. Our eyes met over the board. My insides still felt melty and my brain mushy. We both leaned forward but were immediately stopped by the barrier between us. I tried to shove the board farther into the car, but it got caught on the front seats, not budging another inch, three feet still hanging out the trunk. Theo came around the end, and then my back was pressed against the taillight and my front was pressed against him.

"Do you know how long I've wanted to kiss you?" he asked before his mouth covered mine.

"Three weeks?" I guessed, against his lips, referencing the day in the bathroom. The day I'd realized how hot he was.

"Longer than that," he said, his hands sliding around my waist. "And it was worth the wait."

Chapter
twenty-seven

WE KISSED!!!!

I typed that into the group chat, and as I was about to hit send, I hesitated. I'd just dropped Theo and the surfboard off at his house, where we talked about going surfing in the near future, when the weather warmed up more. Before we could even get through that conversation we were making out. Me, stretched over the center console practically in his lap, his hands in my hair. He was such a good kisser.

Perhaps it was that giddy high coursing through me that had me typing those words into the group chat after he left my car and disappeared into his house. I was still parked on his street, my lips tingling from the kiss. But I hesitated. This wasn't an over-text type of announcement. I had to tell them face to face. Especially when only one, possibly two, of them would be excited about this news. I wasn't ready for my after-kiss high to disappear just yet.

There was a knock on my window, and I yelped.

Theo stood there, hand pressed against the glass.

I powered down my window.

"What are you doing?" he asked. "Texting your friends about kissing some hot guy?"

I smiled. "Something like that."

He leaned forward and placed a kiss on my lips. "Is that why you're blushing?"

"I'm not—it's just hot."

"It's not hot at all," he said. "In fact, I'm a little cold."

I laughed and pushed the upper half of my body out the window to kiss him again.

"For training tomorrow," he said between kisses, "let's go to Cal Poly. Kick through their uprights." Cal Poly was a state college about twenty minutes away.

I sat back in my seat. "We're allowed to do that?"

He shrugged. "I've trained there before. I guess we'll see."

"Am I ready for that?"

"It's time."

"WHAT ARE YOUR COLLEGE PLANS NOW THAT FOOTBALL is off the table?" I asked as we worked our way through the Cal Poly campus the next day toward the football field.

He was quiet for too long, taking in our surroundings. The campus was beautiful, sandwiched between rolling hills; it had a small-campus feel even though it was relatively big. Maybe my relative was skewed, though, since I hadn't been on a lot of college campuses and my high school was on the small side.

I grabbed hold of his hand because I wanted to be closer to him. Ever since we kissed the day before, I'd wanted to be near him. If I was being honest with myself, that feeling had started long before we kissed. "Wait, *is* football still on the table?"

"Yes," he said quickly. "No . . . I don't know. . . . Probably not. I'd have to try for a walk-on position, and even in my prime, walking on is not the easiest way to get on a team. What about you?"

"I don't think I'll play football in college," I teased.

"Maybe you'll get scouted next year," he joked back. "No, but have you thought more about the internship? Sending in your podcast. It's gotten so popular."

"Jensen did that." I said out loud what had been brewing in my brain since last week when he'd told me. "He's the one who shared it on his socials. He'll probably write it as one of his accomplishments on his application."

Anger flashed across Theo's face, and he stopped. I turned and looked at him. "He took credit for your views?" Theo's voice was low.

"He felt the need to point it out, yes. And beyond that, the real star of the show is my grandma. Jensen and my grandma are the reasons the show has done anything."

"Stop saying stuff like that, Finley."

"Stop saying the truth?"

"He doesn't get to claim your successes anymore. And in less than two weeks, he'll be put in his place."

I wondered if that was true. He had easily won the hosting position, he'd get the internship. And he might easily win his kicking spot.

Theo nodded as if that settled it, and we kept walking.

We reached the football stadium and walked through the entrance and onto the field. I stopped in the end zone, breathless. It was huge, and I felt overwhelmed, to say the least. "Not sure this is a good idea for my first time actually kicking through uprights."

"It only seems bigger," he said. "It's the same size as the high school field, there's just more"—he spun a circle while pointing—"other things."

"Right," I said.

"So are you ready?"

"I think so," I said.

He rolled his entire head. "Finley. You know this. You have to get pumped up. Get some blood flowing through your veins. Are you ready?"

"Yes . . ."

"Scream it!"

I laughed and looked around; the field was empty, and the stadium seats were mostly empty. A few people ran the steps, exercising. It was a Sunday, so the campus had been pretty quiet on our walk.

He moved so he was standing in front of me and jumped a few times, then indicated he wanted me to do the same.

I jumped.

"Are you ready?"

"Yes!" I felt like I was on the soccer field again about to start playing. In soccer we'd all huddle together and yell out positive affirmations. Things like *We're the best, We can run forever, Kicking balls is fun, Bury the enemy.* That last one wasn't so positive, but it always made Deja laugh. She was the most supportive teammate ever when working for the same goal. And when we weren't on the same page, like now, in my relationship with Theo, the lack of support was glaring.

"Again!" Theo shouted.

"I'm ready!"

"Good! Then let's go!" He ran to the twenty-yard line, and I followed. There, he took off his backpack and retrieved a football, then squatted down and held it in place. We'd practiced this last time after flag football. Him holding the ball instead of placing it on the plastic ring. It took a while to get used to. I kept thinking I was going to kick his hand. But he moved it out of the way fast enough every time. Right now, he looked at me with a sweet smile. "It's all about muscle memory. Just do what you've been doing. Don't even think about it."

I shook out my hands. *Don't even think about it. Don't even think about it.* I drove forward and connected with the ball. It flew through the air and straight down the center.

Theo's hands shot in the air like I'd just scored the winning points in the Super Bowl. "That was amazing. And it went far! Really far. We can back up ten yards."

Theo grabbed another ball and was already running back to the thirty.

"And did I tell you!" he yelled over his shoulder. "The goal posts are narrower in college. So it will be even easier on our field."

I followed after him, walking, not running like he was. "They're narrower here?"

"Yes!" he said when I reached him. "You are brilliant!"

The wind picked up, whipping through my hair and twisting it around in front of my head. He pushed it out of my face and placed his palms on my cheeks, staring into my eyes in boyish excitement. "There's wind!"

Coach Theo, who had turned to Kissing Coach Theo, was adorable.

With his hands still on my cheeks, I pushed forward and kissed him. "Does that mean I am done for the day? We can make out now?"

He wrapped an arm around my waist and spun me in a circle. "No! It means we get to practice in the wind! You get to learn how to adjust your kick."

I laughed and held a fake microphone up to my mouth. "Coach Theo, how are you feeling after your hard work helped an ex–soccer player make a field goal?"

He brought my hand to his mouth. "I'm feeling like she needs to kick about a hundred more today."

"She thinks fifty sounds more doable."

He laughed. "I'm seriously super impressed. We probably should've come here earlier."

"And does watching her success make you want to kick a ball today?" I asked, fake microphone still in hand.

The giddy excitement that had been on his face melted right off.

I lowered my hand, dropping the reporter act. "Will you?" I asked softly. I'd watched him do so many physical things now, and aside from the occasional wince, and the slight favor he showed his left knee, I sensed what was stopping him was more mental than anything.

"We're working on your kick. In the wind," he said, squatting down to hold the ball in place. "I don't . . . If I . . . Just pay attention to how the wind is blowing and adjust your swing in the opposite direction. It might take a couple attempts to get the hang of it."

I squatted down next to him. "I guess I'm not the only one afraid to put myself out there."

He sighed and shifted so he sat all the way on the ground. I joined him.

"I'm not afraid, Finley. The doctor said . . ." He trailed off.

"The doctor told you not to?"

"No, I've been cleared."

"Then what?"

"I just need to . . ."

"Try?" I said. "See that it's going to be fine? Come on."

"No, I—"

"Please," I said.

"I *have* been kicking," he bit out. "Every day for a while."

I blinked several times in surprise. "You have?"

He nodded.

"And?"

"And it's not good. I'm weak. Unsteady."

221

"I'm sorry," I said.

He ran his hands down his face. "It's fine. Maybe you need to learn when to keep trying and I need to learn when to give up."

I pulled him into a hug. His breaths were short, irregular, like he was on the verge of panic. "I'm sorry," I said. "Maybe you need to take some pressure off. Learn how to kick for the fun of it again. Without your whole future sitting on your shoulders." I knew how heavy that weight was.

"Maybe. I'm just . . ." He held me against him and drew in some air until his breathing was steady and even.

"Yoga?" I asked, resting my head on his shoulder.

He gave a quiet laugh. "You, actually."

"Your charming lines don't work on me," I said even though I was now smiling.

He laughed and pulled us sideways onto the grass. I rolled onto my back, and we both stared up at the sky, our legs and hands interlocked. Clouds floated lazily across the blue backdrop.

Eventually, he propped himself up on his elbow, staring down at me. "Have you ever thought about being a sideline reporter? You'd actually be really good at it. You get this glimmer in your eye during your fake interviews."

I shook my head. I actually had thought of it but always quickly dismissed it. "I'm not good with live stuff. I need the security of being able to edit out my mistakes."

"I think your unscripted commentary is some of the best when you're interviewing your grandma."

"Yeah, but . . ."

"But you want to be perfect?"

222

I looked toward the uprights. "I'm trying to be less hard on myself."

"I get it. I obviously have insecurities too."

"And here I thought you were cocky."

He leaned down and brushed his lips over mine. "It's all for show."

Chapter
twenty-eight

I HAVE TO TELL MY FRIENDS. I HAVE TO TELL MY FRIENDS.
Those were the words that circled my brain as I headed to school
the next morning. I'd been putting it off, but it was time because
they would see us together. I actually wasn't sure what kissing Theo
meant as far as school life went. We had discussed nothing about
how public or private we planned on being with this after spend-
ing the weekend kissing.

The day before, we'd spent another hour at the stadium. Every
ball I'd tried went through. We'd kiss between kicks and water
breaks.

I'd dropped him home that day without either of us saying anything like *So we're cool with the general public seeing us do this or no?*
I wasn't sure how I felt about going public. I still had the very valid
fear that people would think I was only with Theo to get back at
Jensen. Maybe it would be better to keep the kissing to ourselves for
now, like the whole kicking thing.

On my way to sleep, my brain decided that Theo was a private person anyway, who liked to keep his relationships private. After all, I'd never seen him in a relationship. But he was Theo Torres, he had to have been in one. The way he kissed proved to me he'd done it before. But regardless of how little I wanted the school to know, my friends still needed to.

I wanted them to. I wanted them to be excited for me. I wanted Maxwell to squeal and Lee to tell me to trust again and Deja . . . I just wanted her to be okay with this. To not actively be against it. I didn't think that was too much to ask.

I parked my car and waited, my nerves buzzing while I watched for their cars. I'd gotten here early. I hadn't planned on it, but my energy was heightened this morning.

Maxwell and Lee arrived together, only parking a few spots down from me. I got out of my car and waited for them to do the same.

"Hey, girlie," Maxwell said, giving me a side hug. "Looking cute today."

"Thanks." I looked down at my jeans and green sweater.

"How was your weekend?" Lee asked. "How's the training going?"

"Good. I can kick a football."

"Nice," he said. "Operation Revenge is getting closer."

"Yes, for sure. Oh," I said. "Also, I found some pictures of the surfboard this weekend."

"You did?" Maxwell asked. "Show us!"

"Show us what?" Deja asked, joining us.

"The surfboard. I have actual pictures of it." I swung my backpack around and took my binder out. I'd slid the pictures inside the front protective pocket.

Her eyes lit up. "What did your grandma say?"

"I haven't shown her yet." I had wanted to do a podcast the day before, revealing the pictures to my grandma, but she was having an off day. I hoped that sometime this week she would feel up to it, because I was so excited.

I handed Deja the pictures, and she looked at them, flipping through as the boys peered over her shoulders.

"Oh, wow," she said. "It's cooler than I even imagined."

"Right?" I said.

"We have to find it now."

"Where did you get these?" Lee asked.

"Alice answered my DM and told me about a shed her mom had. Theo and I went over on Saturday and looked through it. We didn't find the surfboard but found those."

"You and Theo?" Deja asked.

"Yes," I said. "After training."

She handed me back the pictures. "We wanted to help you find the board."

Maxwell nodded.

"I didn't think you'd want to dig through a dirty shed." The truth was, I was being selfish. I had wanted to be alone with Theo.

"I'm the one who has been listening to your podcast forever. I'm the one who was excited about the board. You took Theo?" She was hurt. We hadn't even gotten to the bigger admission.

"I'm so sorry," I said, realizing my misstep. I really should've brought my friends. I hadn't thought anyone would care this much. I was surprised when Theo asked to join. I tucked the pictures into my binder and zipped my backpack shut.

Then, in a show of terrible timing, a pair of arms wrapped around me from behind and a kiss was planted on my cheek. "Hey," Theo's low voice said into my ear. "Good morning."

My eyes were on my friends who all had varying degrees of shocked looks on their faces.

"And I'm out," Deja said, and with a flip of her hair, she walked away.

"Wait," I started, taking a step to go after her. But Theo's arms were still around me, holding me in place.

"Just give her some time," Lee said, putting his hand on my shoulder.

Theo dropped his arms and slid into place beside me. "What happened?"

"This happened," Maxwell said, pointing between us, his shocked expression turning into one of pure delight. "I need all the details."

"I thought you told your friends," Theo said.

I closed my eyes. If I had to see one more hurt expression this morning, I was going to have to take a sick day.

"I had started to text them but decided it was better in person. I was just about to tell them," I said. "And then . . ."

The first bell rang, and I looked up, like the sky had made that happen.

"I'll work on Deja," Lee said. "You can tell us all about it at lunch."

I nodded as he grabbed Maxwell's hand and they walked away. Maxwell looked over his shoulder and mouthed *OMG* along with a silent scream. I smiled but only halfway. I'd screwed everything up.

"I'm sorry" was the first thing I said when they were gone.

"Do you regret this weekend?" he asked.

I turned to face him. "No. Not at all. Do you?"

"No."

"Theo!" someone called as he walked by. "Scrimmage today after school?"

"I'm busy after school!" he called back. "I'm in for Wednesday."

"Cool!"

Theo turned his attention back to me.

"What are you doing after school?" I asked.

"I'll be with you," he said.

"You will?"

"When are you going to realize that I just want to be near you, Finley? All the time."

My heart leapt in my chest.

He looked at the ground and popped one eyebrow. I had taken a step back when he was talking with his friend. Things seemed to click inside his head because he said, "You don't want anyone to know about us?"

"No, I . . . I wasn't sure what *you* wanted. And I didn't want everyone to think I was only with you because of . . ."

"Are you?"

"No!"

"What do *you* want?" he asked.

"I . . ." I thought I was done caring about what people thought. That I was trying to be more authentic. I knew how I felt and why I felt it. It was time to stop worrying about how everyone else would perceive the things I did and start doing what made me happy. "I like you. A lot." I closed the distance between us, grabbed hold of the straps of his backpack, and used them to pull myself up onto my toes. It wasn't some passionate, tongues-blazing kiss. Just a soft, simple touching of lips. And yet my whole body reacted, every hair standing on end.

The late bell rang, and we pulled apart.

A group of people walking by were staring. I recognized one guy as one of Theo's friends from the library. His eyes tracked back and forth between us, and then he laughed. I averted my gaze.

"You didn't tell your friends either?" I asked.

"I told my friends," he said. "They didn't believe me."

"Why?" I asked.

"After the way you ran out of the library that one day, they figured you weren't a fan of mine. I mean, technically speaking, you weren't."

I laughed. "Yeah, that day I wasn't."

He smirked. "See you later?"

"Yes."

Theo mumbled something about Jensen that I couldn't quite make out, and then he was gone. I scanned the area, but there was no Jensen. He must've known, like I did, that with a school full of gossip lovers, Jensen would find out about our kiss before the day was over.

Chapter
twenty-nine

I WAS RIGHT; JENSEN FOUND OUT I WAS KISSING THEO
Torres sometime between first period and podcast class, because
when I went inside and sat down, he sat down next to me.

"What, Jensen?"

"You really have to ask?"

I stood up and walked around the table to Nolen, deciding to
ignore Jensen. "Hey, I was wondering if we could have a refresher
on editing techniques for ambient noise reduction." I'd thought I
had this down, but it was time consuming and I wondered if Nolen
had any shortcuts for the editing I had to do later.

He answered, "Sure, no problem. That's not your responsibility
on the podcast, you know that, right?"

"Yeah, of course. More for my personal podcast. And I think
everyone could benefit from it," I said, thinking about how Jensen
probably hadn't thought once about how heavy he breathed while
talking into the mic.

I started to turn away when Nolen said, "Finley, I haven't gotten your bid for a regular feature idea for next year's podcast."

That's because I hadn't thought of one. "Um . . . I was thinking about . . ." My mind was all over the place. "Sideline interviews during and after high school sporting events."

Susie, who must've been listening from her spot at the table, said, "Ooh, I like that one."

Nolen gave a slow nod. "I like it too. You could commit the time to watch games?"

"Right, I . . ." I wanted to say yes. Maybe this would help me get an internship. But suddenly it occurred to me that I couldn't watch the most popular sporting event our school had—football. Because if all went well, I'd be a player. Maybe my need for revenge was waning, because suddenly I wanted to say that, yes, I could. If I was being true to myself, authentic, even though the thought of live interviews scared me, that's what I wanted more. My heart pumped so hard I could feel it in my throat and temples.

"Say yes," Jensen said. I whipped my head toward him. I hadn't realized he'd followed me around the table. "I suggested the feature idea for you."

Never mind. I still very much wanted to make him pay. "Yeah, actually I can't," I snapped to Nolen. "I have a conflicting obligation during football games. Maybe someone else could do it, though." It seemed like my ideas were up for grabs anyway.

"What conflicting obligation?" Jensen asked.

"Jensen, can you not," I said, anger surging.

"Think about it," Nolen said. "You deserve a spot."

"Okay, thanks."

I headed back toward my seat, and Jensen was like my shadow. I turned. "Do you even want the internship?"

"What?"

"Next summer. The podcast internship at the community college."

"Oh, is there an internship? Yeah. That would be cool, actually."

I groaned. "Please, just leave me alone."

"Can we talk after class? It's important. I promise to leave you alone after that."

I wasn't sure I believed any of his promises, but if there was a chance he was telling the truth, that this really would be the last time he'd try to talk to me, I decided it was worth it. "Fine."

After class, I remained in my seat as the room emptied out. This room in the library wasn't big enough to house normal-sized classes, so it was empty most of the time. It had large glass windows so Mrs. Hughs could keep an eye on the students that used it.

"My friends are waiting for me," I said. I already had a lot to smooth over there. I didn't need Jensen holding me up. "You have two minutes."

He was across the table from me, and he stood and paced, his arms crossed. "I don't want you to get hurt."

"You mean more than you've already hurt me?"

"Yes. Is that what you want to hear? I don't want you to get hurt more than I've hurt you, but if you keep seeing Theo, you're going to."

I stood. He'd already said this. He thought saying it again would make a difference? "We're done." I headed for the door.

"I didn't want to have to tell you this, but I realize that I have to now!" he called as I reached for the handle.

I turned, and he came around the table and spoke low and fast. "Last month, at that party at his house, Theo told someone that he was better than me in every way possible. That he could kick better than me even with an injury. That he could steal my girlfriend if he wanted to. It would be easy."

I rolled my eyes. "Told *someone*? Who?"

"A friend."

"And you believed it? You know how gossip is. It gets twisted. Besides, I'm not your girlfriend, so there was no stealing necessary."

"But he's just doing this to show me he was right."

"You're the one who lost me, Jensen. All on your own."

"Mark my words, this has more to do with me than you think."

"It has to do with *me,* Jensen. He likes me. Is that so hard to believe?"

He looked at his hands, then bit his lip, his nervous reaction. "I . . ." He didn't want to say whatever he thought Theo's motivation really was for *stealing* me. I nearly rolled my eyes at that thought again.

"You have to believe me."

"Actually, Jensen, I don't."

"He was a jerk to me, Finley. A complete and utter jerk. I told you all the stories. You know. And now you're with him and he's going to hurt you. All so he can get back at me."

"Leave me alone, Jensen," I muttered, and opened the door. "You know nothing."

"You'll see, Finley! I'll prove it to you."

MY FRIENDS WERE ALREADY SITTING AT OUR TABLE IN
the courtyard at lunch. I held in my groan as I collapsed onto a
seat. Deja's full attention was on her phone, and she didn't look up
when I sat. Maxwell squeezed my hand, and it looked like Lee was
squeezing Deja's knee.

"I'm sorry," I said. "I should've told you all everything that was
happening. It all happened so fast, and I've been so preoccupied
with my revenge lately. That's taken over everything."

"We were supposed to be part of the revenge thing too, until
Theo took our places," Deja said.

"I know."

"I thought you didn't trust him."

"Theo?" I asked as the words Jensen spewed flashed through
my mind. *He's going to hurt you. All so he can get back at me.*

"Yes," she said.

I swallowed. "I didn't at first . . . but now I do," I said. Because I did. How could I not? He'd been nothing but kind to
me. Whatever Jensen had heard from some mysterious source
was just his twisted way of trying to get back together with me.
"I kicked the ball through the uprights for the first time yesterday. Easily. And I was good. And I think I can actually make
the team."

"That's exciting!" Maxwell said.

"I still don't understand why he's helping you so much," Deja
said, not able to drop the suspicions.

"Because he's a nice guy," I said. "And he likes me." Was that so hard for everyone to believe?

"He seems nice to me," Maxwell said.

"I know you don't know him very well, and that's entirely my fault," I said. "Will you forgive me for cutting you guys out? I really didn't mean to. You are my favorites, and I didn't mean to hurt anyone."

She put her phone down on the table, finally giving me her full attention. "I just don't want to see you get hurt."

"That's what Jensen said ten minutes ago."

"You're comparing me to Jensen?"

"What? No! I just need you to trust me. You're my best friend. Don't you trust me to know what's best for myself?"

She let out a huff of air, then pinched the bridge of her nose, squeezing her eyes shut. I could tell a million thoughts were going through her head. Lee and Maxwell looked on nervously as well, not daring to interrupt whatever internal struggle she was having with herself. "I trust you," she finally said, meeting my eyes.

"Good, because I need you."

"It doesn't feel like you do."

"I promise I do."

She reached across the table. "You have to include us in your life from now on."

I grabbed hold of her hand and took a relieved breath. "I will. I really think you're going to like him. And I know he's going to like you guys. You're the best."

She looked around. "Well? Where is he? We need to get started on grilling him."

Maxwell let out a squeal, as if he'd been waiting for everyone to be on the same page to properly celebrate. He smashed me into a hug. "I know this part wasn't to get back at Jensen, but it's just icing on the cake."

"DID I RUIN EVERYTHING WITH YOUR FRIENDS?" THEO asked after school later. He'd just opened my car door for me, and now we both stood in the space between the interior and exterior.

"No, it was my fault for not being more open with them. I'm sorry for not telling them. It's not that I'm not proud to be with you."

"Proud?"

"Yes, proud. And happy. It's just I've been so distracted."

"By what?" he teased, kissing my cheek.

"By this guy who is super hot and knows it."

He chuckled. "I've been distracted by a beautiful girl who can kick a football."

"I can do other things too," I whispered.

He pulled me closer. "Oh, really?"

"I didn't mean *that*," I said, playfully pushing his chest.

He kissed me, and someone in the parking lot let out a "Whoop!"

"Can I ask you something?" I said, looking up at him.

"Yes." He took a wide-legged stance so his eyes were more level with mine.

Jensen's accusations flashed through my mind again. No, I wasn't going to give them a voice, put a wedge between us, bring up

236

trust issues once again. I trusted Theo. He'd earned that trust. "Why are you such a good kisser?" I said. "Have you kissed a lot of girls?"

He laughed. "Yes, tons."

"No, seriously, have you had a girlfriend before?"

"I have been very focused on football for a very long time."

"Is that a no?" I asked, surprised.

"I've been on a few dates. Kissed a few girls. You are my first girlfriend."

"Are you asking me to be your girlfriend?"

"Oh." He smiled, and my heart melted. "Yes. Will you be my girlfriend, Finley Lucas?"

I nodded and kissed him again.

Chapter
thirty

"I HAVE A SURPRISE FOR YOU." IT HAD BEEN A TOUGH
week for Grandma, and it took me until Friday to feel like she was
ready to record another episode. I wanted to document her reaction
to seeing the pictures for the first time so that we'd always have it to
listen to. But depending on her reaction, I wasn't necessarily going
to publish it. Some things were just for my family.

I pulled my backpack onto my lap with a wince. It had been
a tough week for me too. Since tryouts were now only eight days
away, I'd been practicing kicking a lot with Theo, and I was sore.
My friends had even joined us for a couple of practices.

"What's the surprise?" Grandma asked now. She wore one of
her wigs today with a robe and house slippers. Betsy had painted
her nails again, a bright purple.

I retrieved the pictures and slid them across my desk to her. "I
found some pictures of you with your surfboard."

She picked them up and studied them close, not saying anything for a long time.

"What do you think?" I asked.

"It's beautiful, isn't it? It was even more beautiful in real life." Her eyes were lit up with joy.

"I believe it," I said.

She turned one of the pictures sideways and held it beside her face so the eye on the board was next to her eye. "He must've stared at my eyes a lot," she said.

I smiled and explained what she was doing into the microphone before I asked, "Did he?" My grandma's story felt even more dreamy after having been thoroughly kissed all week, the romantic feelings in my body heightened.

She seemed almost giddy when she said, "He did. He thought they were pretty."

"They are pretty," I said.

"You have my eyes, baby girl."

I squeezed her hand remembering how Theo had said I looked like her. My cheeks went pink with that thought.

She ran a finger over the board in one of the pictures. "I wish I could see it in real life again."

"I wish that too." Hopefully she could.

Mom's head appeared in my doorway, and when she saw I was recording, she took a step back. I waved her inside.

"We have a special guest today," I said. "My mom. Say hi, Mom."

She leaned over and into the mic said, "Hello, people."

I sucked my lips in to keep from laughing.

Her eyes landed on the pictures on the desk. "What are these?"

"I found them last weekend."

Her mouth formed an O. "These are . . . ?"

"She knew Andrew Lancaster."

"I told you," Grandma said.

"You did," Mom said. *Where did you get these?* she mouthed to me.

I'll tell you after, I mouthed back, and pointed at the mic.

She nodded, then left my room.

"Listeners, I'm going to post these pictures on my Instagram so you can see them too. If anyone has seen this board, please DM me."

"I wonder if I'd still fit into this bathing suit," my grandma said with a smirk.

"I FEEL LIKE A PEEPING TOM," MAX SAID, BINOCULARS pushed to his eyes, resting on his stomach on a flat rock. It had been several more days of intense practices, and I'd told Theo my body needed some rest before tryouts. He agreed.

"I was going to say *sniper,*" Theo said. "We're on a hill after all."

We *were* on a hill. We had parked on the road and hiked up a barely visible trail after we hadn't been able to get past the gate and to the front door of the house across the street. Nobody had answered the intercom box we had found to try to communicate with the occupants. So now here we were with binoculars.

"Apparently I'm not as cool as you," Max said to Theo as he handed off the binoculars to Lee.

"Peeping Tom is more accurate," I said. "We have no guns."

"But we have a mission," Deja said, surveying the house without the help of magnification.

"Do people still say *Peeping Tom?*" Lee asked.

"You all knew what I meant," Max said. "So were there any other clues in the message? Like who owns this place now and how we can get past the impenetrable gates or contact the owner?"

"It almost looks abandoned," Lee said, passing off the binoculars to Theo.

"The message just said this was where Andrew Lancaster lived the last ten years of his life and that maybe the surfboard was somewhere on the property." I'd gotten lots of tips from lots of different people in my DMs this week after publishing the latest episode and posting the pictures of the surfboard to my Instagram. But most of the tips didn't help. They talked about locations in different states where his art installation had passed through. They mentioned people who were impossible to get a hold of or information that was just completely wrong. I wasn't even sure if this tip was right. If we were really looking at the house where Andrew had spent the last ten years of his life.

It was tucked in the hills off a small two-way section of Highway 41, quite a bit off the road. There were trees and greenery obstructing most of the view, but I could see pieces of the house.

"You're a delinquent who doesn't worry about things liked locked gates and security cameras," Theo teased, placing the binoculars in my hand. "What should we do?"

"Funny," I said, bringing the binoculars up to my eyes. It was disorienting at first, having everything in front of me magnified to that level. It took me a moment to find the house, bits of brown shingles poking through the surrounding trees.

"We might not have guns," Deja said. "But the person who lives there probably does."

"What's that?" I asked, adjusting the focus wheel on top of the binoculars.

"I said," Deja started, "that we—"

"No, not that. *That.*" I pointed with one hand, while still looking through the lenses.

"I see nothing," Lee said.

"A corner of light blue. It looks like . . . Is it . . . a lifeguard tower in the back corner of the yard?"

"Huh?" Deja said. "Let me see." She held out her hand for the binoculars, and I gave them to her.

"We need more binoculars," Max said.

"Oh, now you all think my dad's bird-watching hobby is useful," Lee said.

"Yes, tell him to take us next weekend," Max said.

Theo was squinting. "It's probably just a shed."

"I swear it's a lifeguard tower," I said, taking him by the shoulders and turning him in the right direction. He smiled, like my hands on his shoulders were the precursor to a kiss. To be fair, he wasn't wrong. *Everything* had been the precursor to a kiss this week. "Concentrate," I whispered.

"I have no idea what you mean," he returned, his hand brushing my thigh. I was standing behind him, higher on the hill, and I wrapped my arms around his neck. He leaned back into me.

I kissed his cheek.

"I think you're right. That's a lifeguard tower," Deja said, squatting to get a better view.

"Why would someone have that? Their backyard is ten minutes from the ocean." It felt significant. If this really was Andrew's old house, it had to mean something.

"We need a closer look," Deja said.

"Let's go," I said.

The walk down the hill was faster than the walk up it, and soon we were standing outside the gate again. I was looking through the binoculars into the backyard while Maxwell was messing with the intercom box again.

"Hello," he said, his mouth close to the speaker. There was no answer.

I combed over every inch of the yard meticulously until the blue was magnified in my view again.

"Did Andrew Lancaster live here?" Max asked the little silver box now, pressing various buttons while he did.

I gasped.

"What?" Theo asked. He was standing at my shoulder squinting through the iron bars of the gate.

"There are paintings on the lifeguard tower. Ocean and surfing scenes." Andrew painted a lot of things over his career, tires and road signs and trucks. This had to mean we were at the right house. That Andrew used to live here.

"Andrew," Deja said softly.

It wasn't the surfboard, but maybe it meant the board was here somewhere.

Max was now saying "Let us in" over and over again into the speaker.

I lowered the binoculars and was about to suggest a walk around the property to find a weak point, when the sound of something hitting metal rang out. Through the gate I saw a fairly large rock land on the ground, kicking up dust.

Max jumped back, and the others, who had been talking, went silent.

"What was tha—" Theo started to ask, when he was cut short by another rock hitting the iron bars.

Lee ducked and covered his head as another rock came flying, over the fence this time. "There's someone in there."

"Get out of here!" came the rough voice of a man from somewhere behind the trees. The voice was accompanied by another rock. This one landed by my feet, bouncing off the ground and hitting my shin.

I sucked in some air.

Theo pulled me back and behind him.

"We just want to talk!" I yelled. "Did Andrew used to live here!"

"Leave or I'm calling the cops!" A big burly man came out from behind the trees.

"Nope," Lee said, and rushed toward the car.

"Have you seen a surfboard?" I yelled.

We watched the man wind up this time to throw the rock, and we all ran and piled into the car faster than I thought possible.

Lee was laughing in the back seat while Theo started the car. He peeled out, tires kicking up dirt before finding purchase on the road.

After several minutes of silence, Max burst out laughing. "We almost died!"

"We did not almost die," Deja said. "But Theo's pretty car almost got a few new dents."

"*I* almost got a few new dents." I rubbed my shin.

"You okay?" Theo asked. "You still going to be able to kick?"

"The most important thing," Max joked.

"No, I just meant . . ."

I took Theo's hand. "I knew what you meant. I'm fine." It actually didn't hurt anymore, but there was a dirt mark from where the rock had hit. "The ground slowed down the rock."

"That was super exciting," Lee said sarcastically. "Let's not do it again."

I nodded, but what I was really wondering was how I could get that man to talk to me, to let me see that lifeguard tower.

Chapter
thirty-one

"WHY DID YOU BREAK UP?" I ASKED GRANDMA INTO the microphone. I was trying to distract myself from many things: the fact that I hadn't figured out how to get that man to let us see the lifeguard tower, the fact that I had resumed practices after a few days off and my muscles were sore all over again, the fact that in two days I'd be trying out to be kicker for the school football team.

"Me and Andrew?" she asked.

"Yes," I said.

"The first time?" she asked.

"You broke up more than once?"

"We did."

"Then yes, the first time."

"Cheryl."

My phone buzzed on my desk, and I cringed. I usually left my phone in my bag during a recording session for exactly this reason.

But the message on the screen from Theo made me smile: *Good job kicking today. You are going to kill it.*

I smiled and tossed my phone onto the bed behind me; I'd answer him when I was done.

"Wait, Cheryl was the reason you broke up?" I said, finally registering Grandma's answer. "The girl you loaned your board to?"

"It was actually Andrew who loaned her my board."

"He didn't!"

"They were in surf club together and her board had been damaged and Andrew came and got mine without my permission."

"He. Did. Not," I said, this time emphasizing each word. "That little punk."

"It wasn't a good move."

"So you broke up with him?"

"It was the jealousy speaking. I thought he had a thing for Cheryl."

"How did you do it?"

"How did I break up with him?"

"Yes, this was before texting," I said, thinking about how I had broken up with Jensen. Or at least how I had made it official.

"We were far from texting at the time. I guess I could've sent him a telegram," she said.

I laughed.

"No, it was a foggy afternoon. You know how it gets here sometimes."

"Yes, for those not from Morro Bay, sometimes a morning or even an all-day fog rolls in and clings to the big rock by the bay and floats out over the ocean. It's both beautiful and haunting all at once."

"The perfect mood for a breakup," Grandma said. "He was surfing, and I waited for him on the shore. He and Cheryl walked up together, my board between them. She kept walking when she saw me. But he stayed. *You let her use my board?* I asked. He seemed confused, and I pointed at her. He said, *What's the big deal? I'm the one who gave it to you.*"

I gasped.

"Yes," she said. "So I screamed, *Then she can have both of you!*"

"And then?" I asked, anger churning in my chest imagining the scene.

"Then they left. With my board."

"WHAT'S GOING ON?" I ASKED MAX, WHO WAS WALKING beside me. We'd gone to my car at lunch to grab a sweatshirt from my trunk, because even though it was April, it was cold today. It was Theo's sweatshirt, the one he had loaned me before yoga. I hadn't given it back, and I was glad for it. The smell of soapy vanilla still lingered on the soft material, and it made me smile.

An afternoon fog had rolled in and clung to the grass and trees and hung in the air. It made me think of my grandma and Andrew today. We were heading back through campus. I pulled the sleeves of the sweatshirt I now wore over my hands. "I haven't had this many people stare at me since Jensen broadcasted to the whole school how terrible I was a month ago."

"Maybe they're staring at me," Max said, waving. The girl he waved to gave me sad eyes, like she felt sorry for me.

"What was that?" I asked. "Do I have something on my face?"

"Yeah, that was weird. And you have nothing on your face."

"Do you think everyone found out I'm trying out tomorrow? That it got leaked?"

"How?"

"I don't know."

I saw Deja and Lee at our table in the courtyard across the way before I could hear them. They were huddled over, sharing a phone screen. Deja looked up at me, as if sensing I was there, then back at the phone.

Has she seen this? I could see the question on Lee's lips even though I couldn't hear the words.

Deja's eyes were back on me again. *I don't think so,* her lips said.

A wave of panic went through me, my walk slowing to a crawl.

"What's wrong?" Max asked, matching my pace.

I pulled my phone out of my pocket to see if I had gotten whatever mysterious message they were looking at, but I didn't have any notifications waiting.

Deja's shoulders rose and fell, worry etching lines in her face. Max, obviously sensing something now too, cursed under his breath.

"Hey," I said when I reached the table.

"I have to show you something," she said.

I swallowed, sinking onto the metal bench attached to the

table. "Is it bad? Maybe we should wait until after my tryouts tomorrow."

"Yeah, maybe," she said. Her eyes flitted to the phone, then back to me.

"Finley, it won't keep that long," Lee said. "You'll find out. Everyone knows."

"*I* don't know," Max said.

"You will."

"Where did Theo go?" I asked, looking around, feeling the need for his steadiness right now.

Deja's jaw tightened.

"He went to find you," Lee said. "He must've missed you on the walk."

"Okay," I said. "Show me."

"Are you sure?" she asked.

"What is it?"

"A video."

"A video?"

She nodded and handed me the phone without asking me if I was sure again. And even though I wasn't, I flipped the phone sideways and pushed play.

The video started in a familiar backyard. It took me a minute to realize it was Theo's. Someone was recording a pickup football game. Just several guys informally passing, catching, and running with the ball. It was obviously a no-contact-type game. When the runner was touched, he stopped. Almost like flag football minus the flags. The recording went on for less than a minute when the camera focused on something in the distance. It zoomed closer and closer until I saw that something was me. Standing on Theo's back porch with Deja, Max, and Lee.

"Do you believe he invited Jensen's girlfriend?" the phone operator asked with a laugh.

"He has balls," someone else said.

"Jensen stole his spot, so now he's going to steal his girlfriend?"

"It was the last game of the season; I wouldn't really call that stealing."

"Hey, Theo," the phone operator called. "Would you call what Jensen did to you stealing?"

Theo looked over. It was hard to tell if he knew he was being recorded, but his hand rubbed over his knee. "The hit?" he asked.

"Yeah, you think he tackled you that hard after the play on purpose so he could kick in the playoff game?"

I could see Theo's jaw working. "Yes," he said.

"So now you're going to get with his girlfriend?"

Theo's eyes shot to somewhere past the camera, probably to where I was standing with my friends.

"You couldn't steal his girlfriend," someone else said. "I heard she's sworn off football players now after the whole podcast thing." I hadn't sworn off anything at that point, but it didn't surprise me that a rumor like that had been spread.

"Oh, please," Theo said, "I could steal her with my hands tied behind my back and make her think it was her idea."

I sucked in a gulp of air, my eyes immediately stinging.

They all laughed, and something must've hit the cell phone

or the person operating it because the video abruptly changed to a picture of the grass and then some jerky, blurry frames until the screen went black.

"Oh no," Max whispered from beside me. "That's not good."

My heart felt like it was at my feet.

"I'm sorry," Deja said, as if her showing me the video made this all her fault.

I squeezed my eyes shut and took a deep breath. I wanted to run away and not look back, forget everything that had happened over the last few weeks.

"What are you going to do?" Lee asked.

That's when I saw Jensen walk into the courtyard, looking around. A slow fire started in my belly and burned up my chest.

The others must have seen him as well because Deja said, "Remember when he announced to the whole school that you would make a sucky podcast host?"

"Remember when he showed up at your house claiming it was because your grandma texted him?" Lee said.

"Remember when he said the podcast ideas you came up with for him were boring and basic?" Max said.

"Remember when the only podcast idea he came up with, the one he tried out with, was *your* idea?" Deja said.

I knew what they were doing. They were working me up. I was glad for it, but I didn't need any reminders of how he'd screwed me over. "You think I'm going to give up?" I asked, realizing that's exactly what they thought. Knowing that my past self probably would've in the face of this new hurdle. But I'd worked hard for this. And maybe I'd fail, but I wasn't going to give up. I had to see this through.

"No, we . . ." Deja trailed off.

"Maybe?" Max said.

"Don't worry, I'm still trying out."

Theo came skidding into the courtyard, frantically looking around. Before he saw me, he and Jensen saw each other.

Jensen advanced on Theo like he was there to avenge me.

I heard Theo say something like "Not now."

Jensen kept advancing, but Theo was looking past him, at me. A mixture of relief and sadness washed over his face, and that's when Jensen punched him.

The courtyard erupted in screams, Theo and Jensen suddenly surrounded by people. Theo had fallen to the ground with the unexpected punch to the face. I flew to my feet and rushed forward, not thinking, only reacting.

"Get up!" Jensen was saying when I pushed my way through the crowd and stepped in front of him.

"Stop," I said.

"You're going to defend him?" Jensen asked.

"I'm not defending either of you. I'm telling you to stop."

"Get out of the way," he said.

Behind me, Theo climbed to his feet. "I'm sorry, Finley," he said.

I gave a single glance back, but before I could say anything Mr. Whitley was there. "What is going on?"

Everyone around us started talking at once, but Max's voice rang out above the others. "Jensen sucker punched Theo!"

Mr. Whitley looked at Jensen, who was seconds away from, most likely, confessing, but was stopped when Theo said, "No, he didn't."

I gave Theo narrow eyes, but he wasn't looking at me.

"He didn't?" Mr. Whitley asked.

"Nobody punched me. I just fell, bum knee, you know," Theo said in a disarming fashion.

"You okay?" Mr. Whitley asked.

"All good," he said.

"Well, lunch is almost over. Let's disperse," he said to the crowd that had gathered.

As people, including Mr. Whitley, left, Jensen said, "I don't need any charity from you."

"Believe me, it wasn't for you," Theo responded.

I turned on my heel and fled. I knew Theo followed me, but I didn't stop until I was almost to the parking lot. He didn't try to make me. Finally, when there was nobody around, I turned. "Are you too cool to tattle?" I said. "He would've been suspended."

"Exactly," he said.

"Exactly? Oh!" The tryouts tomorrow.

"*You're* going to beat him. Not me."

"Ugh," I grunted in frustration. The scent from the sweatshirt I wore surrounded me, suffocated me. I wrestled it off my body and shoved it into his chest.

He barely caught it as it slid down him. "Finley," he said softly.

My eyes shot to his knee covered by his pants. "Did Jensen cause your injury?"

"He's the one that tackled me after the play, yes." He furrowed his brow. There was a red mark forming near his left eye. "I thought Jensen told you that. I thought you knew."

"I didn't." I took a deep breath. "So that's why you're doing all this? Why you wanted to help me?"

"I'm sorry," he said.

I turned again, needing to be anywhere but here.

"That video! I didn't mean it! I had forgotten I said it because sometimes I say stupid things that I don't mean. Mostly because I'm a cocky fool. I thought you hated me. But I'd liked you long before then."

My back was still toward him, and I closed my eyes. "Know when to give up, Theo," I said, and walked away.

Chapter
thirty-two

SHORT BLASTS OF WHISTLES RANG THROUGH THE AIR as I entered the gates, at the end of the football field, surrounded by my friends. They hadn't left me alone since the day before. I received texts every five minutes all afternoon from at least one of them, and then Deja had showed up at my house about eight o'clock telling me she was sleeping over. I wanted to pretend I was fine, but I wasn't. I had collapsed into her arms and let her talk trash on Theo and Jensen all night. It didn't help. I had cried a lot. But today I had to switch the hurt to anger or I wouldn't be able to function.

Groups of guys were being directed to lines.

"Don't be nervous," Max said. "You're trying out for special teams, so you won't have to do all the tackling drills and things. Just the stuff you've been practicing."

I looked at him, wanting to ask him how he knew that, if Theo had been texting him things to say to me, but I didn't need to. It was obvious. He just gave me an innocent expression.

Coach Wallis glanced our way, said something to the assistant coach next to him, then went back to directing the players. I couldn't make out Jensen in the sea of helmets, so I wasn't sure if he saw me yet, but some of the guys were looking.

The assistant coach jogged our way. "Spectators in the stands, please."

"Yes, sir," Maxwell said, and the three of them gave me a combination of side hugs and hand squeezes before they headed for the bleachers.

I didn't move, and the coach gestured to the stands.

"I'm trying out for kicker today," I said.

He studied my expression as though waiting for the punch line.

"Where should I go for that?" I asked.

Coach laughed, but when I didn't join him, he cleared his throat and said, "Oh, for real? That's . . . actually pretty cool. You any good?"

"Yes," I said with as much confidence as I could muster.

"I'll have you talk to Coach Wallis, then. We need to get you some gear. I'm Coach O, by the way. And you are?"

"Finley Lucas."

"Good luck, Finley."

The head coach, Mr. Wallis, wasn't as quick to be convinced. He stared at me for a long time after I told him I wanted to try out. Eventually he asked, "Why? Is this some publicity stunt or something?"

"No, it's not. I'm good, Coach," I said. "Give me a chance to prove it. I'm not asking for any favors. Just the same chance as everyone else here."

He clapped once. "All right. Let's see what you got."

After gearing up, he directed me to a line, and I joined it.

There was some shuffling to my left, and then Jensen was beside me. "What are you doing?" he asked. His eyes were fire.

"I think I'm going to try out," I said, patting my helmet. Those were the same words he'd used on me in front of the recording studio. They were burned into my memory because of the shock surrounding them. I wondered if my words would be burned into his memory now.

"Wh-what? What do you mean? For football? You can't."

"It looks like I can," I said. He didn't know yet, I realized, which specific position I was trying out for. All the anger I had been feeling toward Jensen for the last several weeks was combined with all the anger I was now feeling toward Theo. I was burning with rage. I felt powerful, like nothing could stop me.

NEVER HAD I BEEN MORE GRATEFUL FOR THE LAST month of butt kicking than I was today after being put through football drills. I was running and hitting standing pads and doing fast feet in and out of the squares of rope ladders lying on the grass. All while wearing bulky pads and a helmet. That wasn't exactly new. Theo had been making me kick in pads and a helmet this last week. I felt hotter today, sweatier, but I was keeping up. Not just because of the conditioning that I'd been doing, but because there was adrenaline coursing through my body that the day had finally arrived.

The sun was burning through the fog as Coach began dividing the group into two different teams.

"Special teams," Coach O called out. "Follow me."

I propelled myself into motion, falling into step beside Jensen.

"Really?" Jensen asked.

"Really."

"I get what you're doing. This is payback. But you're taking the joke too far. You're going to embarrass yourself. And Coach isn't going to be happy."

"It's not a joke," I said. "I'm trying out."

He pointed to the uprights in the end zone. "For kicker?"

"It appears so."

"This isn't as easy as trying out for a podcast."

"Maybe it is," I said, because I wanted him to think I hadn't worked at all for this when I stole it from him.

"The only person this is going to hurt is you," he said. "When everyone is talking about you on Monday."

I shrugged. "I'm used to it by now. Ever since your lovely school-wide announcement about how much I suck as a podcast host, I've been the subject of a lot of gossip."

"That's not what I said," Jensen said, with a scoff.

"That's exactly what you said, Jensen, except you were more specific. You spelled out the exact ways I sucked."

"You're remembering things how you want to remember them."

"Maybe you've altered your memory to help yourself feel better, but I know what I heard," I said. He didn't get to change history because the roles were reversed now.

"Did Theo put you up to this?"

"No, this was my idea. It has nothing to do with Theo." Regardless of the fact that I now realized Theo had a bigger interest in seeing Jensen go down than I originally thought, this was always my plan.

"I wasn't trying to hurt you," he said.

I shrugged. "Neither am I." Except that was a lie. That's all I was trying to do. I wanted this to hurt. Bad. I wanted him to feel it in his bones when I took this from him. I wanted him to be scared. But so far, he only seemed mildly annoyed and distracted.

"Well then," he said, as if coming to some sort of acceptance. "Good luck." He stuck out his fist like he wanted me to bump it. We had never fist-bumped before in our lives. He was pretending he was a bigger person than me because he wasn't threatened yet. I did not fist-bump him. I was obviously not even close to the bigger person.

"We'll start at the ten-yard line and work our way back from there," Coach O said. "I want to see three kicks at each stop. One center, one on both sides of center. Then we'll practice with some defenders trying to block you. Who wants to go first?"

A guy in front of me raised his hand. I assumed he was a freshman or sophomore because I didn't recognize him or the other guy. There were four of us hoping to score the spot. I didn't care what order we went in as long as I was before Jensen. I wanted to get in his head.

"Okay, great," Coach O said. He gestured to someone behind me, and Theo came running up. His left eye was now a purplish black. My heart stuttered for a moment. "Theo is going to help me out today with equipment and ball placement and such."

I clenched my teeth. I hadn't realized that was the case, but that was most likely his role as outgoing kicker.

"Let's see what you have," Coach said.

Theo, who'd been holding a mesh bag, began pulling out footballs.

"Does *he* really have to be here?" Jensen asked. "That's a lot of pressure, Coach, to have the starting kicker here."

"You don't think there is going to be pressure in a game?" Coach said.

"I mean, like, he's judging us."

"*I'm* judging you, kid," Coach said. "Suck it up. All right, Scott, place your ball."

"It's not fair she gets her boyfriend here," Jensen mumbled under his breath. If only he knew how little Theo was helping my mental game right now. I was all over the place.

Theo positioned a ball on a plastic holder on the ten-yard line, and Scott, the first volunteer, approached him. Then he backed up and kicked. It made it cleanly through the uprights. Maybe I had more competition than just Jensen for this. I hadn't really considered I'd have to beat out more than one person. I squared my shoulders. Jensen beat out twenty-four people for my coveted spot; I could beat three. The other new guy kicked with the same results.

"I'll go next," I said, stepping forward.

Jensen had stepped forward as well, and when I did, he stopped and held his arm out to the side like he was allowing me to go first. I didn't say a word; my actions would speak for themselves.

"You got this," Theo said when I approached.

"I need to concentrate, Theo. Don't talk to me."

He nodded, his eyes sad, his jaw tight.

He placed the ball on the holder. From the side I heard a whoop. I knew it was Deja, but I didn't look over. I didn't want Coach to think that I thought of this as a joke. I took my three steps back and one to the left.

I took a deep breath, then released it and drove forward.

Right before I got to the ball Jensen said loudly, "Don't miss."

I stutter-stepped, and my foot hit the ball at a weird angle; it shot straight out in front of me, skidding along the grass. I held back a curse.

Theo growled and went charging toward Jensen. Coach pulled him back by his shirt. "Cool off! Now! Go take a lap."

Theo put his head down and jogged away.

Jensen could barely contain the smug smile on his face.

"Jensen," Coach said. "No antics. But, Finley, there will be distractions during a game; you can't let them get to you."

"I know. I'm sorry."

"Try again," he said.

"She gets to try again?" Jensen whined.

"Of course she does. Now, mouth shut."

This time I put away all thoughts of anything but the ball. I tried to forget the embarrassment of missing. Of other people judging me for it. I focused. This time I connected squarely. It wasn't as strong a kick as I wanted it to be, but it made it, barely flying on the inside of the far right post. That definitely wasn't going to get in Jensen's head as much as I hoped it would. He proved that by kicking it right down the middle and celebrating with an eyebrow raise in my direction.

We each completed our other kicks at that distance, and then Coach moved us back ten yards. By this time, Theo was back from his lap around the field. His eyes were dark, and he glared at Jensen while we took turns kicking again.

At this distance, I got my rhythm and confidence back. I kicked it firmly straight down the center. After that I relaxed. As I relaxed and my kicks became more confident and sure, Jensen's became more wild and weak. By the time we were finishing the thirty-yard line, he'd missed two kicks completely. Each flying far left. The other two kickers had each missed one. Aside from my first botched attempt, I hadn't made another error.

"You haven't given up the wedge kick yet, huh?" I heard Theo mutter after Jensen's miss, making sure he was close enough to Coach so he could hear. Coach was making notes on his clipboard, I wasn't sure what, but I hoped next to Jensen's name it was something like *inconsistent wedge kicker*.

Me winning could be good for ticket sales, I wanted to say, mocking one of the reasons they'd chosen Jensen for the podcast. *I could bring in a new, different audience.* I held my tongue because Jensen was spiraling. He didn't need a push; he was getting there himself.

He missed one more kick at the next distance. After his miss, he picked up the plastic holder and threw it on the ground in frustration. It bounced and tumbled to a stop ten feet away. The new guys missed two kicks at that distance. I still had a perfect record. At this point, I was running on adrenaline and karma.

That energy took me through to the end, when after finishing my last kick, over the outstretched hands of some defenders that had been brought over, Coach jotted something down on his clipboard, met my eyes, then said, "Where have you been? Super impressive."

This time I gave Jensen the eyebrow pop as I freed myself from my helmet and joined the others waiting. I watched Jensen get his last kick blocked. He looked destroyed. He hung his head, and unlike before, when he'd thrown the holder in anger, he just gathered it like he was picking up a delicate egg and then jogged to where the ball had landed.

Next to me Theo said, "You know you did it, right?"

I wanted to ignore him, but instead I asked, "How do you know?"

"First of all, I could read the notes Coach was making. Second, I watched you."

The feelings of exoneration and triumph that I thought would course through me with that knowledge didn't. Instead, I felt like I was crashing down from the rage that had been fueling me. I felt a bit like Jensen looked, walking slowly back toward us, his knuckles practically dragging along the ground like the ball he carried weighed a ton. I felt the weight of sadness over what I had lost weeks ago, over what I had lost yesterday.

I felt lost.

Chapter
thirty-three

COACH BLEW HIS WHISTLE AND GESTURED FOR US ALL to come forward. We stepped into a half circle around him.

"Good job, everyone. We'll have the official list up on the locker room office door on Monday."

I raised my hand. "Um? The boys' locker room?"

"Oh." He cleared his throat. "Right . . . Yeah . . . Um, I'll put a list up in the . . . um . . ."

"The athletics office?" Theo suggested.

"Yes, exactly. Monday morning." He pointed at the gear surrounding us. "Stack gear and pads and helmets back in the bin on the sidelines, please." With those words he left, probably to see if Coach Wallis needed help with the other group, which was still going strong.

Jensen thew his helmet onto the ground, followed by his pads. Before he walked away, he met Theo's eyes. "You played the long game, but in the end, you got me."

"Me!" I called after him. "*I* played the long game!"

He didn't turn around, and my outburst didn't make me feel better.

The others had taken off their helmets and pads and stacked them next to Jensen's, leaving just me and Theo standing there.

"I'm so proud of you," he said.

"Don't," I responded.

"I wish I had a better explanation for why I said that. I didn't even think it was true. I thought you hated me back then, to be honest. I don't even remember saying it. I probably said it because I thought it sounded tough or cool or anything but how I felt. It's how I keep my walls up sometimes. But I'm learning how to drop them. I wasn't trying to steal you. I wasn't trying to do anything but help you get back at Jensen. And while doing that, I fell for you. Hard. Don't quit us, Finley."

"I haven't even been myself these past few weeks. I've been angry. Lost. How could you want to be with this angry ex-girlfriend who only defined herself by her lost dream unless you were doing it to get back at him?"

"You're telling me you haven't been yourself around me? That every second we've been together you've been overcome with rage and hopelessness? Is that your story?"

"No. Ugh." I ran my hands down my face. "But it's been there, simmering beneath the surface, and now it's gone. It boiled over when I saw that video, when I kicked that last ball, and all I'm left with is . . ." What was I left with? I didn't even know. Emptiness? The realization that all this pushing and trying and sacrifice left me with nothing? With even less than nothing. It left me feeling the opposite of fulfilled. "Shame."

"You think I'm a bad person?" he asked. "That I've been using you?"

"No, I think *I'm* a bad person."

"We've been doing this together, Finley. If you are than I am."

"Yeah, maybe we are."

His eyes were glassy . . . or maybe mine were.

My friends surrounded me then, Maxwell tucking me into a protective side hug.

"I knew I shouldn't trust you," Deja said. "And I was right."

"You messed up," Lee said.

"I did," Theo answered.

Maxwell let out a huff, as if he had thought he was going to have to add something to Lee's declaration, but Theo admitting to it so easily took the wind out of his sails.

"We're leaving," Deja said, and I didn't stop them as they pulled me away. I didn't stop them as they led me to the parking lot telling me I did amazing and saying we should celebrate my awesomeness with diner fries.

All I said was "I need to shower first. Can I meet you all there?"

I GOT OUT OF THE CAR BACK AT MY HOUSE THINKING that maybe going to the diner with my friends would make me feel better. Because all I felt now was nothing. I wasn't proud of my performance. I wasn't happy karma gave Jensen what he deserved. I felt emptied out.

I clung to the laces of my cleats as I walked in the house. The living room was full. Mom, Dad, Grandma, and even Corey were gathered around the couch. They were all wearing shirts with sharks on them and headbands with a fin sticking straight out of the middle of their heads. I was confused. "What's going on?"

"We were wondering the same thing," Dad said, pulling off his headband and tossing it onto the coffee table.

"What? Did you go somewhere today?" I asked.

"Did *you*?" Mom returned. She lifted a sign by her feet that had big sparkly words on it that spelled out *GO FINLEY!*

I was even more confused. "Did you try to go to the football stadium?" Had they closed the gates? How had they heard about me trying out for the position? And what did sharks have to do with kicking a football?

"We were in Pismo, loser," Corey said from where he sat on the couch. He had a smirk on his face, but I could tell even he was annoyed.

"Pismo?" And then it hit me like a slap to the face. The triathlon I'd told them about weeks ago. That was today. I was supposed to have confessed by now about what I was really doing. And even if I hadn't, I never expected them to actually go to the triathlon. Especially not my grandma who didn't get out that much. I could tell that the morning exhausted her by how flushed her cheeks were. "Oh no."

"Explain," Dad said.

"I'm so sorry. I was trying out to be kicker for the school's football team."

"Kicker?" Mom said.

"I probably made it," I added, as if that would help this situation. The emptiness that had settled in my chest seemed to be double in size now.

"Jensen's position?" Dad asked.

"Yeah . . . he, uh . . . he made it as host of the podcast." I wished like never before that I had explained the whole situation earlier.

"Oh!" Grandma said with a clap of her hands. "He'll be so good at that."

I bit the insides of my cheeks, reminding myself she didn't understand how much those words hurt.

"I don't understand," Mom said. "He tried out for the podcast?"

"Yes, and made it. And I didn't. I'm sure you remember. And it sucked. And I was angry. So I tried out for kicker."

"And he's cool with that?" Corey asked.

"No! Of course he's not cool with that! That was kind of the point."

My words seemed to be sinking in for everyone in the room except my grandma, whose flushed cheeks were accompanied by drooping shoulders.

Corey's eyes got wide, and then he smiled. "Nice."

Mom's brows shot down. "You tried out for revenge?"

"Revenge?" Grandma said. "Finley wouldn't do that. She's much too mature for that."

"I'm not, Grandma. Obviously, I'm not . . ." My voice trailed off.

Dad cleared his throat. "I wish you hadn't lied to us." He nodded toward the sparkly sign. "We walked around all morning looking for you. We were so worried."

"I'm so sorry. I didn't mean for that to happen. I meant to tell you before now."

"So what now?" Mom asked. "You made it?"

"I think."

"Congratulations," Dad said, but he didn't sound like he meant it.

"Thank you," I responded, but I didn't sound like I meant it.

"Are you . . . ," Mom started, "excited? This is a new dream of yours that you've accomplished?"

"Yes," I said firmly. "I'm super excited." I was not even a little bit excited. This was not a dream of mine. Not even close. The only dream this accomplished was exacting revenge on Jensen. But what was left, a position on the team, was more of a burden than a reward, and I hated that.

"Imagine," Grandma said in an ill-timed moment of clarity, "what you could've accomplished if you spent that much time and energy doing something for yourself."

I swallowed hard. "I'm going to take a shower."

Corey jumped up from the couch and followed me down the hall. "I wish you would've at least told *me*. I wanted to see the look on Jensen's face. Worth it?"

"Yep," I said, still trying to convince myself that it was. That I didn't just waste *more* of my life on Jensen.

I'M NOT FEELING GREAT, I TEXTED THE GROUP AFTER A shower. *Today tired me out. Can we do the diner celebration tomorrow?*

Not as cool, but fiiiiine, Max responded first.

We already ordered fries! Get your butt over here, Deja said next.

Rest, Lee said. *We're good.*

Nothing felt good. My family was disappointed in me. I didn't feel the euphoria I was expecting after accomplishing what I'd been working toward. And Theo . . . My heart squeezed in my chest and my eyes pricked, the first emotions I'd felt in hours. . . . Why did everything about that ending feel wrong too?

I crawled into my bed, pulled a pillow against my chest, and let the tears come.

Chapter
thirty-four

"I'M READY, FINLEY." GRANDMA STOOD IN MY DOORWAY dressed in a colorful dress with one of her wigs on. It looked like she'd put some makeup on as well.

"Ready for what, Grandma?" I was in bed. It was Sunday, well past noon. I'd begged out of the diner with my friends again. I wasn't ready to see anyone. I just wanted to lie in bed all day. Maybe my brain would figure out my life for me if I let it think about things long enough.

"For my interview." She didn't wait for my answer, just sat at my desk where I'd been recording podcasts with her. I hadn't asked her to come in today, but it was possible she was remembering another day where I had.

"Can we do it tomorrow? I'm not feeling my best today."

She tapped her slippered foot on the ground several times, then pointed to her wig. "I'm ready now."

I closed my eyes and hugged my pillow to my chest.

"What's wrong, my sweet girl?"

"Everyone is disappointed in me."

"I'm not."

I wanted to tell her she had been yesterday. But what was the point of that? "Thank you."

"What about you? Are you disappointed in you?"

"I am," I said. Because I was.

"How are you going to fix it?" she asked.

"I don't know."

She patted the chair next to her. "Come tell me about it, dear."

And so I did. I pulled myself out of bed and sat next to her. She handed me the headphones on the desk, and I chuckled but slid them onto my head. She put hers on as well. She'd seen me do this so much that she even knew how to connect them and start the recording. I wanted to turn it off, but it didn't matter. It's not like I had to do anything with the audio. I could be the subject today.

"Tell me what happened?" Grandma said.

"I let anger take over my judgment. I thought I'd feel better if I took something away from someone who took something from me, but I feel worse. And now I have something that I don't want."

"You're speaking in riddles," she said.

"I know." I didn't want my grandma to be disappointed in me. It didn't feel good yesterday, and I wasn't sure I could handle her reaction all over again today. I didn't want her to say that I was too good to do bad things sometimes.

But she surprised me by saying, "We all make mistakes. It's how we deal with our mistakes that really define our character."

"Can mistakes be purposeful, though? I did this very much on purpose. I knew what I was doing."

"You thought it would help you?"

I breathed in. "I did."

"But it didn't."

I shook my head, a podcast error. People couldn't hear body movements. So I held the mic closer to my mouth and said, "It didn't help at all."

"What are you going to do about it?"

"I think I need to start over. I need to hit the reset button. I need to forget the last month even happened. Maybe even the last year."

"Now, now, honey. Don't throw the baby out with the bathwater."

"What does that mean?"

"I'm sure some good things happened in the last month, the last year. Mistakes aren't all-encompassing. Things aren't only black or white."

She was right. I was reverting to what I always did: quit. I wasn't going to do that. I didn't want to do that. "You're very smart, Grandma. Do you know that?"

"Of course I do, dear."

"So I need to keep the baby and throw out the bathwater?" I asked.

"Exactly."

I tried to think about the good parts of the last month or so. They were definitely the things that didn't involve Jensen. Like interviewing my grandma and searching for her surfboard. Even though I still hadn't found it, the process had been fun and interesting.

"Do you remember telling me about the boy who painted a surfboard for you, Grandma?"

"Andrew," she said.

"Yes, Andrew. I tried to find that surfboard, but the owner of his old house ran us off. I wanted to find it for you."

"That's sweet, honey. But I can't surf anymore."

I laughed. "I know, Grandma. I thought you might want to see it."

"You are very thoughtful."

"Sometimes." For some reason Theo's smile flashed through my mind, igniting a new spark of sadness. "You broke up with Andrew when he made a big mistake. But you said you got back together. How did you forgive him? *Why* did you forgive him?"

"Well, for one, nobody is perfect. For two, his mistake injured my ego more than it injured me."

"Oh . . ." I thought about that. I wondered if that was why I felt mostly anger when I thought about Jensen and mainly sadness when I thought about Theo. Because Jensen had injured me, taken something important from me, and Theo had injured my ego. Still wrong, but perhaps my pride was also involved in the equation, was part of the reason I couldn't get past it.

"Thirdly, there was the grand gesture," she said.

"What do you mean?" I asked.

"He did something big to prove that he cared about me. Something that meant he saw me."

"What?" I asked.

"It was a couple weeks after he lent my board to Cheryl. I

275

was walking the beach, like I did most mornings. But instead of watching the surfers, my eyes were on the ground so I could throw stranded sand dollars back into the water before the sun dried them up. I heard shouting up ahead and looked up to see a group of lifeguards surrounding someone by one of their towers. Everyone was speaking in loud, angry voices."

"Why?" I asked.

"At first, I couldn't tell. But as I drew closer, I saw the person in the middle of the group was Andrew. He held a paintbrush, his arms streaked multicolored."

"What was he painting?"

"The tower," she said with a smile.

"The tower?"

"The lifeguard tower where we first met."

My mouth fell open. The lifeguard tower. Was that the one I had seen in the rock thrower's backyard? "What was on it?"

"Surfing scenes, waves, a sun, and when I walked around the back, there was us. Well, not detailed versions of us, but our silhouettes, representing the first time we met. The lifeguards were angry that he had defaced their property."

"What did they do?"

"The police came, drove their truck right across the sand. Andrew had seen me at that point, and he was saying things like *I'm sorry I was so stupid* and *I shouldn't have lent her the board. You mean everything to me. I miss you.* By this time, the cops were pulling him toward their truck and he was yelling, *I love you, Charlotte! Please forgive me.*"

"And what were you doing?"

"I was running after him, saying, *I forgive you! The tower is beautiful!*"

"Did they really arrest him?"

"They took him down to the station and gave him a serious talking-to. And in order to get the charges dropped, he had to repaint the tower back to its normal, boring blue."

My heart sank. "He repainted it?"

"He did."

That meant the lifeguard tower we'd found probably wasn't the real one. Had someone made a replica? "And then you guys got back together?" I asked.

"I showed up on the beach with a paintbrush early the next day because my dad told me that was the day he was scheduled to repaint it. And there he was, blue paint and a mopey expression on. He'd already painted over the front half, like he was saving the back, saving us, for last. *Need help?* I asked him. He turned and looked at me in surprise, scooping me up and twirling me around. Then he carried me up the stairs and inside, where my surfboard was leaning up against the back wall. I was so happy to see it, so happy to be with him that I pulled him into a kiss."

"Of course you did," I said. "You missed kissing the best kisser."

She chuckled.

"Wait," I said. "You got your surfboard back?"

She tilted her head, as if she had forgotten that part of the story until now. And maybe she had. Maybe the more traumatic part of the story, when Cheryl borrowed it, was what had stuck in her memory originally. "I guess I did."

Did that mean she really did lose that surfboard in the house fire? Or that it was unfindable now? "How did he even know you were going to show up that morning?"

"He didn't. He hoped."

"Hope," I said. "That's a good feeling."

"It is."

MY PARENTS WERE IN THE KITCHEN WHEN I WALKED IN that evening, talking quietly to each other. They stopped when they saw me.

"I'm sorry," I said. "For lying to you for the past month. And that you went out to Pismo yesterday and wasted your morning searching for me with your costumes and your signs. I didn't mean to make you worry. I wish I had been there. Your support would've meant a lot." I brushed at an escaped tear. I told myself I wasn't going to cry. "The universe has helped me learn some pretty big lessons, but if you feel like you want to pile on some parent-specific punishments for my actions, scrubbing toilets or weeding flowerbeds or whatever, I understand."

My mom pulled out the chair next to her, and I sank into it.

"We're not horrible parents, are we?" she asked. "Pretty understanding and reasonable."

"Very understanding and very reasonable."

"Then why didn't you feel like you could tell us everything that was going on?" Dad asked.

"Probably because in the back of my mind, I always knew what

278

I was doing was wrong, and I didn't want you to talk me out of it. I was angry."

Mom nodded and then placed her hand over mine on the table. "If the universe has taken care of the lesson portion of your actions, we'll forgo any further punishments."

Dad met her eyes like that was not what they had previously discussed, but he didn't say anything, just joined Mom in patting my hand.

"I'll do some extra chores this week for good measure," I said.

Mom pulled me into a hug. "I know you're hurting and I'm not entirely sure why, but when you want to talk, we're here."

"It's mainly stupid boys," I said. "Being stupid."

She squeezed me tighter. "I'm sorry."

Chapter
thirty-five

I GOT TO SCHOOL EARLY MONDAY MORNING BECAUSE I had a mess to clean up.

The athletics office was on the back side of the front office, but when I tugged on the handle to let myself in, it was locked. I knocked on the door.

The volleyball coach, Ms. Linus, came to greet me. "Hi, did you have paperwork you need to turn in or something?"

"No, I'm looking for Coach Wallis or Coach O."

"They're probably in their office."

"They said they were going to post a list of who made the team here." I scanned the door and window to the right to make sure I hadn't missed it. They were full of flyers announcing fundraisers and game schedules and tryouts. No list of who made the football team.

"They must not have done that yet. Try their office."

"The one in the boys' locker room?" That was the only one I knew of.

"Or just wait here."

"Okay, thank you."

I didn't want to wait here. I needed to catch them before they posted the list, not after. So I went to the locker room. School didn't start for another thirty minutes, and the rows of lockers I passed as I walked through it were free from people. I was grateful for that. The offices were at the far back, and I kept my focus straight ahead, just in case, until I reached the door. As I lifted my hand to knock, I noticed a paper taped to the door. *Varsity Football Roster*, it read. My heart thumped hard in my chest as my eyes scanned the list. At the far bottom I found the word *Kicker*. My finger traced a line from the word to the name listed on the right. *Finley Lucas*. My breath caught in my chest. Even though I'd been expecting it, a small voice in the back of my head had told me maybe it wasn't true. The pride I hadn't felt on Saturday, that I hadn't gotten to feel a month ago with the podcast, expanded in my chest now. I'd made it. I'd worked hard toward something and then accomplished it. There was definitely a deep sense of pride in that.

But . . . after my name were the words *Second String: Jensen Ballard*.

I reached up and ripped the paper down in one fast motion, crumpled it into a ball, and knocked on the door.

A muffled "Come in!" sounded through the metal.

I opened the door to find Coach O sitting at his desk. Coach Wallis's was empty.

"Finley," Coach said. "You're here early. I was just about to hang another roster at the athletics office. Congratulations."

"No," I said. "I mean, thank you. But I can't." I walked the ball of paper I held to his desk and set it on top. "I'm sorry. I can print and hang another one, but I need you to take my name off it first."

"Why?"

"Because I don't belong on the team. I have zero desire, and I tried out for all the wrong reasons. My heart isn't in it, and I know how much work it will be. I want to spend my senior year on *my* goals, not on something that I only did to hurt someone."

"I'm disappointed," Coach O said. "You were good out there. The team could use you."

"Jensen is good. The team doesn't need me." I needed me.

He stared at me for a while, and I could see why players might be afraid of him. But I'd already made up my mind, and this tactic of intimidation, if that was what it was, wasn't going to work on me. I wasn't scared of losing my place on the team. That was exactly what I was trying to do.

A voice came through the open door behind me amid the serious staring. "Coach, is the list going up soon?"

I turned to see Jensen's big body standing in the doorway. His face went dark when he saw me.

"Just about," Coach said. "Maybe you can talk Finley into—"

"Leaving," I interrupted. I gave Coach a look that said, *Jensen doesn't need to know.* "I'm going. You don't need to tell me again."

But Coach wasn't having it, and he surprised me by saying, "You might want to thank this girl, because she's turning down the starting spot for you."

"No," I said. "Not for him." I turned to face Jensen. "Not for you. For me. I'm turning it down for me."

His eyes shot to the ground, then met mine. "You don't have to. You earned it."

"Like I said, this has nothing to do with you. I don't want it. But good luck next year." I swiped up the crumpled paper on Coach's desk because I decided I wanted it as a memento. "Sorry again. And thank you for the opportunity to try." With those words, I left the office.

Footsteps followed behind me, but I kept going.

"Finley, wait up," Jensen said.

"Nothing has changed," I said. "I still don't want to talk to you." My anger may have expended itself on Saturday, but that didn't mean I was suddenly a fan of Jensen's again. What he had done was still messed up, and it said everything I needed to know about him.

"I'm sorry," he said. "I shouldn't have done it."

I stopped in the middle of the locker room and turned to face him. "No, you shouldn't have. But you did, so it's done."

"Do you want me to drop out? To talk to Nolen? Is that why you did this?" He pointed back toward the office.

"What? No. Once again, Jensen, not everything I do is about you. Keep both your spots. I was being truthful. I did this for me."

"But now I feel bad."

I let out a single laugh. "Now?"

"Yes. I didn't see what I had done as being wrong before. I didn't see it until Saturday, when you tried out."

I studied his demeanor. He seemed sincere. Maybe he *had*

learned a little empathy. "And what about Theo?" I asked, not planning to, but the words came spilling out. "Can you see what you did to him was wrong? What you took from him? Have you said sorry to him?"

"*That* was an accident," he said.

I didn't think that was true, but still, I said, "Then you should feel even sorrier."

He huffed out a breath of air.

"Bye, Jensen," I said, and left.

"NOLEN, CAN I TALK TO YOU?" I ASKED. HE AND SUSIE had just finished morning announcements, and he was putting papers into his backpack, getting ready to head to first period.

"I told him he could," he said. "Did he change his mind? Talk to you already?"

"What?" I asked, confused, then remembered what Jensen had said twenty minutes ago in the locker room. Had he approached Nolen about dropping out after our talk? "No, not that," I said now. "I didn't earn that. I want to commentate the football games next year. Do live calls during the game and interviews after the game. Teachers do it right now, but I think it should be a student responsibility. And I actually think I'd be pretty good at it. Not perfect, but I'd be willing to try." That was new for me. Putting myself out there when I felt unsure. When I didn't have the ability to edit

284

out my mistakes. "I just spent the last month learning all the rules and regulations and terminology and plays and more than I ever thought I wanted to know. I even learned to kick."

He slung his backpack onto his shoulder, not saying anything, and together we walked out of the studio. "You learned how to kick? Like through the uprights?"

"Yeah, Theo taught me. I'm pretty good," I said.

He laughed. "Cool. And yeah, that's a really cool idea. So you don't want your podcast research spot? Is that why you're telling me this?"

"Yes, I don't," I said. I was quitting, but for all the right reasons.

"Okay, I'll reach out to the runner-up."

"Thanks," I said.

"You talked to Mr. Whitley about the commentator idea?"

"I did," I said. He liked it.

"Nice. So did you forgive him?"

"Jensen? Yeah." Because I did. I didn't have to like him, but I was done with the anger.

"No . . . I meant Theo."

"Oh." I took a deep breath. "I don't know yet."

Chapter
thirty-six

"IS THIS STILL ON?" CAME A VOICE THROUGH THE speakers.

I was sitting in seventh period, ready to be done with today. I felt like I had been in school for weeks, but not because anything major happened. After talking to Coach that morning and then Nolen, the day had actually been really slow. I found myself searching the halls as I walked, in classes I found myself unable to concentrate, and at lunch Deja had said, "Why don't you just text him? Find out where he is? Go talk to him?"

The *he* she was referring to was Theo, of course. I hadn't seen him all day. Not even a glimpse of him. Had he stayed home? After telling him I didn't want to talk to him on Saturday, he had, in fact, stopped talking to me. I should've been happy he was respecting my boundaries, but maybe I had wanted him to try just one more time. Wanted him to talk me into forgiving him. Not give up like I had told him to. But maybe he was trying to grow too. Accept what was in front of him. Maybe he had assessed our relationship and found that it was based on anger and revenge and decided that wasn't a great way to start anything. Maybe it wasn't.

To Deja at lunch, I had said, "You don't even like him. Why would you want me to text him?"

"Will you kill me if I say that I think I actually do like him. That he owned up to his mistakes, that he's just an occasional punk, and that you two were good together?"

"Yes, I will kill you," I'd said.

"Yeah, probably a good choice," she'd said.

But now, in seventh period, sitting next to me, she whipped her head around when she heard the voice being broadcast into the room through the speakers.

"Yes, it's on," Nolen said. "Theo has one more announcement to make for the day."

"Yes," Theo said. "I would like to invite anyone who can to come to the football field after school."

"As in right now?" Nolen asked.

"Yes, right now. Especially if you have been listening to or host a podcast called *It's About Us.*"

"What is he doing?" Deja asked next to me.

I wasn't sure, but maybe it was what my grandma had referred to as a grand gesture.

IT WAS HARD TO SEE MUCH OF ANYTHING AS I WALKED through the open gates of the football stadium because I was surrounded by people. Apparently, the whole school decided to come see what Theo was up to. Max held one of my hands and Deja the other as we walked. Lee was on Max's other side.

"What are we hoping for?" Max asked. "So I know how to react."

"Seriously," Deja said. "You've been so quiet since his announcement. What do you want to happen now?"

"I don't know," I said, because I didn't. I was just holding on to the hope that whatever this was, it would make me feel better.

"I don't think all these people have listened to your podcast," Max said. "I think they're liars."

"He didn't say it was a requirement," Lee said.

My feet hit the rubber of the track that surrounded the field, when I started hearing people say, "What is that? Why is it here?"

I tried to stand on my tiptoes, but my view was still obstructed.

Deja started to drag us through and around people. We followed along like train cars to her engine.

"Hello, everyone," Theo's voice said into a microphone. There was feedback after his words, and everyone groaned. "Sorry, sorry. Is this better? Hello. I'm not really good on a mic. It's not my thing."

This time there was no earsplitting whine. He was right; his thing was hiding in earbuds and not talking, watching school relays he was supposed to participate in from the sidelines, maintaining his privacy.

"I didn't think this many people would come. Is Finley here? Has anyone seen Finley?" he asked.

A low mumbling of voices sounded, as if everyone started looking for me at once.

"She's here!" Deja said, throwing up her hand.

And then I was surrounded even more, pressed in the middle of a group ushering me toward what I could only assume was the middle of the football field. Was he going to tell everyone I could kick? Make me kick in front of the whole school? Did he not understand how I felt about that? Just as the thought went through my mind, I caught a glimpse of bright blue through the bodies surrounding me.

"Is that . . . ?" And then I was in front of it—the lifeguard tower that I had only seen through binoculars and an iron gate at Andrew Lancaster's old house. It took my breath away. It was just like my grandma had described. A series of ocean scenes. And I knew if I walked around the back there would be a silhouette of her and Andrew. I thought he had painted over all this fifty years ago. But then at the right corner of the face of the tower, next to the door, I saw his signature and the year *2015* followed by the words *in memory of first love.* I was so preoccupied with the structure in front of me that it took my brain a minute to wonder how it got here.

As if Theo could read my mind, he was speaking into the mic again. I looked around and found him on the far side of the tower, a microphone in hand, staring at me with soft eyes. "For those of you who haven't listened to Finley's podcast, you might want to so you can understand what this is. It is a piece of her grandma's history. And I hope it can become a piece of hers too, because right now it serves as the symbol to an apology I owe her.

"Most of you saw the video of me being a jerk. Of me acting

like Finley was a thing to be had or owned or stolen. She's not. She has been hurt in very public ways over the last several weeks, and I felt like she needed to be apologized to in a very public way as well. Finley, there is no excuse for how I behaved, and I am sorry. But now I would like to talk to her in private, so excuse me while I find out if she's still speaking to me."

He handed the mic to Deja. When had she left my side? Then he was walking my way. Nerves and butterflies battled it out in my stomach.

When he reached me, he looked at the ground and then at me again. "I'm . . . I . . . You don't have to talk to me, but there's . . . something more . . . up in . . . Will you . . . ? I don't know why I can't speak."

I'd never seen him this nervous before. "I have that effect on people," I said, quoting his line from weeks ago.

He gave me a slow smile, probably unsure if we were allowed to joke with each other anymore. I wasn't sure either. He pointed to the tower.

Behind him, Deja had started a song on her phone, and she held the mic up to it. I knew that was her way of giving us privacy, but suddenly it was very loud. Theo's lips were moving, but I couldn't hear what he was saying.

"It's really cool!" I yelled, nodding to the paintings.

He shook his head. I'd obviously gotten whatever he'd intended to say wrong. He held out his hand. I stared at it for several long beats. Someone bumped into me, pushing me closer to Theo. I placed my hand in his. He led me to the tower steps and then up them. He opened the door and guided me inside. The door shut and did a surprisingly good job of muffling the noise outside. I could still see all the movement and bodies out the tinted windows, but it felt like we were in our own world.

There wasn't a surfboard inside like I was expecting. But painted on the wall was a life-sized version of the board I'd seen in the pictures. It was better preserved than the paintings outside, more vibrant and beautiful. It made my eyes prick with tears.

"How did you . . . ?" I had so many questions I didn't even know where to start. "You got Nolen to let you make an announcement today? You talked to the rock-throwing man?"

He nodded. "Nolen was easy. The rock-throwing man—Cliff is his name—took some work."

"And how did you get this here? Mrs. Carpenter let you put a lifeguard tower on the football field?" Mrs. Carpenter was the principal.

He cringed. "I didn't exactly ask for permission. My cousin owns some heavy lifting equipment. I might be suspended now. But totally worth it."

I widened my eyes. "Theo. You didn't have to be so dramatic about it. You could've put it in the parking lot or on the beach or something."

"This felt more right. This, the football field, is what brought us together. And besides, if I'm not willing to take a risk, I don't deserve a reward."

"What kind of reward are you looking for?"

"Forgiveness. I'm so sorry for what I said and how I acted in that video. And I'm sorry for not telling you about my injury and the revenge I personally wanted against Jensen. You were right.

What we did wasn't good, and it was for all the wrong reasons. And I wasn't trying to lie to you, but I can see how I did."

"You told me from the beginning you hated him and that you wanted to get back at him. It shouldn't have surprised me that you had a really good reason of your own. Like I did," I said.

"But the other part . . . ," he said. And I knew what other part he meant, the stealing-me part.

"I know," I said.

"That wasn't about him. I started liking you when you argued with me about the correct order of pool lights in my backyard over a year ago."

"I don't know that I was *arguing*," I said.

"Whatever it was, you were adorable."

"I am adorable," I said.

He smiled. "You are."

"Forgiveness," I repeated. "That's all you want?"

"It's not about what I want. This is for you. What do *you* want?"

"You."

As soon as the word exited my mouth, he pulled me against him. Our lips found each other, smashing together in a not-so-gentle kiss that sent waves of pleasure through my body.

My arms wrapped tightly around his neck, and his were holding me firm around my middle, my toes barely brushing the floor. It felt like I was where I was meant to be.

I smiled against his mouth as something occurred to me.

"What?" he said with a smile of his own.

"I haven't posted my latest episode."

"Yeah . . . ," he said, not following. He released his grip on me, and my feet found the ground again. We stayed close, my hands on his chest, his at my waist.

"So you have no idea that Andrew used this for his grand gesture too."

"What do you mean? This wasn't painted until 2015," he said, referencing the date on the outside.

"It was repainted in 2015."

"Really?" he asked.

"You are amazing."

He pressed his lips to mine.

Chapter
thirty-seven

SOMEHOW, THEO HAD CONVINCED MRS. CARPENTER TO let him leave the lifeguard tower on the football field through spring break, referencing art history and local legends. Whatever he said, it worked, and now, on a Tuesday afternoon, we were standing in front of said tower waiting for my parents and grandma to arrive because another miracle had happened over the weekend, as well—Alice had messaged me that she found the board in the shed. Which meant that somehow Cheryl had ended up with it again, and I didn't want to know how.

I'd hang on to the story of Grandma and Andrew in love in the lifeguard tower forever . . . or at least until she met my grandpa.

My friends and I had gone and collected the board and placed it in the tower. We weren't the only ones in the field. A few families walked around the structure, looking at the somewhat-faded paintings. Yesterday a news crew had come out and done a piece on it where they actually referenced my podcast.

"Are you going to wait inside or right here?" Deja asked as I nervously wrung my hands, pacing in front of the steps. At first Theo tried to hold my hand, help me relax, but then he stopped and just smiled at me sweetly with each pass.

"You want her to wait inside and do what?" Max asked. "Jump out and yell surprise, scare her grandma?"

"*Is* it a surprise?" Deja asked.

"I mean, no?" I said.

Lee gave me a confused face.

"I told her," I clarified. "But she might not remember."

"Oh, right," he said just as I saw Grandma, flanked by my parents, walking our way. Corey had come as well, home for spring break.

Grandma's eyes were on the tower, a smile on her lips.

"Do you want me to record with my phone?" Theo asked. "So you can be in the moment?"

"Yes, please." I rushed forward to meet her halfway.

"This is amazing, Fin," Mom said. Dad and Corey agreed.

"Isn't it cool?" I said.

Dad gave up his place next to Grandma, and I hooked my arm in hers.

"Why is it here?" she asked.

"Long story," I said.

"I like long stories."

"My boyfriend used it as a grand gesture."

She squinted her eyes at me. "Are you confusing our stories?"

"No, I'm not."

"Is this your boyfriend?" she asked as we reached Theo. She'd

295

met him at the house both yesterday and the day before, along with my parents and brother, but new people were harder for her to remember.

"It is," I said.

"Hi, I'm Theo," he said, shaking her hand. "Nice to meet you."

A rush of gratitude washed over me at how sweet he was.

"Well, aren't you handsome," Grandma said. She'd said that at both their previous meetings, and he gave me a smirk at the compliment.

"Grandma, he already has a big head. He doesn't need any more encouragement."

"I need all the encouragement."

He really was handsome.

"Don't mind my granddaughter," she said. "She's a sassy one."

"She definitely is," Theo said.

"Are you ready to go inside?" I asked.

"I am."

We slowly climbed the stairs, me and my grandma first and everyone else trailing behind. I opened the door, and she stepped inside.

The sun shone bright through the windows, creating a hazy warmth. Her bracelet caught some light and rainbows bounced off every surface, but she was focused on the board straight in front of her as the group piled in behind us.

"Isn't that something?" she said.

It really was. We'd shined up the board as best we could, and the colors were vibrant greens and browns, like my grandma's eyes. Not only did he capture the shape and color perfectly, but Andrew had captured her character too, her kindness, her curiosity. He obviously knew her and loved her.

"Should I give her a spin or no?" she asked, and everyone laughed. Then she pulled me into a gentle hug. "Thank you, my thoughtful girl, this is very special."

I looked around the small room, where everyone I loved now stood, laughing and talking, and I couldn't remember if I'd ever been happier.

Two months later

"DO I HAVE TO TEACH YOU ALL THE RULES AND REGULA-tions of the game you want to play?" I teased, quoting him from the first time I'd gone to his house to learn to kick.

Theo barked out a laugh and picked me up by the middle, marching toward the ocean.

"Don't you dare!" I scream-laughed, struggling to get out of his hold.

We were on the beach with our friends and a bunch of girls from the soccer team. They'd started a game, and Theo had nodded in their direction. "Should we play?"

"Soccer?"

"Yes," he said.

"Sure."

"Do they play by the book here? Call out of bounds? Keep score?" he asked.

He didn't dump me in the ocean now, just set me down, twirled me toward him, and kissed me.

"Keep it PG!" Max called from where he sat under a beach umbrella layering on more sunblock.

"Do you really need more of that?" I asked as Theo and I joined him.

"I'm a ginger. Yes, I do."

"He does," Lee informed me from where he sat on a blanket, a book in his hand.

"Do you two want to play soccer?" Theo asked.

"Unless we need to become stellar goalies to avenge some wrongdoing, we are staying right here with our books and snacks," Maxwell said.

Lying next to our beach blanket was the foam surfboard we'd found in Cheryl's shed. We were going to take it out later, try our hand at surfing. Grandma had told us to take her board when we left today as well, but we'd donated that one to the Andrew Lancaster exhibit. That way it could be preserved and appreciated by more people. Grandma had been part of the decision, but she forgot things like that.

"I need to think of a wrongdoing for you to avenge," Theo said to Max. "Because I would like to see you become stellar goalies."

"I would like to see that too," Max said. "But I don't want to do any of the work."

"You guys playing?" Deja called from twenty feet away.

"Yes!" I called back.

We joined the game. Watching Theo kick a soccer ball made

me happy. He'd started kicking for fun. Had taken some of the pressure off his shoulders. And doing that opened him up to trying out for a kicker position at the community college next week. He still didn't feel like he was back to his pre-injury self, but he wasn't giving up. Not yet. And I was glad because he was a beautiful kicker. I was probably biased, but the way he moved was like dancing on air.

"Stop staring at me," he said now, passing the ball to Deja and pulling me into a hug.

"But I don't want to," I said. "And you were staring too."

He placed a slow kiss on my lips. "You're right. Never stop."

Acknowledgments

I don't normally give life lessons or advice in my acknowledgments section. Mostly because every reader has their own takeaway from a story that is sometimes different from anything I ever thought of or intended. And whatever you took away from this book is valid. But if I were to give one thought after writing this story, it's this: Karma > Revenge. Protect your peace of mind.

And now to the thank-yous. First, thank *you*. If you're reading this, if you read my whole book and now want to hear more from me, you are amazing. Whether this is the first book of mine you've read or the seventeenth, I appreciate you. I couldn't do this without you. Your messages and comments and support over the years help so much, and I am happy you love my books. It means the world to me.

To my agent, Michelle Wolfson. You are truly an amazing agent. Your advice and guidance over the last ten-plus years have been invaluable. I couldn't have done this without you. I'm so grateful to have you in my corner, not only as someone who knows your stuff, but as a friend. I never take for granted how lucky I am to have you.

To Wendy Loggia, who seriously whipped this book into shape. I know what it looked like before your spot-on suggestions and what it looked like after, and I'll take the after every time. You have been amazing to work with. Your experience and expertise are unmatched, and my stories are better because of you. Thanks as well to Hannah Hill, who also had phenomenal advice. And to the entire team at Delacorte: Alison Romig, Lili Feinberg, Kristen Guy, Erica Stone, Casey Moses, Megan Shortt, Tamar Schwartz, Colleen Fellingham, and Shameiza Ally. I appreciate your help and support and work on my behalf.

My family has provided me with unwavering support through the years. My husband, Jared, gets my odd hours and inconsistent writing schedule and cheers me through all my highs and lows. And my kids, Skyler, Autumn, Abby, and Donavan, who have grown into amazing young adults, are my very favorite people.

I have some of the best friends ever. Friends who read my books and give me advice. Friends who cheer me on. Friends who help me to stay focused and motivated. Those people in my life are: Stephanie Ryan, Candi Kennington, Bree Despain, Jenn Johansson, Renee Collins, Natalie Whipple, Michelle Argyle, Elizabeth Minnick, Brittney Swift, Mandy Hillman, Jamie Lawrence, Emily Freeman, and Misti Hamel.

And last, but definitely not least, thanks to my family, who have always been there for me no matter what. It's so fun to have a big family! It has helped me to write big, authentic family relationships. So thank you: Chris DeWoody, Mark Thompson, Heather Garza, Jared DeWoody, Spencer DeWoody, Stephanie Ryan, Dave

Garza, Rachel DeWoody, Zita Konik, Kevin Ryan, Vance West, Karen West, Eric West, Michelle West, Sharlynn West, Rachel Braithwaite, Brian Braithwaite, Angie Stettler, Jim Stettler, Emily Hill, Rick Hill, and the twenty-five children and numerous children of children that exist between all these people. I love you all so much.

Author Question & Answer

Q: The title of this book is a Taylor Swift song title. And you dedicated this book to her. You're obviously a huge Taylor Swift fan. What's your favorite era? What T.S. song best represents this book?

A: I'm a massive Taylor Swift fan. I've been dropping references to her in my books for many years. I'm in awe of her talent and her business brain. Her songs are forever inspiring me. I absolutely adore her. My favorite era changes on the regular. For a long time, it was *Evermore.* And then *The Tortured Poets Department* came out and I've been listening to that on repeat for many weeks. So right now, *TTPD* is my album. And speaking of that album, two songs that always remind me of this book are: "imgonnagetyouback" and "Who's Afraid of Little Old Me?"

Q: This is your second book featuring podcasts. Do you love podcasts? What's your favorite? Do you secretly wish to host a podcast?

A: I secretly wish I could do a lot of things. So yes, hosting a podcast is on my short list of things I would love to do that I will probably never do. I guess that makes it a not-so-secret wish now that I've typed it for the world to see. I love true crime podcasts, like *Crime Junkie.* That's one of my favorites. I also secretly wish I was a detective.

Q: Your readers are always asking you, and we'll ask again: Will there be a sequel to this book?

A: This is a question I love even though my answer is generally no. Because that means people loved the book so much that they want more of it. But I have also learned to never say never, because you never know. If a book really takes off and demands it, I would consider a sequel. I do love all my characters, and it's often fun to think about what they might be doing now or what they did after the end of their book.

Q: Have you ever gotten revenge (or at least pulled a petty prank) on someone?

A: I wish I had a super-fun, harmless story to share with you about this. But, no, I'm a true Scorpio in that I can hold an epic grudge if I feel like I've been wronged, but I generally just walk away from relationships/situations that aren't right for me. I barely have enough energy to run my own life; I can't be destroying someone else's. Ha.

Q: Are you a football fan? Have you ever kicked a football like your main character?

A: I am a casual football fan. I watch big games, like the Super Bowl, because I like to get together with people. And I do enjoy supporting my hometown college team because the energy at in-person games is unbeatable. But for the most part, I do not watch football. As for kicking a football, I had never kicked one before writing this book. But then, for a promo video I did, I went out and kicked one (barely) through some uprights from as close as I could possibly get. It was fun but also hard, and I have a lot of respect for my main character now. She's a stud.

Q: Can we—and hear me out—get a full-length prequel to this book featuring Finley's grandma and her high school boyfriend, Andrew?

A: Oh! That could be fun. I don't know if I know enough about the '60s to pull that off. I am not a historical fiction writer. Although, I guess, technically I wrote it into this book, so maybe I need to give myself more credit. I do love Grandma and Andrew. They were so fun to write about. A whole book about them would be swell (is that a '60s word? I need to do some research).

Q: What inspired this idea?

A: Revenge. The idea of revenge. The idea of being wronged so bad that a person would be driven to act. I asked myself what that would look like in high school. What might drive someone to feel that way. And I didn't want it to be cheating. Not that cheating isn't an action that has driven many a person to seek payback. But I wanted it to be something deeper, in a way. Someone's life dreams, the thing they were resting their entire future on. That felt big enough to me. The rest of the story was born from there.

Q: Easiest part of this book to write? Hardest part?

A: Maybe this is a bad thing to admit, but the easiest parts were the revenge plots. What she was going to do to get back at him and the conversations she had with her friends about it. In fact, those parts were so easy that I got a little wordy in her talks with friends and ended up needing to cut quite a bit of friend time/plotting. Oops. Hardest part to write was Grandma's story. I needed it to be compelling enough that readers would be rooting for her, but not so long that readers would get annoyed that they were being pulled out of the main story. It's hard to write a very short love story within a love story. I ended up revamping it quite a bit in edits.

Q: A lot of your books take place on the central coast of California. What about that particular area do you love?

A: I love the Central California coast. It's such a unique area of the state. It's not as crowded as Southern California. I really do get why people flock to SoCal—the perfect weather and restaurants and beaches and attractions—but it is so crowded, and sometimes it can take hours to get from point A to point B. The Central Coast is sleepier. It's slower. It's colder (but still great weather). It feels older, in a way. The beaches are gorgeous. The people are nice. The hiking is perfect. And the shrimp tacos are amazing. I'm a big fan of the entire place.

Q: Finally, tell us what you're working on next.

A: I have at least three more YA contemporary romances to come. One is in the works right now. It may or may not involve being trapped together in a tight space with your enemy. Keep an eye out! And thank you so much for reading my books! I hope you enjoy reading them as much as I enjoy writing them.

About the Author

KASIE WEST is the author of many YA novels, including *Borrow My Heart, Places We've Never Been, Sunkissed, The Fill-In Boyfriend, P.S. I Like You, Lucky in Love,* and *Listen to Your Heart.* Her books have been named ALA Quick Picks for Reluctant Readers, JLG selections, and ALA-YALSA Best Books for Young Adults. When she's not writing, she's binge-watching television, devouring books, or road-tripping to new places. Kasie lives in Fresno, California, with her family.

KASIEWEST.COM